breeds

FOXES

EDITED BY THURSTON HOWL

A THURSTON HOWL PUBLICATIONS BOOK

BREEDS: Foxes

Copyright © 2018 by Thurston Howl
Individual copyrights for each story belong to the respective author.

First Edition, 2018. All rights reserved.

A Thurston Howl Publications Book
Published by Thurston Howl Publications
thurstonhowlpublications.com
Lansing, MI

jonathan.thurstonhowlpub@gmail.com

Cover design by Thurston Howl
Cover art by Joseph Chou © 2018
Profile illustrations by Joseph Chou © 2018

Printed in the United States of America
10 9 8 7 6 5 4 3 2 1

Contents

INTRODUCTION
Thurston Howl

Thurston Howl is the editor-in-chief of Thurston Howl Publications, an editor for Weasel Press and Sinister Stoat Press, and an occasional formatter for Armoured Fox Press. Howl self-identifies as a slut, and there is a very clear reason—as evidenced by his profile illustration above—that he is part fox. He once thought of himself as a much wolfier person, but everyone around him insisted otherwise. When he is not writing, editing, or fucking, he is curled up in bed with a good cup of coffee and a good book in paw.

Foxes are submissive bottoms. This is one of the most frequently disseminated clichés of furry erotic literature. (And from experience, there's at least a grain of truth in the stereotype!) Starting this call for writers, I knew the volume would be fairly popular. Hell, several of the stories contained in this volume were likely just resting in the writers' filing cabinets from years past. Everyone has a fox story. Maybe it's our devilish smiles that attract people. Or maybe our fiery fur. Or even the famed elasticity of our tailholes...

As you read, you will notice each piece has an illustration with it, done by the gracious Joseph Chou. Most of these illustrations involve both the author and the author's characters in the story. But that's not all! I encouraged the authors to have some foxy, yiffy fun with their bios, so make sure to read those before diving into the stories themselves!

I like to think of myself as an editor knowledgeable in many genres, and I hope you will see some of that diversity achieved throughout this book. If I had to summarize each story in two words a piece, as a series of quickies, if you will, it would look something like this: butler butts, love letters, caged fox, fine dining, brothel bonding, bondage guide, wish fulfillment, yiff accounting, lesbian pup-play, coffee noir, truck stop, and cooking oils. Perhaps, these tags at least make you curious to read the full stories!

This variety will include the many faces (and groins...and tails) of the anthropomorphic fox in furry erotica: the submissive bottom, the clever trickster, the passionate lover, and the incoherent sounds of their mating that lead us to question, ultimately, what it is the fox is saying. On one paw, it's your fault for putting the gag in his mouth. On the other, maybe it's best to leave it in. As the point of this series is to showcase some of the best species-specific stories, I hope that, when you go back to shelve this book in your personal library, you feel just a little bit foxier...or at least start craving your local fox furries.

Ever onward, dear reader.

Thurston Howl

THE TREACHERY OF IMAGES
WhiteClaw

WhiteClaw is a Tiger/Panther hybrid who enjoys the warm embrace of a fox...And we're not necessarily talking about hugs. Like countless others, he developed a crush on Robin Hood, and from there, his fate as furry trash was sealed. He was severely disappointed when he grew up and discovered the cartoon fox couldn't be his boyfriend, but he found like-minded companions when he stumbled upon and joined the furry fandom. As an outlet for his frustrations in being denied a real-life prince of thieves, he decided to start writing bad, furry romance stories. And while his characters are rarely outlaws, he'll always hold a special place in his heart (and pants) for a morally dubious fox.

Trey sat alone in the booth, flipping through social media on his phone. The tiger had come to the bar straight from work but had ditched his button up shirt in favor of the white tank top he wore underneath. The undershirt showed off Trey's striped, muscular physique, but the image was somewhat ruined by the tiger's frazzled appearance. His short black hair stood up at crazy angles from where he'd run his fingers through it a few too many times.

Trey had just finished his second beer and was contemplating getting another when someone plopped down into the seat across from him. The tiger's ears flicked forward slightly, but he didn't bother looking up. He knew only one person that was bold enough to walk up and casually sit with someone uninvited. The scent of pomade confirmed his suspicions.

The person across from him cleared their throat loudly. Trey tried to ignore it, but when they did it again, he sighed and lifted his gaze. A thin, red fox with slicked-back, dark-brown hair was sitting across from him. The fox was still dressed in his work clothes, a navy-blue blazer and a light-green dress shirt. He had a beer in one paw and was leaning forward over the table to peer at Trey's phone.

"Huh, it sure looks like your phone is working," said the fox. "Which is weird, because you haven't called or texted me in three weeks."

Trey rolled his eyes. "Hi, Jonas," Trey said.

"Oh, 'hi, Jonas'?" said the fox, raising an eyebrow. "That's all I'm getting?"

"Hi, Jonas. What do you want?" Trey elaborated, crossing his arms across his chest.

Jonas frowned, his pointed ears folding back as he took a sip from his beer. "So, I take it you're still mad?"

"Mad?" replied the tiger mildly. "What do I have to be mad about?" Trey feigned confusion for a moment. "Oh yeah," he said with mock surprise, "I remember, now. You outed me to everyone I work with and told the entire company we'd slept together."

"Not the entire company—" Jonas started, but Trey cut

him off.

"Mr. Bartlett himself probably knows you fucked me," Trey said dryly.

"Okay, so first of all," Jonas said, holding up a long, nimble finger, "I'd be flattered if the CEO of a multibillion dollar company were talking about my sex life. Second," he added, holding up another finger, "technically, it wasn't me that told everyone. I just kind of told the person who told everyone. And, third,"—he finished holding up a third finger—"I already fixed all that."

"You call what you did," Trey said slowly, "'fixing' it." The tiger's tail lashed against the booth, belying his calm tone.

"Uh, yeah," Jonas said, grabbing his beer and knocking it back. "I started three different rumors that completely over-shadowed us having sex. Everybody has practically forgotten about us."

Trey let out a deep sigh. "Okay, so let's run through those. One," Trey said, holding up his own finger, "you started a rumor that Kim in scheduling was having Mr. Bartlett's secret love child."

"She had that coming, too," Jonas said with a sly look. "Bitch refused to approve my vacation time last month."

"Two," Trey said, ignoring the fox's comment and holding up a second finger, "you somehow convinced five different women to claim they'd slept with me and that I was amazing in bed. Which has since spiraled into me having slept with nearly every woman in the building."

"See?" Jonas said, spreading his paws and grinning. "Nobody thinks you're gay anymore."

"And then there's three," Trey said darkly, a low growl entering his voice as he held up a third finger. Jonas actually winced at this, his big fluffy tail curling protectively around his body on instinct, but he didn't say anything. "Because now, the current rumor is that Kim, who it turns out is actually pregnant, is having not Mr. Bartlett's child, but mine."

Jonas's ears flattened back against his head again. "So…"

"The current theory is that she was sleeping with us both,

but the kid is definitely mine."

"Ah," Jonas said. "I mean, it could be worse."

Trey narrowed his eyes, his fur bristling slightly, and started to get up, but Jonas reached out across the table to put a paw on the tiger's bicep. The thin fox didn't have a hope of actually restraining the tiger physically. Trey was quite buff, and, when the tiger was angry, his muscles had a habit of really standing out. Jonas would have found the sight arousing under different circumstances.

"Wait, please. I'm sorry. If it makes you feel better, you can hit me again."

Trey grimaced and froze. He'd been pretty angry when he'd found out that Jonas had told everyone about the night they'd spent together. Trey normally would have never done something so violent, but he'd been storming out of the building when he'd run into the fox. The tiger had charged up to Jonas from behind, shouted at him, and, when the fox had turned around, Trey had punched Jonas right in the face. Even now, it was something he regretted. The memory of Jonas sprawled out on the floor and looking up at him in fear was something he couldn't quite forget.

For his part, Jonas was pretty sure the tiger wouldn't actually try to hit him again. He'd made his peace with what had happened and, upon reflection, decided he'd had it coming. He knew he was being manipulative bringing it up like this, but Jonas actually would have let Trey hit him a second time if it meant the tiger would forgive him and start talking to him again.

"I'm not going to hit you," Trey said, sagging slightly.

Somewhat reluctantly, Jonas released his grip on the tiger's bicep, his paw lingering a second longer than was strictly necessary. "Then, does that mean you'll give me another chance?" asked the fox hopefully.

"A chance at what?" Trey asked.

"I was thinking maybe an actual date. Followed by…" Jonas trailed off, a mischievous gleam in his eye.

Trey couldn't help but smirk at that. "I meant want I said

last time," Trey said. He leaned across the table, grabbed the front of the fox's shirt, and pulled him forward. "The next time we fuck, your ass is mine."

Jonas felt a little thrill go through him and quietly churred. "So, does that mean there will be a next time?" asked the fox, practically panting at the idea.

Trey released the fox and leaned back into the booth. He had to admit, he liked the idea of sleeping with the fox again—at least this time around, there would be nothing new to reveal if Jonas blabbed the details—but this talk of going on a date was something different. "What did you have in mind?" Trey asked cautiously.

Jonas just grinned. "I'll take that as a yes," he declared with a little yip of victory, "and trust me. I've already got it all planned out."

For some reason, that made Trey feel even more troubled.

This was bad. Really bad. Trey's sense of unease had grown when Jonas had informed the tiger he would need to dress up for their date. That had been three days ago, and it had given Trey ample time to worry about what the fox had in store.

But, the tiger's fears had not included this.

The art gallery was packed full of men and women dressed in elegant evening wear. Waiters in white tuxes made their way across the floor with serving trays full of champagne and hors d'oeuvres. There was music coming from somewhere…Oh, God, there was actually a string quartet playing the music live. This was really happening.

Trey's gray blazer was old and ill-fitting. He was pretty sure the last time he'd worn it was to a wedding, back before he'd really started hitting the gym and when he was a lot smaller. The only dress shirt he owned was the white, short-sleeved button-up he wore to work, and he hoped no one noticed his tie was a clip-on.

Jonas, however, was actually wearing a full-blown black tuxedo, his red fur glowing brightly in contrast. The outfit looked like it had been tailored specifically for the fox's small frame and showed virtually no signs of wear. He even had a little bowtie that Trey surreptitiously checked and confirmed was the real deal.

"So," Trey said, trying to sound casual and doing a very bad job at it, "why, um, an art gallery?"

"Hmm? Oh," Jonas said a little sheepishly, his long tail swishing back and forth a little in embarrassment. "Do you remember that first night back at my apartment?"

Oh no.

"You know, when we first..." the fox trailed off.

Please don't say it.

"You were really interested in that painting I had."

Son of a motherfucking bitch.

"So, I thought since you were so into art, you might enjoy this."

Well, shit.

In a way, it was actually really sweat. It had been such a small, inconsequential detail of their night together, and Jonas had remembered it. More than that, he'd planned an entire evening around something he thought the tiger might enjoy. That actually spoke to something deeper, and, for the first time, Trey realized that this was more than about sex for Jonas. The fox actually liked him.

Trey decided to a put a pin in that thought, however, because, unfortunately, the fox had wildly misinterpreted the situation. Trey hadn't been staring at the painting on Jonas's wall because he was interested in art. He'd been staring at it because he'd been mentally comparing how nice Jonas's place was to his own. Trey's walls were covered in posters devoted to movies and video games.

Of course, it was too late to correct the fox's assumption. Or, at the very least, now wasn't the time. So, Trey said, "Oh...that's really nice of you," as he tried to process his conflicting emotions.

"So, what style of art do you prefer?" Jonas asked, glancing around. "I've always really liked surrealism. I think Rene Magritte is my favorite."

Trey tried to swallow and found his mouth suddenly very dry. "Oh, you know," said the tiger, his voice a bit thin, "hard to choose."

"Well, what area do you want to start in?"

"You know, I think I'll just wander and look around," Trey said, trying to keep a polite smile on his face.

"Oh," Jonas said. His tone sounded a bit hurt, and Trey found himself opening his mouth to confess everything right then and there. But, before he could, Jonas just shrugged and said, "Okay. I'm going to grab some champagne and wander a bit too. Meet me over in the impressionism section in a little bit?"

"Sure, sure," Trey said, his smile verging on manic now. He turned away from the fox and stiffly walked towards the least populated area he could find. Turning a corner, Trey leaned against the wall and clutched his paw to his chest. Oh, God, what was he doing?

Trey took a deep breath and tried to relax. He had no idea what was going on here. It was like he'd been stranded on another planet. Except, he'd actually have some idea what to do in that situation, since it typically involved fighting aliens with laser pistols and flamethrowers.

He knew what he needed to do. He would go back out there, find Jonas, and explain that he knew absolutely nothing about art. He'd tell the fox that it had all been one big misunderstanding but that he really appreciated the gesture. Then, they'd go back to Jonas's place and have sex. Maybe afterwards, they could find something they actually had in common and could both enjoy.

Trey pushed off from the wall, intent on this new plan of action, when he spotted something. There was a small collection of paintings nearby that no one else seemed to be paying attention to. It was one painting in particular that caught his attention, however.

The painting showed a lion in a chariot, his mane billowing behind him as he raised a hammer high into the air. Lightning forked down from the sky, and various figures seemed to be falling before the lion's attack. The style of the painting was odd, and there had certainly been some artistic liberties taken with the outfit, but it was clearly a painting of Thor.

Next to it was another painting of a nude wolf, bound in chains. A female deer stood next to the wolf holding a basin and collecting something dripping from the mouth of a snake. Trey had no idea who the deer was or what the snake was about. But, despite his shorter hair, the wolf on the ground was clearly Loki.

There were other paintings here, too, but Trey didn't recognize the figures in them. For a moment, he wondered if he was mistaken. He moved closer to the painting of Thor and peered at it. No, that had to be him.

"A fan of Winge, are you?" asked a gruff voice.

Trey turned to spot an old grizzly bear dressed in a tux and leaning heavily on a cane. The bear's fur was patchy and almost solid gray in areas, but there was still a hint of brown here and there. Trey had no idea what the bear meant, so he just smiled.

"Not too many people still interested in the old boy's work," said the bear. "Very classical in his style."

"Oh, um, yeah, very classical," Trey agreed with a nervous smile. "I was just looking at this picture of…Thor?"

"Ah, so it's the old legends you're a fan of, is it?" said the bear. "Yes, mighty Thor and his hammer."

"Mjolnir," Trey supplied, feeling on slightly more stable ground now.

"Quite right," said the bear, impressed.

"It's a bit of a strange design," Trey said gesturing towards the paintings. "Same for this one of Loki."

"Ah, yes, not quite how I pictured them myself," agreed the bear. "Always nice to meet a young person interested in the classics, though. Tell me: what draws a young man such as yourself to the story of Thor?"

That seemed like an odd question to Trey. Most people probably weren't familiar with the comics, and, when Trey was younger, he'd had a difficult time finding anyone else interested in superheroes. But now that the movies had come out, everyone knew about characters like Thor.

Then again, maybe that was just on the internet and in Trey's own circle of fellow geeks and nerds. The bear was old, after all. Did he even own a computer? It was hard to guess anymore, though Trey had a hard time picturing anyone who wasn't plugged in one way or another.

"Well, I mean, Thor's pretty cool," Trey said. "He's got the hammer and can summon lightning. And, there's the whole mystical realm of Asgard with everyone flying around. I wasn't personally a big fan of the romance part, but I guess that's what sells."

"Romance?" asked the bear, confused. "Ah, I see. You're more a fan of the action."

"Oh yeah," Trey said, feeling more at ease. "The fight scenes are my favorite." Trey pointed to the painting of Thor. "I mean, this is okay, but kind of tame."

"Ah, you prefer the works with a bit more blood, do you?" asked the bear.

"Well, not necessarily that," Trey said hastily. "Just…I don't even recognize this scene. And, it's weird that there's just a painting of Thor and Loki here. You'd at least think there'd be a few of Iron Fox and Captain America."

The bear frowned at that, confused. "Ah, I'm sorry. What was that, young man?"

"I mean, I get they're popular," Trey continued obliviously, "but it seems weird not to include the other Avengers, you know?"

The bear stood there in silence, his bushy brows knit together in confusion. Before either he or Trey could say more, however, someone nearby started snickering.

Trey turned, following the sound. A white and brown rabbit, his ears pointing down, stood nearby holding a glass of champagne. He stood almost a full head taller than Trey and practically towered over the stooping figure of the bear. The rabbit's shoulders were quite broad, but the frame under his tux was clearly leaner than Trey's. His hair was either dark-brown or black and had been swept forward and gelled such that his bangs rose up like a wave.

"Oh, Peters, you doddering old fool," said the rabbit, addressing the bear.

The bear seemed to hesitate, his body language suggesting he didn't wish to engage this new figure. Nevertheless, he turned towards the rabbit and said, "Ah, young Master Quilt. How good to see you again."

"Looks like the senility has finally set in, huh?" Quilt said, taking a drink from his champagne.

"Ah, you'll find I'm still quite sharp, Master Quilt," Peters replied casually, but the bear's expression seemed troubled by the comment.

"Wouldn't be so sure of that," Quilt said, "not given the company you're keeping." The rabbit eyed Trey, his critical gaze traveling up and down the tiger. Trey had no doubt the rabbit was fully aware of every imperfection in the tiger's outfit.

The bear gestured towards Trey. "Ah, this young man and I were just having an enlightening conversation about Norse mythology," Peters replied.

"Think again," Quilt said sardonically. The rabbit turned to Trey, the look in his eyes making it clear that even addressing the tiger was beneath him. "Since you're such an expert on art, could you tell us when this was painted?" he said, gesturing to the painting of Thor.

"Oh, um…" Trey said trailing off. There was something very cruel in the rabbit's gaze, and Trey had a terrible feeling he wasn't going to like the answer.

"Try reading the plaque on the bottom," Quilt said with a sneer.

Trey looked at the painting of Thor and noticed there was a small gold plaque long the bottom of the frame. The text printed on it was small, and he had to lean in to read it, but he saw now that it clearly listed the name of the painting, the artist, and…the date. The date said 1872.

Quilt laughed as he saw the tiger's eyes widen. Peters just looked between them both, confused. "Master Quilt, I'm really not sure—" Peters began, but Quilt cut him off.

"This slob doesn't know anything about art, Peters," Quilt said. "He's been talking about a movie this entire time."

"Movie?" Peters said, looking at Trey.

"Barely even that," Quilt said. "Certainly not fine cinema. It's mindless drivel manufactured for the idiot masses. The poor things save up their pennies to visit the theater, too stupid to realize they're being shown garbage."

Trey's ears turned red in embarrassment. The old bear was looking at him with confusion but also disappointment. Grimacing, Trey turned to leave, determined to find Jonas and get the hell out of here.

As if summoned by the thought, the fox suddenly rounded the corner. "Hey, there you are," Jonas said with an excited yelp, smiling as he spotting Trey and walking towards him. "You never showed up."

Trey moved quickly towards Jonas, gently grabbing the fox's arm and turning him around. "We should go," Trey said, trying to lead Jonas away.

"Huh, what?" Jonas asked, his lean body twisting as he tried to look over his shoulder at the rabbit and bear.

"Oh, how cute," Quilt called after them. "Our art connoisseur has a little friend."

Jonas struggled and managed to slip out of Trey's grip. The fox spun back around to look at Peters and Quilt. "What's going on?" said the fox with a frown.

"Oh, not bad," Quilt said, eyeing Jonas's suit, "certainly a step up. Hmm, but still a bit on the low end. I suppose trash can only do so well. Garbage in a suit is still just garbage, after all."

Trey had been struggling to grab back ahold of Jonas, but he suddenly stopped, his brawny form going still. Jonas was looking back and forth between Quilt and Trey, the fox's muzzle open slightly as he let out a surprised, high-pitched bark. Standing off to the side Peters just shuffled uncomfortably.

Quilt was smiling, a look of superiority on his face. It was a look that quickly faded when Trey turned around. The tiger was walking towards him—no, stalking towards him with a dark look on his face and his tail lashing back and forth angrily. Trey's shoulders were hunched, and his muscles seemed to stand out in sharp relief. Despite being taller than the tiger, Quilt was suddenly afraid.

Quilt took a step back as the tiger approached, raising his free paw to ward off an attack. Trey didn't take a swing at him, however. Instead, the tiger snatched the champagne from the rabbit's other paw and splashed the drink right into Quilt's face.

Sputtering in shock, the rabbit looked down at his ruined suit and back up at Trey. "How dare you—" began the rabbit.

Trey grabbed the front of Quilt's suit and pulled him down and forward so they're faces were level and only an inch apart. "If you ever insult my boyfriend again," Trey said quietly, "I'll show you what real art is by painting the walls with your face."

The rabbit blinked, opened his mouth to say something, met the tiger's gaze, and closed his mouth again. A long, tense moment passed and then Trey let go of the rabbit. Quilt stumbled back, his nose twitching slightly in fear. He glanced at Peters, but the old bear just had a paw over his muzzle. There was a gleam in the bear's eyes, however, that made Quilt suspect Peters was laughing behind that paw.

Trey turned and walked towards Jonas, pausing briefly when he reached the fox's side. "We're leaving," Trey said evenly. Then Trey disappeared around the corner.

Jonas stared after the tiger, and then looked back at the scene he'd left behind. "Uh, nice meeting you," Jonas said to the rabbit and bear before he turned and quickly scampered after Trey.

An awkward silence hung in the car as Jonas drove Trey back to his apartment. The tiger had uttered only four words when they'd reached the car, "Please take me home," and had said nothing else since.

When they'd finally reached Trey's place, the tiger just sat there, staring down. By this point, Jonas was starting to get worried, but he wasn't sure what to say. Something had happened back at the art gallery, but he wasn't really clear on what. It seemed the longer the silence stretched on, the harder it was to speak.

It was Trey who finally broke the silence, looking up to meet the fox's gaze. "Can I show you something in my apartment?" Trey said.

Normally, Jonas would have made a suggestive comment at that, but he tamped down that response. From the tiger's tone, it was clear he wasn't inviting Jonas up for sex. "Sure," Jonas said, trying to smile.

Trey just looked at him with an unreadable expression and then got out of the car. The tiger led Jonas up a flight of stairs and to the front door of his apartment. Trey paused here as though he was contemplating something. "Trey, is everything—" Jonas started to say.

"I want to show you something," Trey said, interrupting him. The tiger unlocked his front door and turned on the light as he walked in. Jonas was right behind him.

The apartment was…Jonas wasn't sure he had words for it. Most of the living room was taken up by an entertainment center and a computer desk. A large, flat screen TV sat atop the entertainment center. A computer screen almost as big as the TV sat on the desk. There were colorful, plastic cases scattered everywhere that looked like the kind DVDs came in. Beneath the entertainment center were multiple electronics and a nest of tangled cords.

Posters dotted the walls, many showcasing brightly colored images. Most seemed to be for movies that Jonas had never heard of. There was one entire bookshelf devoted entirely to DVDs and another full of magazines—no, Jonas realized, they were comic books. There were some regular books there too, but they were greatly outnumbered.

Trey said nothing. The tiger just sat down on an old couch, the fabric worn and threadbare in places. The entire thing seemed to sag under his weight. Leaning forward, Trey rested his elbows on his knees and stared down at the floor.

"Um, what did you want to show me?" Jonas said, glancing

around the room bewildered.

Trey sighed. "This," said the tiger, looking up. "This room. Me."

Jonas shuffled his feet nervously. "I'm not sure I—"

"I don't know anything about art," Trey said. "I was looking at that painting because...I don't even know anymore. I just was. But, this is the kind of stuff I like. Superheroes. Video games. Comic books. Ever been to a comic book convention? Or a sci-fi con? I've been to dozens. I think tonight is the first time I've ever set foot in an art gallery. Maybe I went to one on a school field trip once. I honestly don't remember."

"Oh," Jonas said, frowning. "I'm sorry. I didn't realize—"

"You don't have anything to apologize for," Trey said. "I actually thought it was nice. That you thought it was something I'd enjoy, I mean. But..." Trey looked at Jonas, the tiger's expression lost. "Do you know what any of this is?" he said, gesturing around the room.

Again, Jonas glanced around the room with uncertainty. "Oh, hey, um, that movie," he said, pointing at a poster. "It's part of some big superhero thing, right? I think I saw one of them."

"Which one?" Trey asked, perking up slightly.

"Um..." Jonas grimaced as he tried to remember. "I actually don't know. I...I wasn't that into it."

Trey sagged back onto the couch. "Ah."

"Okay. What's this all about?" Jonas said, walking around the tiger to sit next to him on the couch. "I mean we don't— Um, hold on." Jonas frowned as he realized he'd sat on something. He reached down and pulled up something shiny and black. "Uh, is this some kind of dildo?"

Trey stared at the fox. "It's a controller." The fox's expression remained blank, so Trey elaborated. "A video game controller?"

"Oh," Jonas said twisting it about in his nimble paws. "I guess...Oh, okay. I guess I see. Shouldn't there be a cord?"

"It's wireless," Trey said, frowning. "You've never seen a video game controller? Have you ever even played a video game?"

"Oh, um, Pac-Man?" Jonas said sheepishly. "Oh wait, actually I remember. When I was a kid, I had a friend that had one of those video game systems. I really like Mario."

Feeling wary but hopeful, Trey said, "Oh, well, okay. I actually have some downloads of older games. Which Mario games do you like?"

Jonas blinked. "There's more than one?"

"Please tell me you're joking."

Jonas set the controller down on the floor and then pulled one leg up on the couch so he could turn and face the tiger. "I don't understand," Jonas said, confused. "Why does it matter?"

"It doesn't. I mean, not just this," Trey said, letting out a frustrated sigh. "It's...everything. We're just...different."

"So?" Jonas said

"So, we have nothing in common!" Trey snapped. He immediately regretted the outburst when he saw Jonas flinch. "I'm sorry," the tiger said, his voice softer as he reached out to put a paw on Jonas's knee. "It's not your fault. It's just not been a great night."

Jonas looked away. He was a little hurt by that, but did his best not to dwell on it. "We don't have to go to any more art galleries," Jonas said, turning back to the tiger. "We could go to a play, or a restaurant, or..." the fox trailed off. Trey was already shaking his head.

"Jonas," said the tiger, "I've never seen a play outside of high school. And this," he said gesturing at his current outfit, "is the nicest thing I own." Trey popped off the clip-on tie and threw it on the floor. "You think they'd even let me into a fancy restaurant wearing this? You're missing the point."

Jonas let out a little high-pitched bark as he started to become frustrated himself. "What point? What is this all about?"

"That it was one thing when it was just sex," Trey said. He gave the fox's knee a little squeeze before removing his paw and leaning back. "But this...You want more. Don't you? I mean, asking me out on a date? Trying to get me to go to a play or dinner with you? I like you, I do. But I think you're trying to go somewhere with this, and I just don't see how it's supposed to work. What do you enjoy? What do you do for fun?"

"I don't know," Jonas said helplessly. "Yes, I like art galleries and museums and plays and fancy restaurants. But, I like other stuff too. I like to stay in and read sometimes."

"Somehow, I don't think you read comic books," Trey said. "And, I spend a lot of my time either at the gym or playing video games. I like super hero movies. I also spend way, way too much time online. How is this supposed to work? Actually, before we even get to that, you never answered my question. Are you wanting something more?"

Jonas wrung his paws together in his lap and curled his tail around himself. He hadn't let himself think too deeply about it. He'd just gone with what felt natural, which had involving asking the tiger to spend time with him. "I missed you when we weren't talking," he said slowly. "I kept thinking about how I wanted to see you again. And, yeah, a big part of it was about sex." A ghost of a grin touched the fox's muzzle. "But, I guess, yeah, I thought maybe it could be more."

Trey nodded sadly. "It really was sweet that you tried. I was actually kind of surprised you even remembered me looking at that painting in your apartment. But, I mean, look around," Trey said waving his paw at the room around them. "Even our apartments…I don't think we fit."

They both sat in silence for a few moments while the words sank in. Jonas glanced around the room searching for anything familiar, but everything here felt so foreign. He didn't know it, but the thought he had now was the very same one Trey had had while in the art gallery. He felt like was stranded on another planet.

Jonas frowned. "*Star Wars*," he said suddenly.

Trey blinked in surprise. "What?"

"*Star Wars*," Jonas repeated. "I like it."

Cautiously, Trey asked, "Which ones?"

Jonas made a face. "Oh, I didn't like when they started making the new ones. Too flashy. But, the first three, I liked."

Careful not to get too excited, Trey leaned forward a little.

"Really? So, you like science fiction?"

Jonas's expression was pensive. "It's not so much that. But, the movies are kind of like an opera. Minus all the singing, obviously. But, love triangles and long-lost family members with big dramatic showdowns and battles? That's basically what operas are all about."

"Oh. Huh, I guess I didn't realize," Trey said, thoughtfully. "I've never been to an opera. I really like *Star Wars* too. The original ones. I thought I just liked it because of all the sci-fi stuff, but I guess I liked the opera parts too."

"Well, with operas, a lot of times they're in other languages, but even if you don't know all the words, you get the gist of what's going on. Maybe we could go see one?"

Trey was hesitant. "Well, maybe…You said you like to read? What kind of books do you like?"

"Oh, um, I really liked *The Lord of the Rings* and *The Chronicles of Narnia* when I was a kid."

Surprised, Trey said, "Really? You know they made movies out of those. I have the DVDs."

"Oh yeah, I kind of remember that," Jonas said. "I think I wanted to see them but never got around to it." The fox gave Trey a hopeful smile. "Maybe you could show me them?"

"Heh, well, I guess if you're willing to sit through three four-hour long movies with me, I could sit through an opera."

Jonas's eyes widened. "They're four hours long?"

Trey chuckled. "*The Lord of the Rings* ones are. Extended release version. But, hey, you said you read those when you were a kid. What do you like to read now?"

Jonas looked embarrassed. "You'll laugh."

"Is it trashy romance novels?" Trey asked with a grin.

"No, it's…" Jonas hesitated. Then, in a small voice he said, "I like detective novels."

Trey just nodded. "Hey, that's kind of cool."

"Really?" Jonas asked. "Most people I've talked to consider them schlock."

Trey shrugged. "Actually, if you like that kind of thing, I have a couple of detective video games."

"That's a thing?" Jonas asked, confused. "I thought video games were more…I don't know, shooting and jumping?"

Trey chuckled again. "Well, a lot of them are, yeah. But, some are more about puzzle solving and talking to people. Sometimes you have to figure out the right questions to ask them or remember things they said. Or, you have to search an area for clues. Basically, you are the detective."

"Oh, wow," Jonas said, genuinely intrigued by the concept. "That actually sounds like a lot of fun."

"I could show you one," Trey said standing up.

Jonas reached out and grabbed the tiger's sinewy arm before he could move away. "Actually, I was wondering if you could show me something else first."

"What's that?"

Jonas looked up at the tiger. "Your bedroom," said the fox slyly, a slow grin spreading across his muzzle.

Trey was confused by Jonas's request for a full second before the fox's meaning dawned on him. He returned Jonas's grin and leaned over the still sitting fox. "I suppose we could start there," Trey said.

Jonas started to stand, but the tiger suddenly reached down and lifted the fox up. "Whoa," Jonas barked, his eyes going wide in astonishment. Trey cradled the fox in his powerful arms, and Jonas couldn't help but smile as the effortless way the tiger carried him.

Trey carefully navigated them around a corner and into his bedroom. Jonas had a brief impression of more posters on the walls and some slightly roughed-up furniture before Trey set him gently on the bed. Then, all of Jonas's focus was on the tiger as Trey leaned down and kissed him.

Jonas ran his paws over the tiger's thick arms and chest. He was already getting hot in his suit, but Jonas didn't want to take his paws off Trey's body. Trey slipped his tongue into Jonas's muzzle and the fox felt his cock start to stiffen.

Trey let out a little growl before breaking the kiss and standing back up. Shrugging off his blazer and unbuttoning his shirt, the tiger nodded towards Jonas's suit. "There are way too many buttons on that thing. You'll have to either take it off yourself, or,"—Trey undid his pants and let them and his boxers fall, revealing his already thickening cock—"I'm going to rip it off you."

Jonas felt himself go from semi-hard to fully erect. "Maybe, I'd like that," Jonas said slyly.

Trey raised an eyebrow. "Oh?"

For moment Jonas honestly considered letting the tiger rip the suit off him. Then, he remembered how much he'd paid for it. "Okay, well maybe not rip it off me," he said quickly as he undid his tie and began tossing each piece of his suit to the floor. "But maybe you could be a little...rough?" he asked shyly.

Trey blinked. "Oh! Well, I've never...but I could try."

"I promise I'll say if it's too much," Jonas said. He was now completely naked on Trey's bed. The tiger bent down, reached under the bed, and pulled out an old shoe box, the lid flipping open. Trey pulled out a bottle of lube and started to close the box, but not before Jonas spotted something. "That is definitely not a video game controller," Jonas said, raising an eyebrow.

Trey grinned. "Still just as fun to play with. Maybe next time I'll show you. But, right now..." Trey paused and then in a more commanding voice, he said, "Roll over."

Jonas's eyes widened a little and his cock twitched. He rolled onto his stomach and lay flat on the bed. A moment later, he felt Trey's powerful paws grab his hips and lift him up, forcing his ass into the air.

"Raise your tail," Trey commanded. There was a slight warble in the tiger's voice as he tried to make himself sound harsher. Part of him thought he sounded silly doing this, but Jonas seemed to be getting into it.

Jonas lifted his tail and felt a little shiver run through him as he exposed his hole. A thought occurred to him as he realized the position he was in and what he'd asked for. "Ah, just, maybe go slo—oh!" Jonas let out an exclamation of surprise as he felt the tiger's tongue run across his hole.

Trey gently lapped at the puckered flesh, his tongue working around the edges of Jonas's hole before plunging into the center. Jonas squirmed a little, but Trey grabbed the base of the fox's upraised tail and yanked it up.

Jonas let out a little gasp, and, for a moment, Trey thought he had pulled too hard. "Don't stop," Jonas said, his voice slightly strained.

Trey kept his grip on the fox's tail as he continued to probe his tongue into Jonas's hole. Occasionally, he would slide lower and lick the underside of the fox's balls, but he always returned to the soft, vulnerable flesh just beneath Jonas's tail.

Jonas was dripping now, his cock leaking precum onto the worn comforter. His head was down, his face pressed into the bed as he moaned into the fabric. He felt Trey release his tail, grab his cheeks, and spread them apart as far as they would go. A moment later, the tiger's muzzle was practically buried in his ass, working his hole with surprising vigor.

Jonas whined and panted into the comforter. He didn't think he could take it any longer and was about to reach for his own cock when he felt Trey pull back. Slick fingers replaced the tiger's tongue and began gently worked Jonas's opening. Lube and spit mixed as the fingers slid inside him.

Then, the fingers disappeared and Jonas felt the bed dip as Trey took position behind him. Jonas started to lift his head when he felt the tiger's paw on the back of his neck, forcing him down. "Stay," Trey ordered. The tiger leaned over the fox, Trey's massive bulk completely covering Jonas's smaller frame. Trey's muzzle came down to gently whisper into Jonas's ear. "You still okay?"

Jonas couldn't help but smile at the tiger's slightly worried tones. "Yeah, keep going," Jonas said.

Trey straightened up, positioned himself, and pushed his hips forward, the tip of his cock slipping just inside Jonas. Despite Jonas's insistence, Trey tried to move slowly, his cock carefully sliding into the fox.

Jonas didn't wait. He wiggled his hips and pushed back, letting out a gasp as the tiger's entire erection filled him. Trey froze at the sound, suddenly unsure. But Jonas swallowed as he felt himself adjust around Trey's dick and repeated, "Keep going."

Still hesitant, Trey started rocking his hips slowly. Jonas was tight around him, so Trey tried to keep his thrusts slow and shallow. Jonas didn't let up, however, the fox pushing back with each thrust, impaling himself on the tiger, and urging Trey on.

Encouraged, Trey grabbed both of Jonas's hips and began to pound into the fox harder. With each push, his hips slammed into Jonas's backside, making a steady slapping sound. If Trey had any doubt Jonas was enjoying this, he only had to listen to the sounds the fox was making. Jonas could barely speak, the only words Trey could make out being, "Yes! Yes!" The rest were gasps, moans, and half-formed syllables.

Throughout it all, Jonas's cock remained untouched, though it was still leaking a steady stream of precum. Feeling mischievous, Trey released his grip on one of Jonas's hips and reached down to very lightly caress the fox's length. Jonas whined and his hips bucked slightly, prompting Trey to lean forward and push the fox's head down again. With his cock fully sheathed inside Jonas's hole, Trey stopped thrusting and once more reached under the fox. Gently, he stroked a finger from the tip of Jonas's cock down to his balls. The fox's entire body shuddered, but he was effectively trapped, barely able to move. Feeling Jonas's hole clench around his length, Trey flexed his cock a few times inside the fox.

Jonas's entire body was shaking now. His own cock was twitching constantly, begging for release as it pumped out an obscene amount of precum. And still, Trey held him down and only gently traced a finger along the fox's length.

"Please," Jonas finally begged, "cum in me."

Trey pulled back and straightened up, some of his length slipping out of the fox's hole. The tiger put both his paws back on Jonas's hips and yanked the fox backwards, forcing Jonas's ass to slam into Trey's hips and the tiger's cock to once again fully slide inside the fox.

The force of being pulled back so suddenly was enough

that Jonas's top half was momentarily airborne. But, before the fox could fall back to his paws, Trey's large arms slid around Jonas's middle and pulled him up straight.

When they were both on their knees, Trey wrapped one arm around Jonas's chest to hold the fox against him. His other arm circled Jonas's hip, the tiger's paw grabbing and beginning to stroke the fox's hard length. Jonas moaned and arched his back, reaching up and using both paws to grab onto the arm around his chest.

Trey held on to the fox tightly, his muzzle buried in Jonas's neck fur. Trey began to once again pump his hips harder and harder, the feel of Jonas's body against his and the tight warmth of the fox's hole pushing the tiger to the edge. Trey breathed in Jonas's scent and found his cock swelling even more. A sudden urge overtook him, and Trey opened his muzzle and gently bit the space between the fox's neck and shoulder.

Jonas's immediately let out a high-pitched cry of pleasure. Trey's paw furiously pumped at the fox's erection, and Jonas's entire body shivered as he felt the tiger's dick go rock hard inside him. The thrusts deepened until Trey's length was fully buried inside Jonas, and the tiger let out a long, deep groan. Jonas felt Trey's cock twitch inside him, followed quickly by a spreading warmth.

Trey bit down harder as he shot load after load inside Jonas, the fox's tight hold milking him for all he had. The tiger felt his balls draw up tight as the last of his cum pumped out of him and his entire body spasmed with the wave of his orgasm. His arm still tightly wrapped around Jonas, he felt the fox suddenly stiffen and let out a wordless cry.

The feel of Trey's teeth on his neck had sent the fox over the edge. With both paws still holding onto Trey's arms, Jonas came hard into the tiger's paw. The first few shots went wide, long ropes of sticky, white seed flying from his cock and spreading out across the comforter. The rest dripped down to coat Trey's paw.

Trey gently released Jonas's neck but kept his arms firmly wrapped around the fox's body. They were both breathing hard, their hearts hammering in their chests. When he finally caught his breath, Trey said, "Here, lay down on your side." Slowly, his length still fully inside the fox, he guided them both down onto the wet comforter.

Jonas pressed his back to the tiger's broad chest and felt Trey slip his arms back around the fox's body. Laying there, Jonas could feel the tiger's heartbeat against him, and, for a few seconds, he forgot about everything but how good it felt to have Trey holding him like this.

Trey started to pull his hips back, but Jonas reached back and grabbed the tiger's hips. "Wait," Jonas said with a little gasp. "Just stay there, please."

Trey gently licked the spot on Jonas's neck where he'd bitten the fox. "Okay," whispered the tiger. They lay there, not speaking for several minutes. Jonas closed his eyes and let himself just enjoy the feel of the tiger holding him while Trey continued to lick and softly nuzzle the fox's neck.

Finally, Jonas said, "I think I ruined your comforter."

Trey let out an amused snort. "Don't worry about it. It'll dry." Trey took a deep breath, inhaling the fox's scent. "Maybe it'll smell like you."

"Heh, I came a lot," Jonas said. "The biting was a surprise."

"Good surprise, or bad surprise?" Trey asked nervously.

"Oh, definitely a good surprise," Jonas said, giving Trey's arms a little squeeze. "I wasn't expecting it. But, it was nice."

"I'm not used to being like that," Trey said, tensing up a little. "I mean, I'm glad you enjoyed it, but I hope you don't think—"

"Hey, hey, it's cool," Jonas said. "In case you forgot, I like seeing big guys like you on your back sometimes. I had just as much fun being on top. I'm not expecting some big, brutal dom."

"Sorry," Trey said relaxing. "It's just some guys…because of my size…"

"No, I get it," Jonas said. There was a brief pause, and then slowly, Jonas said, "There is something I've been wanting to ask you, though."

Trey's ear's perked up. "Okay?"

"It's about that rabbit at the gallery."

Trey groaned. "Well that's killed the mood."

Jonas chuckled. "It's not so much about him, but...I thought I heard some of what you said to him."

Trey's expression turned sour. "I really doubt that. If you had, you wouldn't have come home with me."

"Well based on the way you grabbed him, I figured it was a threat. But...I thought I heard you say 'my boyfriend.'"

"Oh, I—" They both grunted as Trey's softening cock slipped out of Jonas, interrupting the conversation. Trey released his grip on the fox and Jonas lifted himself up and rolled over so that they were facing each other.

Jonas reached out and trailed his fingers through Trey's chest fur. Face to face, it suddenly felt harder to talk, but Jonas wasn't quite willing to let it go. "I thought about you a lot the past few weeks. Even after that first night, before I accidently told everyone about us, I knew I wanted to see you again. And then...with everything that happened, I thought I should give you space."

Trey sighed. "If I'm honest...I think I really hated you for a while," admitted the tiger.

Jonas tried his best not to wince at that. "I am really sorry—"

"It's okay," Trey said, reaching out to stroke the side of Jonas's muzzle. "I was angry at you. But, I know you tried to help. And, you did keep me from getting fired. I wasn't sure how to feel about you after that. And tonight..."

Jonas gave the tiger a little half smile. "I promise, no more art galleries."

Trey shrugged. "I don't know. Maybe I could get into it. But...not so fancy? Like, no suits and ties?"

Jonas nodded. "What if we just took things slow?" said the fox. "In general."

Trey smiled. "I think I'd like that."

"Except...we can still have lots of sex, right?" said the fox hopefully.

The tiger grinned and leaned forward, giving Jonas a kiss. "How about you stay over tonight and watch one of those movies I was telling you about. And then...."

"And then?" Jonas asked, licking his lips.

"I actually have more than one shoe box under my bed," Trey said with a smirk.

It was a long movie, but an even longer night.

GHOSTED
Lou Treblé

Lou Treblé is an ottaur (i.e. horny otter) who appreciates coffee, epistolary narrative, parentheticals, and brevity (except of course when [content redacted]).

January 12, 2017

Dear Horten,

Hello! I found your profile on Pen Paws and would like to start writing to each other. I notice that we live in the same city; how strange that we have never met before!

Allow me to introduce myself: My name's Kit. I'm a fox. I live on the west side of town. I work at a local coffee shop, I speak French fluently (I majored in it at college), and I love to read Victorian English literature. For fun, I like to go downtown to rival coffee shops, and I like to play Galaga at the arcade—I've even got the high score there! Of course, I enjoy many other things that aren't quite as "niche." I know people sometimes use Pen Paws to find mates. In the interest of full disclosure—although I would be open to finding a mate—I really just joined because writing letters has always fascinated me, and I hoped I would make some friends in the process. Regardless, since we live in the same city, I am definitely interested in meeting in person sometime!

I hope you'll write back to me and tell me a little bit about yourself!

Sincerely,
　Kit

Hey Kit,

So yeah, that's so crazy that we live in the same city, and I can't believe we never met before because I go downtown all the time. I work at the antique shop just a block down from the arcade. You should definitely stop in sometime! And, yeah, I'd really love to meet up for some coffee, or preferably some craft beer!

Anyway, yeah, you found my profile, so you already know my name is Horten and I'm a lion. Let's see…I didn't go to college and have no plans to go, but I thought I should read and write more, so I signed up for the Pen Paws thing. Only been on there like a month, so I'm surprised I already got a letter—writing letters seems so weird and old fashioned, but it's kind of cool. I repair and sell antiques, so I kind of dig old-fashioned weird vintage things like that, haha. I live pretty much right outside downtown, so don't make it over to the west side a whole lot, but if you're around downtown, we should totally meet up. We get a lot of antique cameras at the shop, so one of my hobbies is vintage photography so…I'm sending along a polaroid of me, haha. Also, a lot of the antiques I work with have French names, so I'll probably ask you for help pronouncing some of them because I don't know any French. It's kind of embarrassing when customers ask about them and I have no idea how to say it.

So, yeah, write me back and send me a pic if you have any? Also, yeah I'm just looking for friends, but who knows what could happen right?

Horten

Dear Horten,

Thank you for your letter! I also like old-fashioned, vintage kinds of things too! I've even been into the antique shop you work at before, but it's been a few years; you probably didn't work there at that time.

Thank you also for the photograph of you. It's rare that people take pictures with film these days, and I definitely appreciate it tremendously! It's a good photograph; you're quite attractive, and I really like the nerdy James Dean look you've got in it...Leather jacket over bare fur and those suggestively low-waisted jeans...Let's just say the imagination wanders, and I've already put the photograph to good use, as it were...I have enclosed a photograph of me. It's not a genuine polaroid like yours—sadly I have no film cameras, but it's a hobby I would be interested in learning more about—so I'm sorry it's just a printout on glossy paper and not something more "authentic."

I will be downtown for sure next weekend; would you like to meet up at the coffee shop on Walnut & Main around 3:00 on Saturday the 28th? We could get some alcoholic beverages afterwards if you feel up for it!

I look forward to hearing from you again, and (hopefully) seeing you in the near future!

Yours,
        Kit

Kit,

Oh my God, were you implying that you pawed off to my picture? 'Cause I totally did the same with the one you sent, haha! You look so cute in this picture!! That scarf totally goes with your russet coat, and that smoldering grin you've got, haha—I love it. Makes my imagination wander too. I wouldn't mind tying you down to a bench with that scarf and going to town on your tail, haha. Yeah, we can definitely meet up for coffee at 3:00, but you better be ready to go out and get wastey-faced afterwards; I'm gonna take you to my favorite brewery after coffee. And then my second favorite. And my third, haha. I live near downtown, so you can crash at my place if we get too sloshy ;3.

It's been a helluva week, but I'm not gonna write about it so we have stuff to talk about when we meet up Saturday. Can't wait to see you cutie!

Xoxo Horten

Dear Horten,

Thanks again for a wonderful time on Saturday! I had a lot of fun talking to you at the cafe! And, I'm glad we decided to keep writing each other letters even though we exchanged phone numbers; it's really exciting to find somebody who shares my strange fascination with obsolete communication. And, it doesn't hurt that you also happen to be ridiculously attractive (and such a good kisser…When we left the coffee shop and you just grabbed me, squeezed my ass, and kissed me…wow). I also enjoyed the breweries you took me to; I usually don't drink that much, so I'm glad you let me stay at your place so I didn't have to drive after that (well, that's not the only reason I'm glad, of course; I thoroughly enjoyed making out with you and cuddling).

I know I told you that I was too drunk to have sex with you that night…but to tell the truth, I wasn't. I've just had some bad experiences with guys recently…so I wanted to wait until after at least the first date. There's been a long string of guys that I've gotten really attached to and really close to, and, as soon as we have sex, they block my phone number, block me on social media, just kind of completely ghosting me…Part of me is afraid that you'll end up ghosting me too, but…It's hard to explain. I just have a good feeling about you and think I can trust you…so I definitely want to see you again, and…I definitely want you in me, and soon! I recall you mentioning something about tying me to a bench with my scarf? You could do a hell of a lot more to me…if you still want to after the other night, that is. I guess that's one thing about us deciding to keep writing letters instead of texting—I just have to wait to find out instead of finding out instantly whether you're still interested or not. It's sort of like torture, but there's also a kind of solace in the silence and uncertainty between letters that perhaps we miss out on these days of instant communication.

God, leave it to me to start philosophizing when I get

horny. Anyway, I hope you write me back and still want to see me, because I could feel how hard and massive you were against my back when you were spooning around me, and I would love to take that in me.

Yours, truly,
 Kit

KIT!

There you are! Haha, took you a few days to write me, and I know we said to write each other, but God it's been hard not to just text you. I've been checking my mailbox like three times a day since you left. YES I want to see you again!! Even without sex, that was the best night I've had all year. Just getting to hang out with you was quite simply awesome. As I kinda mentioned at the coffee shop, the last year was pretty shitty for me, and you made me smile bigger than I have in such a long time. You're also funny as Hell which is a big plus; omg, when we were at that first brewery and you spoke in that Norwegian accent to convince that annoying guy you didn't know any English so he'd leave us alone! I died, haha! And, don't worry, I promise I literally will never ghost you, even if things don't look like they'll work out, but I think they will.

But, yeah, haha, I was pretty hard that whole night, and, yeah, I def rubbed my cock up against your back after you fell asleep before pawing myself off and going to sleep myself, haha. God, you're sexy though. I guess since we've decided we're not gonna text each other, how about we just go ahead and make plans for Valentine's Day next Tuesday? I mean, I guess we could go out for dinner or a movie or whatever, but we've already gotten coffee and drinks at a few different bars, so you might as well just come straight over to my place. How about, like, 7:00?

Say yes, sexy,
   Horten

p.s. Yeah I really mean it when I say it was fun even without sex, but obvs. if you come over again I'm defs gonna strip you naked and fuck you hard. Just so ya know ;3

February 06, 2017

Dear Horten,

Definitely a "yes" to Valentine's Day at 7:00! I'm glad that you enjoyed my company as much as I enjoyed yours; and I guess we've both had pretty rough years. You want to tell me about yours when I see you again? In any event, it looks like things can only get better for both of us! And, next time I will be happy to help you paw off (and more, of course). I've been thinking about that massive hunk of leonine meat you've got all week, and I can't wait to take it in my tailhole; it's been a while since I've taken anyone that way, so it'll be nice and tight for you...

The anticipation is killing me, waiting for these letters to arrive! It's only a few days in between, but it always feels like an eternity. I'm so used to getting immediate responses from other people via text messaging. I still like it, though, the waiting. I don't really get excited about text messages the same way I get excited about checking the mail and finding a letter from you. It's something physical, something...intimate. I also feel like there's something sort of magical about having physical copies of things, like letters and like your polaroid. Even though pretty much all digital communication is, at least in theory, permanently stored and filed on thousands of different servers for marketing and data mining purposes, somehow these physical letters feel less ephemeral and more everlasting, despite the fact that the material they're written on will one day deteriorate and vanish into nothing while the inaptly named "cloud" constantly shifts and moves and evolves so the data on it can theoretically last truly into eternity.

There I go getting philosophical again. In my defense, I'm horny as fuck right now. And, I really, really like you.

Can't wait to be yours,
    Kit

Kitkat,

Yeah, I'll tell you about my year if you really wanna hear about it...I kinda told you I'd lost a lot of friends and had some financial difficulties...Well, it's because I've been kinda struggling a lot with some serious drug addiction, but been clean for a few months now and just trying to get the pieces back together. I'll tell you more when I see you if you want, but either way, I just can't wait to see you and move forward in my life!! Also, next time I see you...I kinda plan to grab you and pull you close, lay a thick wet kiss on you, grab your paw, and guide it down my pants so you can feel my massive lion cock growing bigger and bigger as you stroke it...I'll pull your pants down, then mine, and push you back against my bed...lift your legs up in the air, spit on my dick and slide it right into your foxy tailhole, haha.

I'm sure you've picked up there's no philosophy from me when I'm horny, haha, but it's so damn cute when you do it...you can talk all the philosophy you want to me while I ram into your tight little foxpussy XD. But, yeah, horniness aside...I really, really like you too. I hope you coming into my life is a sign of things getting better, but from my own experience, I know that things can always get worse, haha. Just gotta take things one thing at a time, and right now, the thing I wanna take is you ;3.

Just in case this wasn't clear, very much expecting to abuse the Hell out of your hole on Valentine's Day, and for many, many more days to come after, I hope.

Horten

February 10, 2017

Dearest Horten,

Valentine's Day with you sounds like Heaven :-). I look forward to feeling your cock throb deep inside of me, and fully expect you to fill me up with hot lion cum from BOTH ends, so be prepared to deliver.

And, I'm very sorry to read that you've been going through so much hardship with drug addiction. From what you said at the cafe, I kind of thought that might have been what was going on, but wasn't certain. I'm here if you need any kind of moral support; I know that kind of problem can be difficult to talk to people about, but just know that I'll never judge you and I'll always give you a sympathetic ear...in addition to a couple other sympathetic orifices...Anyway, congratulations on being clean now! I'm sure we can think of a lot of fun and sexy ways to celebrate!

Valentine's Day is approaching soon, probably too soon for me to hear back from you between now and then. Once again, I'll have to just take solace in the silence and uncertainty until the 14th...so I'll just plan to see you then, handsome!

Almost yours,
    Kit

My Dearest Horten,

I don't even know how to begin processing last week. I guess that's why I'm writing this, just to kind of sort through my own thoughts…so, here goes, I guess.

I pretended to be upset with you when you broke our "no texting" rule on the 13th. I guess I should have made that more obvious that I wasn't really mad and was just teasing you. I was actually really excited, and, to be honest, I was about to break down and text you first, you just beat me to it. I couldn't wait to see you either. I mean, even though I pretended to be annoyed, I'm sure you figured out that I wouldn't have driven downtown with fifteen minutes notice if I hadn't wanted to see you just as badly as you wanted to see me.

By the time I got the brewery downtown, my cock was already hard and my heart was racing at a thousand beats per minute. That's the kind of anticipation we've built up with these letters, I guess, even if we broke it a day prematurely. And, God, you looked so handsome waiting outside, smoking a cigarette, wearing a tight t-shirt, skin-tight jeans, and, somehow, you made the nerdy fanny pack look sexy and masculine as Hell (and, yes, I noticed the bulge threatening to burst straight out of your skinny jeans). Shivers went down my spine when you took me by the paw and led me up to the bar. You ordered a beer for me, one of those IPA's you like (and I told you I hated). I drank it anyway as you rubbed the fur on the back of my head and breathed warm against my neck and into my perked up ears, telling me that things with me just felt perfect. They felt perfect with you too.

You held my paw, and yours felt so soft and warm against mine. Then, we kissed, and even though it was not for the first time, somehow it *felt* like the first time all over again. You must have noticed as you held me close to you that my cock was just as hard as yours, and you forever had my heart when you led me to the bathroom and started unzipping your jeans, pushing me down, not aggressively, but firmly, to greet your throbbing little (big!) lion. I sniffed it inquisitively, and began licking your tip thirstily, tasting the saline pre that was already leaking out. It wasn't long before your paws gripped the back of my head to hold it steady and you thrust your member down the back of my throat. My eyes bulged out, and I gagged a little, but I wanted it so bad I didn't push you away; instead, I wrapped all around your cock with my tongue, tightening it every time I felt your cock pulse and gently bobbing back and forth once your grip loosened enough to allow me. But, you didn't let me move too much; you wanted the control (and I wanted you to have it too), and so your thrusts and your firm grip on my head kept me in check.

I was lost in time, and this might have gone on for hours, or forever. More than likely, it was only a few minutes before your veiny pulsating organ shot load after load of your warm, sticky seed into my maw and down my throat. Like an expensive and rare aged whiskey, I had never tasted finer; I could have drunk your spunk all night and never been sated.

You pulled your pants up, and we left the bathroom. You paid for both of us at the bar and then led me out of the brewery. You asked if I wanted to come over to your place for more fun. God, I wanted to. But...I wanted the anticipation, that extra day, that little extra wait till Valentine's Day to make it all the sweeter. And, I wanted to tease you a little bit more. So I said no, not tonight, but you'll get a very special treat tomorrow at 7:00 like we planned; just like we have to do with the letters, we'll have to wait, just a little bit. You smiled and said that was fine, and then leaned in for a kiss. Another eternity of five minutes as I got lost in your scent and your tongue and your paws wandering down my spine, playing with my tail, squeezing here and caressing there, and all I could do was dissolve into you. At last, you pulled away, and with that leonine smirk, you said, "Hey, fuck you for getting me so light-headed when I'm about to drive home!" I laughed, just as hard as you, and then we kissed again, briefly, softly, sweetly, and said good night.

I raced home and straight to bed. I've never slept so well as I did after that, knowing the next day held even more excitement in store; Valentine's Day I would be yours and all yours. I drove to your house, timing it perfectly to arrive at 7:00. I knocked on your door, expecting to see you answer wearing nothing at all—or maybe some heart-patterned boxers. I knocked again, and no answer came. I texted you, breaking the rule myself this time, and waited. And waited. And knocked again. And waited.

And then I left. I tried calling you. Your phone apparently was no longer accepting incoming calls, at the subscriber's request. Had you really ghosted me? But what could I do? So, I went home. And went online, and saw the post on Facebook from the local news station.

```
Lion killed in car crash: Hor-
ten Llewellyn, say police, was
traveling at an excessive speed
away from the downtown area at
12:40 am...
```

You only drank one beer. I was with you—you weren't drunk. But, you were driving fast. Because you were excited about the next day, like I was, maybe? Did you just want to get home as fast as possible, want to go to sleep and not wake up until it was time to see me, just like I did? I guess. I don't know. I'll never know. I really don't know why I'm writing this, because you'll never get to read it. I might still send it, though. Even if you can never respond. Because I still find a kind of solace in the silence and uncertainty.

Forever yours,
Kit

CAGES AND JAGUARS
Kuroko

While we can probably blame Spellsinger and Disney's Robin Hood for Kuroko being a furry and a fox, respectively, there's no excuse for the way he tends to fox things up regularly. An unapologetic nerd and gamer, he lives in Montana with more animals than people.

Icon stepped out of the sedan and opened the trunk. Just a briefcase inside, unremarkable. A bit worn—old leather. After closing the trunk and blowing the driver a kiss, he turned to face the building and his assignment.

As an assistant at Kuroko's Finest, his job was quite simply to help customers unwind. Sometimes, that was just having a drink with them while they spoke of their troubles. Sometimes, it was holding them, cuddling into the night and morning, to give them relaxing, soothing sleep.

Neither of those were really his specialty, although being five feet even and lush-furred, he was quite good at cuddles. Cross foxes always had bright and distinctive markings. Sometimes poorly suited to discreet meetings, but, sometimes, when you really need to let go, a professional is what it takes, regardless of possible lapses in discretion.

One of those customers was his, today. Midafternoon on a Friday in late May, that time of day when the wage-slaves were counting minutes and trying to stay awake, dreaming of the warm air and sunshine and a cold beer or twelve. A good time for him to stroll into the skyscraper and up to the security desk.

"Hello, miss." The security guard gave him a bored glance, then a second, sharper one. Might have been the distinctive cross fox coloring, might have been the sleek silk dress, might have been the cockatiel crest of black hair, might have been the intensely blue eyes. Probably wasn't the cheerful smile, but hey, could happen. Foxes got attention for less. Something about a species-wide reputation for loving…fun—call it fun.

"I'm expected. Mister Étoile has me as his 3:30."

The security guard typed a few things into his console, then gave Icon another confused look. His general androgyny and the dress probably accounted for the, "Mister? Newton?" response.

A little grimace of distaste crossed the fox's face. "Icon, please. Mister Newton was my father, and he made some very poor choices when he named me. Would some ID help?" He set the briefcase on the guard's kiosk and opened it up. One ID card, all fields in order and, yes, there was an M in one particular spot. Not that the dress or wide-eyed smile was going to help. But, after some more scrutiny, the guard shrugged.

"Seems to be in order, and, yes, you're in for a 3:30. Take this visitor pass. Mister Étoile's office is on floor 86, to your left as you come out of the elevator. Do not lose that pass—the security systems are very picky."

Icon nodded and clipped the pass to the left shoulder strap of that slinky dress and made his way to the elevator.

The ride up was uneventful and isolated. No one else to join him or make small talk with. Plenty of time to muse over the briefing he'd had for this job.

"Your clients are Mr. and Mrs. Étoile, a combination of stress relief and…call it marriage therapy," Kuroko had explained. "They're not first-time customers, but their usual, Janice, is on holiday. Jaguar couple, high-power business folks, and they need someone they can kind of cut loose on. Expect sexual, and they've paid your fee for heavy S&M stuff. You're off for a week after this as they sometimes play pretty rough, but they also understand that you have to be able to walk out afterward. They've been informed of your do's and don't's, and your safeword, and, as long-time customers, they've been thoroughly vetted. Ah, and they left some things and instructions for you, as well."

The 'things' had included the dress he was wearing now, and the panties under it, and one more item under *those* as well. A shiny steel chastity cage, low profile, not a bulge to mar the smooth lines of the dress. It wasn't a real problem for him—he often wore one for his own amusement when he went out. The instructions weren't even all that ominous, though they might have been for someone less comfortable with this kind of play. Two days prior to the appointment, he'd started a repeated cycle of edging and stopping without release. They obviously wanted a very pent up fox on their hands, though to what end was still a mystery. Wouldn't be one for long.

Just thinking about it all was enough to make that little cage distinctly uncomfortable, and make him very, very sure that he wanted to get this party rolling. He took a deep breath as the elevator beeped his arrival on the 86th floor and he stepped out. Big hallways. Lush carpet. Wood-paneled walls and brass nameplates beside the doors. And, as promised, just to the left was *Samson Étoile, CFO*. He knocked twice, then waited.

There were a few moments of quiet, then a soft chime. A distinct 'clunk' as a lock disengaged, and he pushed the door open, stepping inside the office.

Large office, too. The same lush carpet that had him wanting to just take his shoes right off and luxuriate in the feel of it under his paws. One whole wall was nothing but a single seamless window, high enough up for sunlight and a sprawling view of the city. And seated behind a truly massive desk was one of his clients. Mister Étoile, certainly, the jaguar true to type: a solidly-built man, square-jawed, maybe a bit stocky, though, seated, it was hard to tell. Tie and waistcoat, tailored shirt, and the matching sports coat to finish the three-piece suit that was hanging on a hook beside the door. Short black hair and yellow eyes behind square-lensed glasses. An affectation— no one needed corrective lenses anymore—but there was still a peculiar sense of culture to them.

"Hm. Well, you're not Janice, but you're pretty enough in that dress. Set the briefcase down and come over here." His voice was soft, gentle almost, and calm. Not someone in a hurry. "Have a seat." He gestured at the desk, which had been cleared of paperwork. Recently, Icon supposed. However luxurious, this was a working office, with bookshelves, file cabinets, and almost certainly a console built into the desk.

Icon sat on the corner of the desk and crossed his legs. "Well, what can I do for you, sir? As I'm sure you know, we— I, will do whatever you like to help you relax."

Samson just grinned a little. "Is that so? Well, you're small enough to fit under the desk. Get down there and figure out a good way to relax me, then."

Not a bad way to start, really. Icon slide off the desk and crawled under it. Closed in, and flush to the floor, he'd be all but invisible to anyone not behind the desk. Which wasn't bad. Mister Étoile might have other appointments this afternoon.

Still, once he'd gotten comfortable on his knees, it was time to earn his pay. Fingers undid that belt, opened the fly of those trousers. Nothing worn underneath, but—"Oh wow. That's...thick," he murmured. It was, too—not overly long (and thankfully not barbed), but, God, almost as thick as his wrist. A few licks and a good deep breath told him things.

This male was going to be tough to swallow, but worth it. Maybe pent up or maybe just eager as a matter of course from the way he shivered when Icon ran his tongue from base to tip in one slow stroke. Well...help him relax, alright. The fox opened wide and started to suck. Careful of fangs, only lightly letting them touch, never catch, just slow and easy, up and down, bobbing an inch or so on that cock. He heard shuffled papers above, the low hum of a console coming to life. Then, a huff of breath as his sucking got results, a bead of salt-slick on his tongue. Not pent up, he decided, just excited.

He pushed forward to put his nose in the other male's fur and drew back quickly, fighting his gag reflex down to a quiet cough. This was going to be just as hard as he had thought.

"You've got three seconds to get your nose back there. And, keep it there." Just as quiet and deep, considerably less calm, that voice. A faint, hard edge to it. Not one to be disobeyed.

He slid forward again and gagged around that thick cock, pushing hard to get it in far enough to swallow, tears in his eyes. One of his hands tightened on the hem of his dress, the other rose to slide under the other male's shirt and splay fingers in that thick, white belly fur. He held it as long as he could, fighting that rebellious throat, but finally just couldn't stop. He had to pull back, coughing and choking, to catch his breath. He pushed right back on, back to place, nose in that thick fur, tongue out to lap at his balls.

"Well, that's disappointing. You couldn't hold it. Here, I suppose I'll help." A hand landed on his head, tangling in his hair, grabbing tight and holding him in place, cock in his spasming throat. The other hand curled up under, wrapping that big mitt around his throat as well. Gagging and choking helplessly for an eternal minute. There was some mercy in that hand as it pushed him away, giving just long enough to suck in a breath before dragging him back down, over and over, until finally he hung on tight, pulled him down hard, and poured jet after jet of cum down his throat. All he could do was swallow, hard.

As soon as that hand let go, Icon lurched back, coughing and sputtering, swallowing that spunk down, though some had drooled down his chin, splattering his lap. "Clean up your mess, fox," came the growl from above, and he set to lapping up, cleaning that still-stiff shaft.

Just as he was finishing, he heard the door open and shut, the muted thud of the lock securing, and hushed footfalls in the carpet. A new voice, lighter by an octave, just as calm and easy. "How's your last appointment coming, Sam?"

"He's...alright. Just cleaning up. Want to see?" More hushed steps, and then he saw a face. Much like Mister Étoile, a jaguar, leaner and lighter, but those same luminous yellow eyes. Black hair as well, a matched pair, but hers was worn long, curls and ringlets falling well past her shoulders.

"Oooh, very cute. Crying much? Have you been choking him?"

"How could I not? His throat's even tighter than yours. Alright, I'm clean enough, come out of there." The fox crawled out from under the desk, but stayed on his knees, giving a little stretch here and there. He could feel damp on his cheeks, too, there had been a lot of those choking tears.

"Have you checked him out to see if he did as asked?" she asked. "Suppose if he's one of the professionals, he did, but it never hurts to check." The lady (jaguaress?) leaned down and cupped a hand under his dress, feeling the bulge of that too-small cage for far longer than necessary, fondling and caressing, making him strain and throb in the confined space. "I guess he did. I'll bet silk panties were a real tough thing, sliding all smooth against you with every step."

Icon nodded, breath quicker and sharper after all those touches.

"I'll bet you want out of that thing, don't you?"

Another nod.

"Too bad. You're going to *hurt* for us before you get any pleasure." Not unexpected, but still…the fox's ears dropped, and a worried look crossed his face. He wasn't actually worried, but foxes had a type to play to, and he was both a very good actor and the kind of fox who relished the role.

The jaguar stood from his desk and undid his tie, waistcoat, shirt, stepping out of shoes and pants to stand bare. Somewhat older, with that stubborn bit of paunch that older males tend to get. Fit, though, muscles visible through short, dense fur. Icon heard something from behind him, and realized he'd been staring when the lady grabbed his wrists and started knotting them together behind him.

"What are we going to do with you? Well, you liked my husband's cock so much, I'd say it's only fair to give you more of it. And, it looked like you *enjoyed* crying, so we'll let you do more." Clearly, they'd studied his file as thoroughly as he had theirs. Whatever was going on with their own likes and desires, they were just as intent on giving him a good time as getting their own. Granted, a good time wasn't going to be easy on him at all.

Mrs. Étoile took the tail end of that rope and lifted, forcing him to lean forward, then stumble to his feet as she kept pulling. Bent over at the waist, hands up behind him in a position that his shoulders were not liking at all, he was suddenly aware of how damned short the dress was. Those panties were certainly showing behind him.

He squeaked in surprise when they were yanked down, and each foot lifted to let him step out of them. Any further protest was stifled by the wadded ball of silk being stuffed in his muzzle. "Drop those and you're going to be in a lot more trouble than for not keeping your nose where it belonged." Mr. Étoile's voice was amused more than harsh. That 'failure' of his had simply been part of the plan, Icon guessed.

Still, he was in for a rough time—almost certainly, with how thick the jaguar was. And, given the admonishment to keep his mouth full of silk, there was really only one place that cock was going to go. Suspicion that was confirmed when someone—he was pretty sure it was the male-dribbled cold, cold lube on his pucker, and started working it in with two fingers, rubbing circles there. That was worth a healthy, delighted little groan. He couldn't help himself. It felt really, really good.

"Hmph, eager thing," Mrs. Étoile remarked. "I bet he'll cum even without taking the cage off."

"Oh? Mm...probably right, but we'll make a wager of it. How about: if he doesn't cum, I get to punish him, and if he does, you get to."

This was not a bet that Icon wanted either side to win, but his input was not being asked, nor could he make suggestions with his mouth full of damp silk.

"Deal. I'm going to enjoy making him cry."

One of those rubbing fingers pressed in, opening him, rubbing more and more lube in, drizzling it on that finger before it was pushed in. Sheathed claws, thank god, so he wasn't in danger of anything other than not being able to sit right for a few days.

A second finger joined the first, slowly spreading him wider, prompting more enthusiastic groans from him. Eyes shut, focusing on the feelings, he was surprised to feel something settling on his muzzle. Icon opened his eyes to see... fur, creamy-white, short and dense and velvety. Oh, and a flash of pink flesh, too, the lady straddling his muzzle with her pussy. He could smell her, her arousal, her excitement, and it was an excitement he shared. Whatever else, he could tell that both of his customers were having a great time.

Mrs. Étoile started to rub herself, grinding along the top of his muzzle, getting it damp. Her fingers, too, just rubbing there, strumming side to side, grazing her clitoris. She knew best how to pleasure herself, and he was going to get an education on it, right up close and personal. Though it was proving hard to focus as that second finger got fully inside him, spreading, stretching. A little ache of protest at stretched muscle, but he wasn't going terribly fast, still giving him time to adjust, to stretch. Which was good—that thick tool would split him in half otherwise.

He found himself, absently, wondering what these two got up to between each other. Was it as rough as he suspected, with torn patches of fur, bitemarks and blood, broken furniture? Or were they soft and tender? It was hard to tell—people tended to behave differently when a third was added in. And, there weren't many people better to cut loose on than a fox.

His muzzle was soaked on top, the smell of jaguar arousal and lust all he could inhale, and those fingers left, leaving him empty and wanting. Not for long, though. There was, quickly, a hand around the base of his tail, and a blunt, thick cock tip against his anus. Pressure, insistent, very, very eager. He had slicked himself as well, thoroughly, for which Icon was very grateful. He tried to push back, but the grip on his tail and the rope on his wrists didn't let him do much of that. But still, it was electric, shocks of pleasure up his spine. God, that cage was too, too tight, painful as his cock tried to swell but had nowhere to go.

He groaned protest and pleasure, arousal and pain, as that thick, too thick cock slid slowly in him, stretching him wide. So wide. He knew it wasn't splitting him, but God, it felt like it. And, suddenly, while he was distracted by the growing fullness of his ass, Mrs. Étoile came. Sweet, lustful nectar dripping down his muzzle as she yowled pleasure above him. Dropped the rope, at least, in her distraction, which let his shoulders relax. A profound comfort, made all the more pleasant by Mr. Étoile's hips coming to rest against his ass. Full, his face soaked with cum, cock aching in the cage, everything held still for a moment.

And then the jaguar pulled back, slowly, and pushed, just as slow, easy, gentle. It wouldn't stay that way, he knew, and feeling that rub against his prostate, he started to wonder what would constitute cumming for their bet. Because he was already dripping precum into a little puddle between his feet and knew damned well that he was almost certain to be dripping thicker stuff, without actually getting off, very soon.

The lady's recovery, still straddling his muzzle, was marked by hands on his hair. He was pulled up, looking at his customer and captor, his own eyes hazed and half-lidded with pleasure. "You're not squeezing on my husband, are you? Staying relaxed for him? Good boy. Oh, and look at all that dripping. Did you cum already? No?" She seemed amused more than anything, but he didn't have time to wonder. The jaguar behind him suddenly grabbed his thighs and just lifted, leaning back, so that all his weight was above that cock in his ass.

Icon was *bounced*, there, short, forceful thrusts and that iron grip holding him up, bouncing his aching cock in the cage, his balls so full after days of denial and edging that they, too, ached. That was the idea, probably, to make him ache and need and hurt. It was working pretty damn well.

Samson let him sink down, full, the jaguar's cock nice and deep in his ass, and just held him there. The fox was light enough to carry without trouble for almost anyone, more fluff than mass, and not all that much of that, either. So, holding him still, panting and dripping, dress all disheveled and hair at least as much so wasn't at all hard for someone as muscular as the jaguar. But, through a stray tousled lock, he spotted a lovely sight as Mrs. Étoile, bare from head to toe, was correcting that, putting on long, fingerless gloves, thigh-high stockings, a garter belt, panties, and an under-bust corset. Which had to have been done up just right ahead of time, since no one could lace and tie it themselves. She just hooked the fasteners in the front, settled it, and there it was, cinching her waist just a bit to take the already feminine and powerful shape and make it more so.

"Elisabeth," Mr. Étoile huffed, chin between the fox's ears, "are those new? I don't think I've seen this ensemble before. Very nice. What've you got in mind?"

"Cheating," the jaguaress purred and leaned in close. A hand went to Icon's throat, and she squeezed lightly before stepping in to trap him between two bodies. Quite a bit of time (or only a few heartbeats, but he was in no shape to count) passed with the two kissing around him. He could feel in him and around him both of their passion's rising. In Samson's case, literally rising, that rod in his ass getting even harder as his wife kissed him ferociously.

The kiss eventually broke, and there was a whispered exchange of 'I love you' over his head. And then she sank to her knees in front of him and put her tongue to use. That shiny little cage was…not much protection, not against a dexterous feline tongue. And, it was already much, much too small for his liking. This wasn't a blow job, not really. There wasn't much of anything for her to really suck on, but she was lapping, sliding her tongue between the bars, lavishing attention on him.

Some signal must have passed between the two of them because Mr. Étoile started to thrust again as soon as his wife had their toy in her mouth fully. Every bit of him, cage, balls and all, in that sharp-fanged maw. Singing tension all through him, his belly trying to tense in that amazing pre-orgasm way. Samson was certainly enjoying that if the growls and huffs behind him were any sign. But, Icon was, understandably, focused on the woman in front of him, and the prospect of her punishment when he came. Because she wasn't giving him a choice.

She put a hand up, splayed in the fox's black belly fur, holding, still tonguing around that cage, then suddenly stopped and opened her mouth, removing all touch from his aching, caged shaft. Her husband kept going, and Icon groaned a cry around his mouthful of silk. How had she known exactly when to stop to give him release without relief. He felt it, could see it, cum pouring like a leaky faucet from that cage, but there wasn't the rush of pleasure and delight, just a gnawing need for more.

"Aw, look at that. I'll bet you thought you were going to enjoy that before punishment, little fox—" she was interrupted by an explosive growl from her husband as he got his release, pulling Icon down hard, filling him again and bucking hard, blowing another load inside him. That rush of liquid heat inside him was…soothing, at least. Frustrating still, to feel someone else get that release and be left achingly wanting.

"And, you've made a mess of the carpet in here, too." Never mind that at least a third of the puddle underneath him was her husband's doing, dripping down those jaguar balls. "Well, I guess it's time to punish you. Once Samson's done getting out of you, anyway. And, after you've cleaned him thoroughly."

That took a bit of time, as that stand-and-carry position was a little difficult for dismounting, but they managed, and a dripping Icon got his wrists untied and took several minutes and a few sanitary napkins to thoroughly clean and polish that ink-black jaguar shaft—and clean any mess from his balls, too. After he was done, it was like there hadn't been any sodomy going on. Well, for him, anyway. Icon was still leaking and messy and sore.

"Lay down on your back, fox." Elisabeth instructed while Mr. Étoile ducked through a door into another room. The fox hadn't much choice but to obey. "And spit out your panties." That, he was grateful to do. The taste of silk had gotten old pretty quickly. She took those and tossed them onto the desk, then spent a little time. His wrists were re-tied, then secured over his head to one of the legs of the desk. Another few lengths of rope found his ankles and spread them, one attached to a coffee table, the other to a decorative bit of fretwork on one of the bookshelves.

"There. Now you can't cover or protect yourself. You're helpless. But that's okay. You want to be helpless, don't you?" That warranted a kind of 'well duh' grin and a nod. Really, it was a silly question to ask. "Good." She shifted around to straddle his face. Once again, his nose was filled with the scent of lusty jaguar, and, once again, he didn't mind in the least. He could hear footfalls again, coming near, but that wasn't much important to him.

"Just your teeth and tongue, boy. You're going to move my panties aside and eat me out. If I don't think you're trying your best, or if I want to motivate you, or if I just want to, I will hurt you, punish you." He felt a hand cupping his balls, then felt it curl and squeeze. Gently, carefully, but enough pressure to hurt, to ache. "And, if I like what you're doing enough, I might just unlock you. Don't bet on it, though."

Icon wasn't going to bet on him enjoying the next…however long this took. Or, perhaps he would enjoy not enjoying it? Sometimes being a bottom required some weird mental gymnastics. Whatever the case, he needed to start, and that involved getting his teeth to grip on those beautiful black panties, pulling and tugging and working them aside to expose the next step of his task. Familiar territory, at least to sight and smell, and, as she started to slowly squeeze again, he hurried to work.

He wasn't sure how long he worked, licking at her, stuffing his tongue inside and dragging it out. One careful, questioning nip was met with a squeeze and an admonishment not to try any more funny business. He wasn't at all sure if the squeezes and pressure were really meant as guidance on his technique, or if she just wanted him to squirm and moan and whine. She was doing a lot of squeezing, even when he felt her flutter and spasm in pleasure.

And then…her hands were off of him, and he didn't know why. She was still sitting on his face, still having those pleasurable flutters and leaking delicious tastes on his tongue and chin, but…and then it dawned on him, the sounds outside his little world of jaguar pussy. Her husband was standing over him and she was in the middle of sucking him off.

At least she wasn't going to be squeezing him for a moment or two, and he took that opportunity to work his jaw, stretch and arch and wiggle a bit, let tired muscles and joints adjust a little. Then, back to licking and nuzzling and stuffing. Suddenly, he heard a huffed growl from above, then another from closer, and felt her spasm, tense, felt his work rewarded as she came. Quietly, because at that moment, so did her husband, and she was busy swallowing that, trying not to choke on his seed.

Moments later, as all were panting to catch their breath and both jaguars had seated themselves to either side of him, Samson grinned down at him. "Okay…okay that was…good stuff. Beth?"

"Oh, yeah. Foxy, you have more than earned whatever they pay you. One last thing." He was still bound, but a key was rooted out from his briefcase, and that cage undone, removed. "Together?" she asked.

"Together," her husband replied, and they each took the little fox's cock, stiffening proudly now that it was out of that cage, in hand. Samson held his knot, giving gentle squeezes, while Elisabeth stroked the shaft itself, rubbing her thumb over the tip to spread his pre along that slick red rod. Still bound and helpless, all he could do was moan and push his hips up, the pleasure such a welcome relief, gentle and persistent.

It didn't take long, as wound up as he'd been, for his belly to tense up. He darted a pleading look to Mrs. Étoile, wondering if she was going to ruin it again, but she just grinned and worked her hand faster. Catching that grin, her husband squeezed tighter around that knot, and that was it. The little fox bucked and thrust in their hands, spending himself in exuberant jets onto his own chest and stomach, one even splattering on his nose. Then, down, dizzy with euphoria, hazed with pleasure, aware of the pair kissing, holding hands over his body.

They untied him and spent quite a while petting and talking to him. That, too, had been in the file, surely. Aftercare was always important, and Icon's version tended to be heavy on physical contact and reassurance. Conversation, too. Nothing important, just discussing what had gone on. His questions got a grin from both of them.

"Oh, for sure, you got picked on. A lot of times. Both of us alone? We'll fight hard for dominance, and that can get tiring. We discovered that with a third, we can share that dominance over them, and it's a lot easier for us to be...equal."

"Samson's right. Having a playmate lets us cut loose without worrying about the other one feeling walked on, or subordinate, or...whatever. We don't have to do it often, but a session like this is worth every penny, both paid to you and to the cleaning staff."

Taking a glance around, Icon was quite sure they were right. The carpeting was going to need a thorough cleaning before there was any sort of important meeting in here.

After another forty minutes or so, Icon was settled and recovered enough to fix his dress up, settle himself, and head for the elevators. It was well into evening now, the sun going down over the horizon, and his car was there waiting for him. He smiled tiredly at Leo and let him get on with the business of driving him back to the blocky building occupied by Kuroko, his company, and whoever happened to have booked an overnight stay. He was going to need a long bath, and probably an ice pack for his ass, but it was very, very worth it. The session had been rewarding in itself, and the paycheck wasn't bad either.

SPICY WITH A HINT OF FOX
Colin Leighton

Colin Leighton is a coyote historian from Idaho. He has never eaten a fox's ass, but foxes and rimming are among his favourite subjects to write about in erotic stories. Given foxes are often portrayed as submissive twinks, he enjoys creating vulpine characters with more dominant, masculine personalities. Assorted yapping on history, literature, rimming, and other nonsense can be found on twitter at @ColinCoyote.

On the fourth day of my vacation in New Zealand, I decide to go to a wine tasting.

While a more experienced wine connoisseur would likely have selected a winery to visit based on the repute of its vintages, I choose Villa Serafina for purely aesthetic reasons. It lies on the shores of Lake Wanaka, with vineyards sloping gracefully down almost to the water's edge while behind rise arid hills and a blue cloudless sky. I admit that after seeing the photo on Google images, my mind is made up long before I actually look up Villa Serafina's website. As it turns out, they offer some of my favourite wine strains, but the setting in itself is enough to make me think, *That's the one.* Unlike wine-tastings I've been to in America, this one does not welcome walk-in guests but instead offers tastings based on personal reservation, so I use the booking system on their website to reserve a spot at 2:30 in the afternoon.

When I drive my rental car up the drive to Villa Serafina that afternoon, it's immediately clear that even the photos online have not done the place justice. The drive is lined on either side with Italian cypresses, giving it a vaguely Tuscan appearance, and it winds through a variety of vineyards, curving upwards towards a low rise on which are more trees and a scattering of buildings. Through the rolled-down windows of the car drift scents of dust and pollen and the elusively resonant fragrances of the vineyards themselves. It is that clear kind of afternoon when songbirds are still singing, and even the crunching of the car's tyres over the gravel of the drive has a pleasant air to it. I drive without urgency, breathing in the cool fresh fragrant air of the countryside and taking in the view of Lake Wanaka, extraordinarily scenic, before the drive turns away from the vineyards themselves and up through a small orchard, past landscaped gardens and a small sparking pond, to a level area marked with signs designating visitor's parking.

It is perhaps evident now why the winery took tastings only by appointment, given there is room here only for maybe a half-dozen cars, but, as I switch off the ignition, I reason that, in reality, crowds might have spoiled the effect. Before me rises the grey-green walls of a large bungalow, constructed with a long veranda seemingly encircling it, above whose double-doors a large wooden sign bore in crimson letters the winery's name: Villa Serafina. There are a few tables and benches on the veranda and hanging baskets of poppies and geraniums in full bloom, while more flowers blossom up from flowerbeds alongside the veranda. To the right of the building stands a few trees, while to the left of the parking area extend green lawns, trees, more flowerbeds, and a stone path which I assume leads to the home of the winery's owners.

There is no sign of life in the parking area or on the veranda, so I get out of the car, not bothering to lock it given the seclusion of the place. From the photos on Villa Serafina's website, I know that this bungalow is the wine-tasting centre. Its doors squeak modestly as I enter, instantly met with the scent of wine and fresh bread…and vulpine. More spacious inside than it appears, the bungalow is an open, airy building, its walls on either side lined nearly from floor to ceiling with racks of wine bottles. To either side of the door are sales counters cluttered with cash registers and a scattering of tourist pamphlets and brochures, while the other end of the chamber seems to be arranged for the tasting itself, with round tables and wicker chairs.

The fox I had scented is standing to the side of this tasting area, taking wine glasses out of a big oak cabinet and stacking them on a tray, but, at the click of the door behind me, his ears flick my direction. Oh, Lord, he's gorgeous. Tallish and broad-shouldered, he's bigger than average for a fox, I observe. Not 'heavy,' certainly, but stronger-built, somehow, in a subtly masculine way that belies traditional vulpine stereotypes. Black ears rise over a orangey muzzle and softer creamy cheeks and chin, below which he has on a forest-green waistcoat worn over a tannish short-sleeved shirt, and, below that, slacks of a sea-greenish colour vaguely reminiscent of WWII military uni-forms. Somehow, the assemblage seems fitting for a wine merchant. I guess his age as perhaps forty at most; significantly older than I, certainly, but not so much as to be considered 'old.' "Hello," he barks, "I'll be with you in just a minute."

Yes, I admit, I am attracted to him almost instantly. I guess if you're a gay guy, you can't really help noticing an attractive man whenever you see one, and I can't deny always having had a thing for guys slightly older than me. There's a sense of dominance and confidence some men have that just seems to grow with age, if you know what I mean. Anyway, that quality has always been deliciously appealing to me, and this fox seems to ooze it almost from the moment I laid eyes on him.

"Hey," I say, unsure if I ought to wait here lest other people have booked the same time slot (and, yes, nervous with that self-consciousness you can't help feeling when just having met a hot guy). "I'm here for the 2:30 wine tasting." The fox has put down the tray of wine glasses on a side table and is approaching.

"I thought so," comes the reply. "Actually, you're the only one booked in for that slot, so we can go ahead and get started, if you like."

Just us then. "Yeah, that's fine."

The fox's ears are perked curiously, which I wrongly interpret as being a reaction to my American accent, or, perhaps, because he does not see coyotes often. "Well then. Welcome to Villa Serafina. Usually with these tours, we talk a little about the history of our vineyards and the kinds of wines we offer, then I take you through to the tasting itself."

"Sounds good to me," I agree, tail wagging. The sight of so many wine bottles is starting to make me thirsty for a refreshing sip, but, likewise, the handsome fox before me is stirring other cravings, or at least putting thoughts in my head. Of course, in that moment, I have no real expectations whatsoever that anything will happen between the fox and I, but eye-candy is eye-candy just the same.

The fox smiles softly. "Swell. I'm Gordon Napier, by the way." He holds out a big black-furred hand.

I've not expected introductions. "Oh, uh, Berkeley." I shake his hand. His grip is firm, a contact that for some reason seems to send a shiver through me. We are close enough I can catch his scent, that tangy foxish maleness characteristic of vulpines. *This is what you get for not jerking off for a week,* I berate myself.

"Given our wine-tastings offer a somewhat more personal experience than those provided by some of our competitors, I usually introduce myself to our guests," Gordon explains. His brown eyes are warm and friendly, and his tail is wagging too—just a farmer's enthusiasm at talking of his trade, or something more?

"Given you don't take walk-in customers, I assumed it might be a little different than the average wine-tasting establishment," I say.

Gordon flicks an ear towards the seating area. "We try not to be average. But, really, the booking requirement is mainly because we're a family-run affair, and, since our business is entirely based here at our home, we prefer to be able to control who comes here and how many people do so at a time." As I follow him past rows of wine racks, my eyes inevitably drift to his butt; those slacks don't hide much. He's got a fine ass, no doubt about that. I can only imagine what it looks like without clothing in the way. Too bad he doesn't give tastings in the nude...

"It's worth it, though," I reply, eyes on his ass, "the view here is much better than at the wine shops in town." But then he opens a door, and I follow him out onto the back veranda. My ears fly up again, not because of his ass this time. The view from the veranda is spectacular: Immediately behind the deck, the land drops off somewhat and the vineyards begin, sloping away towards the water. In the midday sun, Lake Wanaka is a glistening cobalt blue, and, beyond it, the mountains of the southern alps seem to beckon and stir up notions of adventure and wanderlust. Gordon and his family really are incredibly lucky to live here, I realise, surrounded by a bounty of vineyards, with mountains and lake as neighbours.

"You were saying something about a view?"

"It's marvellous," I murmur, glancing at him with a slight tail wag. "You guys are blessed. If I lived in a place this beautiful, I'd never want to leave." A warm spring breeze is blowing up from the vineyards; it feels pleasant and calming against my fur. When Gordon offers me a wicker chair next to a wooden patio table, I take it without thinking much about it, absorbed in the idyllic setting.

"We thought so too." He takes a chair across from me. "Winemaking is not necessarily as glamourous an occupation as some may think it, nor is it an easy undertaking, but it's worth it just the same." His eyes flick towards me, and, in his cool gaze, I get a delicious hunch he's checking me out. "My husband and I moved down here wanting to try a different path from what most conventional careers offer, and, though it hasn't always been smooth sailing, I think we found what we were looking for."

My ears flick up. "Oh?" I stop myself before I can repeat 'husband,' but the effect of the word upon me is probably unmistakable, especially to a fox, known as they are for being decidedly observant.

Gordon grins; I can hear his floofy tail rustling against the back of his chair. If I'm not mistaken, he is pleased with my reaction. "My husband, Percy. As I said, we're a family-run business. It's just us and our kids. Oftentimes, all four of us contribute to the tours. Being given a wine tasting by a couple of gay foxes with twin daughters adds to the novelty, I suppose, but, today, Percy had to go into Wanaka to have a tooth worked on, and Tamsin and Eileen are visiting their grandparents up in Perth. With just you to serve today, though, one fox is enough for the job."

I've processed this all quickly: my intuitions were right for once: he is gay—not only gay, but married and raising kids with his husband. His last sentence sounded vaguely flirtatious, though. Perhaps he has a thing for twenty-something American coyotes. "That's cool. It's pretty swell living in an age when 'family-run business' can describe a family with gay parents too." My tail wags as again my eyes drift over the vineyards, the lake, the mountains. "Especially in such an idyllic setting."

I half-wonder if I sound too enthusiastic, such that my ears splay a little, but Gordon doesn't seem to mind. His calm confident smile, rather foxlike, if in a very masculine authoritative kind of way, doesn't falter. "We think so too. When Percy and I founded Villa Serafina in 2006—it's named after a place in Tuscany we stayed at during our honeymoon—we aimed to establish a farm that would be a great place to raise a family and that would contribute some new notes to the symphony that is the wine world." He flicks an ear at the vineyards. "What you see is the result."

"Well, you've succeeded as far as I can tell." Really, the environment is incredibly relaxing. I feel like, in the right time and space, I could drift off to a nice nap here, with a breeze in my fur and the scent of the vineyards in my snout.

"Thank you." The fox nods modestly. "I imagine you are starting to get thirsty, though." The confident brown eyes are watching me again, black ears pricked forwards.

"A bit, yes," I say, my ears tilting a little under his cool gaze. This time, the reaction is unmistakable; almost a smirk. "Very well then." My eyes follow his ass as he gets up and goes back into the bungalow. I'm starting to suspect he's been subtly flirting with me, and, at any rate, my cock is already partially erect within my jeans. How lucky could I be? Getting a private wine-tasting offered by a gorgeous dad-fox who is not only gay but seemingly attracted to me. Wine isn't the only thing I'd appreciate a taste of, this afternoon...

He returns a moment later with a tray full of wine glasses. "Here at Villa Serafina, we specialise in white wines; they tend to grow best in this climate—which is, after all, one of the southernmost wine regions in the world," he tells me, setting the tray on the table. "Most wineries in the area grow more Pinot Noir than anything else, but we personally specialise in Riesling and Gewürztraminer." He sets six glasses in front of me, each a quarter-full of wine, and identifies these as being two Rieslings, two Gewürztraminers, a Chardonnay, and a Pinot Noir. In the shade of the afternoon sun, the wines look vaguely golden, like liquid saffron.

Gordon places a small metal beaker, empty, next to me.

"That's in case you don't like any of them, for discarding. I won't be offended if you spit any out…winemakers have to get used to that, given people's tastes vary."

I flick my ears. "Thanks, but I wouldn't like to waste any. I always swallow."

As the words leave my mouth, I immediately realise the implied innuendo, too glaringly obvious even for a coyote to make without shame. My ears start to splay, but Gordon only grins. "I'll keep that in mind. For the record, I feel the same way." He sits down across from me while I struggle to decide whether to feel embarrassed or aroused. In the end, I distract myself by taking up one of the glasses, a Riesling, and sipping it. It's a very crisp wine, sharp and faintly sweet.

The refreshing zest is just what I need to surrender again to the pleasant relaxation that in this setting is so impossible to resist. "This one's lovely," I observe. Not necessarily wanting him to pick up on how little I know about wine, I decide not to comment further, genuinely delicious and refreshing though it may be.

"My daughter Eileen nicknamed that Riesling 'elves tears' because of the colour," Gordon tells me, "and, given Lord of the Rings was filmed near here, I suppose the name is as fitting as any. We find that one pairs well with fish dishes, though if you don't like fish, it'd also be a nice accompaniment to poultry like pheasant or partridge."

"Oh, I'll eat any kind of meat." I shrug, sipping the Riesling again. It's interesting, this underlying play of words between fox and coyote, two species both famed for cleverness; generally, I would of course argue in favour of my own species, but, in this case, its undeniable that Gordon is the more assertive of the two of us. I wonder if my experience of the tasting is different from the average visitor's; certainly, he probably doesn't flirt with his guests generally, but perhaps a gay American coyote is an exception rare enough to warrant deviations from the norm.

Our eyes meet. "Good to know. I like men who are open-minded in their tastes," says the fox. That sly foxy grin is still there, as if telling me that he knows I know he's flirting with me, and that there is potential for this afternoon to get much spicier indeed. I flick my ears and reach for another glass of wine...

As I finish off the Riesling and move onto the Chardonnay, a terrific thrill seems to be seeping through me; undoubtedly, the wine plays a role in this, but with it is that enchanting quiver you get when flirting with a handsome, sexy guy, the anticipation and hope that is in itself almost as enjoyable as the outcome. Gordon is still watching me, but, after a moment he stands up. "Excuse me just a moment, Berkeley," he says with a grin. "I need to check something." God, there's a bulge in his slacks; I am almost sure of it. And, a sizable one too. He seems to notice the direction of my gaze and smirks before turning to go back into the bungalow. I'm pretty sure he can tell my eyes are on his ass again, and, honestly, I've mostly lost any desire to conceal my interest. The Chardonnay is tasty, but noticing his, ass I can't help but imagine what it'd be like to pull down the slacks, lift his tail, and press my muzzle between those firm cheeks.

Okay, my jeans are definitely getting uncomfortable now. Gulping another swallow of wine, I adjust myself so my cock is no longer pointing down, glancing out over the vineyards lest any third-parties be watching, but, as far as I can see, there's no sign of life beyond the trees and vines and the sparkling lake. Not a bad place to be if you want to fuck outdoors.

The door clicks. "Sorry about that, I thought I'd check the computer and see if any other tastings had been booked for this afternoon." When my head spins round, I see he hasn't sat down again. Instead, he's just standing there with his hands folded behind his head, stretching a bit, the fluffy reddish tail swinging lazily. The outline of his erection is easily detectable in his pants, a thick longish swelling jutting to the side over his hip. He's definitely not making any attempt to hide it.

I swallow, daring to hope. "Oh?" A part of me wants to stand up and put my hand on that bulge, feel it pulse and throb. But really, I prefer being lead to leading.

"As it stands, you are the last person booked for a tasting today," Gordon says, the characteristically sly fox grin never leaving his muzzle. "Given we are therefore unlikely to be interrupted, I wonder if you'd like to taste a vintage most of our guests don't get to try."

Under my gaze, his imprisoned cock seems to throb, pressing harder against the fabric of his slacks. "A different tasting?" I glance at the wine selection on my table. Suddenly feeling oddly shy, I raise my eyes again to meet his intense gaze, and nod as my ears fold back submissively. "That sounds…fun."

"I think you'll like this one even better than the wines you've tried." The fox smirks as he steps up closer to me, while I twist sideways in my chair to face him. I don't know what's more thrilling, that thick bulge getting all the closer—and I can scent it now, too, his arousal, soft and tangy, undeniably manly—or the way he's looking at me. That commanding, confident gaze conveys so much dominance just in its intensity that I feel explicably motivated to get up, yank down my jeans, and lift my tail for him right there.

But, I don't get a chance as he reaches down to take my wrist, then puts my hand against his imprisoned cock. Despite myself, I whine; I can sense the heat of it through the slacks, feel his hardness and the way it throbs intermittently. "For a cute coyote like you, I can offer a tasting on tap," he growls, thrusting his hips ever so slightly to grate that bulge against my hand.

From anyone else, the teasing phrase would sound corny, but something about the confident rumble of the words makes the rising sensation of arousal and submission all the more powerful in me. "I've been hoping you would offer one," I admit, and he chuckles, releases my hand, and unbuttons his trousers.

He's wearing very tight black briefs underneath, but I don't get long to study these as he immediately reaches inside them…Damn! His cock is as striking as I envisioned it. Long and thick, its veiny pink surface damp with pre and long since unsheathed, it flops out to wave rigidly for a few seconds, ending up pointing upwards, vaguely in the direction of my snout. Even as I watch it, a drop of pre forms on the tip. I am indeed being offered a tasting straight from the tap, it seems.

Of course, he doesn't even need to give the command. I lean forward in my chair and lap away the drop, caressing the head of his cock with my tongue. A growl of approval rewards me as I lick my lips. "A good vintage?"

"Soft and sweet," I agree, reaching out to grasp the stiff shaft around the half-swollen knot. He feels so amazingly hard as I pull him to my muzzle; maybe he hasn't got off for a few days, or maybe he *is* a stereotypically nymphomaniac fox after all, just a dominant one instead of being eager to lift tail. I get another hint of the sweet zest of his pre as I slide him into my muzzle, pressing my tongue up against the hot rigidity; he does indeed taste good. A reassuring hand settles between my ears, gently pressing downwards as inch after inch of pink fox cock slips into my muzzle.

We settle into a rhythm. I've got one hand on his hip and the other still grasping his knot, the size of which is not lost on me either; I half expect him to at any moment command me to get on my feet and lift my tail. Even big as the knot is, I wouldn't hesitate to obey. But at the moment, we're both content with things as they are; I'm bobbing my head on his dick, swallowing down every little drop of pre—I swear, he's more leaky than any other man I've ever sucked off. Maybe it's a fox thing, but he tastes so good I'm hardly complaining, swirling my tongue around the sides of his shaft in a way I can tell he likes, given his occasional sighs of contentment, or the way he is rubbing my big coyote ears, or the lowly growled "good boy, Berkeley," I am rewarded with.

Mostly, he just lets me suck on him, but every so often he gives a subtle thrust of his hips, humping at my muzzle. He's so thick—whoever knew foxes were so well hung—I have to struggle not to gasp and choke; I'm not really that practiced at deep throating. My eyes bulge out as he humps inward, and I have to resist the urge to gag as his cocktip jabs the back of my throat, but he seems able to adequately gage just how much I can take. His scent is fantastic, foxy and masculine but not overdone, and with my nose so close to his groin, it's hard to smell anything else. Oh, and every time he growls "good boy," I feel a shiver of delight, in that happy bliss of being put into my place by a dommy fox stud. That we're doing it outside with the warm spring breeze still ruffling my fur just adds to the sexiness of the moment, just as does the table of sample wines next to us; it's wickedly thrilling to reason that it's only natural to move from sampling Gordon's wines to his cock. And, if I had to choose between the two…As much as I love wine, fox cock is better.

Indeed, his cock is undoubtedly a fun toy, the kind that given command or opportunity I'd play with for as long as he allowed it, but as he continues to leak pre onto my tongue, my mind inevitably wanders to wondering if I can get him off. Thoughts of 'tastings' makes me want to taste his cum, drink it all down just like I did the wine he offered me, so I start massaging his knot with my fingers, aiming to send it into that full state of swelling knots get just before climax, while my tongue tugs at his shaft, seeking to draw out his orgasm.

Gordon has other ideas, however, as he releases my head and slowly pulls back, extracting his slick bone from my muzzle. As it bobs back into the air, a line of saliva briefly connects its tip to my muzzle, a symbol of our coupling I'm hesitant to break. "You were doing a fine job there," the fox tells me approvingly, "but, before we finish, I wonder if there wasn't one more thing you'd like a taste of…"

I lick my lips. "Your ass?"

"You've only had your eyes on it from the moment you walked in the door," Gordon chuckles as his tail swishes sensually.

My ears splay slightly. "I don't know whether to be embarrassed you saw through me so easy…or glad you did," I admit, "but I can't deny you have a gorgeous ass."

"Oh, I just have practised gaydar." I watch as he briefly sticks his cock back inside his briefs, then slides both briefs and slacks down onto his hips, leaving his groin and ass entirely exposed. "I had you fixed as being gay the moment I laid eyes on you, and you were so cute and obviously interested. Didn't take long before I was imagining bending you over a table."

Knowledge that he's been scheming of seducing me from the moment I arrived sends another thrill though me, and makes my trapped cock twitch. "I won't complain if you do," I admit, watching him turn around. "Do you always seduce your guests?"

I was right: his ass looks even better outside of clothes than in. Orangey red fur gives way to much lighter cream nearer the cleft between his two big mounds, between which the plumy tail twitches, teasing me; I want so much to brush it aside and thrust in my muzzle. I can already catch stronger hints of his scent again, maybe even better than near his cock. "Oh, no, you're the first, actually," he tells me, smirking over his shoulder. "This is a very special tasting, just for you. Now, get on your knees." I scramble to obey, slipping off the chair and onto the floor; kneeling behind him, my face is about level with his butt. Then, his floofy tail sweeps aside, I get another whiff of his scent, and he leans forward, putting his hands on the table, and arches his ass outwards towards my muzzle.

The view is so lovely I can't help but whine again. Really, I like the view of his ass best with the tail arched away as it is; this way, I can easily admire those white-furred low-hanging balls, probably quite heavy and full given how worked up he's got while I sucked his cock, and just as good or, perhaps, better, his ass itself. He's got a really beautiful asshole, which I know sounds incredibly weird and kinky to say, but it's true; there's something real pretty about his round pink rosebud, nestled in there between the creamy fur of his cheeks, the way its little creases lead into a central indention that seems to beckon my tongue in for a taste. "Your asshole is so pretty," I murmur, almost absently, and then I shove my muzzle in, take a quick sniff of his hole—oh, he smells divine—and kiss him there, a sweet and affectionate kiss that quickly morphs into wet lapping slurps.

"Good boy, Berkeley," he growls again, and without warning his hand settles between my ears and pushes my muzzle deeper into his ass. This show of dominance makes my own cock throb harder than ever; my nose presses up under his tail where his scent is so intense as I make out with his asshole; he tastes fine here too. He holds my face in there firmly, not letting up the pressure against my head, but I don't care; I can still breathe through my nose, if faintly, and, regardless, his ass is so great I'd gladly stay down here an hour if he wanted me too.

I'm swirling my tongue around his hole, teasing my tonguetip over the soft surface, along the creases, down towards the centre; prodding, testing. My hands go up to his rump cheeks, gripping the sides of his ass as I eat him out, feeling the firmness underneath my fingers. My own cock is still trapped, feeling achingly hard; maybe I'll just get off in my underwear at this rate, but I almost don't care. After all, this afternoon has gone so marvellously well, what with getting seduced by a stunningly attractive dad-fox, whose ass my snout is presently buried in. As my tongue swirls inwards, pressing tentatively at the centre of his hole, he continues to rub at my big coyote ears, a subtle sign of approval and appreciation. This encouragement just makes me all the more passionate in my licking; I mouth at his hole, pressing my tongue inward into his hot passage, as deep as my tongue can reach. He must like being tongue-fucked as for perhaps the first time I hear him actually groan, and then my ears catch another sound, a faint glint of palm against shaft, and I realise he's started jerking himself while I eat his ass.

Maybe he's going to get off now, with my tongue in his ass. Of course, I want to make it a good climax for him, so I continue to thrust my tongue inwards, lapping at his asshole lovingly; really, rimming is about my favourite thing to do to a man, especially to really manly studs like Gordon. There's something terribly thrilling about having your muzz buried in a man's ass, your snout filled with his scent, your tongue caressing his hole; how better can you convey your affections? Even more so when it's obviously having the effect of driving him closer to climax, as, though I'd love to get to taste his load, I'm happy to keep eating his ass right up to the point he cums. His hand is holding me in just as firm and steady as ever, seeming to suggest in its subtle dominance that this is my place, this is where I belong, with my tongue darting into him. From the moment I started licking his rump, my tail has been wagging incoherently, an expression of my happiness in the moment, although I can't say I'm putting much thought into controlling it. Show love to his ass; help him get off, that's the priority.

Except, that apparently isn't his plan after all. Suddenly my pricked ears pick up a catch in his voice, and he releases my head, that firm pressure finally disappearing as he straightens up, his ass pulling away from my muzzle. "Here's your last tasting," he growls as he spins round, and there before me again is his big leaky cock, its angry redness seemingly more intense than ever. Instinctively, I open my muzzle, just in time for him to calmly press my head down. I welcome his throbbing shaft back into my mouth eagerly, realising with a burst of excitement he's about to cum; after all our varied innuendos about drinks and tastings, I am very keen on tasting his cum, a product not of grapevines but of this fox himself, or, rather, of those big balls I was admiring earlier. And now, I don't have long to wait. He shoves my head down, I hear him groan, his cock pulses in my muzzle, and, at last, I feel the first hot spurt gush onto my tongue.

He does taste good, but I hardly get a chance to savour him as I did with the wine, because that first spurt is followed by another, and another—clearly, he's extremely pent up—and soon, my cheeks bulge. I struggle to swallow down his load as his cock continues to throb and gush cum, but there's no pulling back now; his hand remains firm on my head, and even if it weren't, I want to drink down it all. Indeed, when his cock does slow from rapid bursts to relieved seeping, I resume sucking on it as I had earlier, keen to get every drop out while he moans again, probably from that increased kind of sensitivity a guy's cock gets immediately after orgasm. Gordon's panting, though otherwise quiet now as he's probably momentarily dazed with afterglow.

As I expected, he had a big load, shooting seven or eight times at least, though I was really too busy swallowing to count, but now his climax is over, and the pressure on my head relents. His cock is still hard, knot enflamed and swollen, as it flops out of my muzzle. I lick my lips, savouring the last taste of him, then look up. Gordon's holding out a hand, which I take, and he pulls me back to my feet. Our tails wag casually as we grin at each other. "So, Berkeley," he begins, having regained his voice, I guess, "how would you rate this wine tasting you've just attended?"

My ears tilt back as I pretend to put on a thoughtful expression of consideration. "Well…the Riesling and the Chardonnay were both delicious…but my favourite vintage was the last." I reach down and lift his sac, still heavy even after having just been emptied into my muzzle. "The most natural taste, provided by you."

The fox smirks. "That's about what I expected. Good thing for you is there's more where that comes from. But, for now, you'd best finish up that wine before it gets too warm."

Clearly, wine is not necessarily the most pressing matter on my mind at the moment, my own cock is still terribly hard, and I've got that awfully tingly feeling in my balls I get when my libido is running full speed ahead, but he's right that the wine will get warm, and I did pay for it, after all, so I slide back into the chair. Post-coital, you'd half-expect Gordon to immediately pull his pants back up and take the conversation somewhere more mundane—it's how unexpected hook-ups often end, after all—but he just watches me sip a Gewürztraminer, not even bothering to pull his pants back up; maybe he enjoys the feeling of the breeze against his groin. His cock has deflated somewhat now, and slid about halfway back into his sheath. My eyes still dart down to it or his balls, occasionally. It seems that actually fulfilling my fantasies of getting acquainted with his cock and ass up close hasn't diminished my attraction to him even slightly, only increased it. I'm kind of sorry that when I finish up the wine, I'll have to leave.

Standing there now, though, his expression is thoughtful, ears quirked somewhat to the side, fingers stroking the underside of his muzzle. "Berkeley...question for you. Do you have anything else planned for the rest of the day?"

My ears swing up curiously. "Nothing in particular. I was just gonna go back to Queenstown and walk around some, then check out one of the restaurants for dinner."

Gordon's querying look transforms back into that sly grin he pulls off so charmingly. "I was going to say, given no other tastings are booked today, you're welcome to hang out here a bit longer. You can try some other wines, if you like, or..."— He reaches down and fondles his sheath and balls casually— "...other things, if you'd prefer."

A jolt of excitement shoots through me and leaves my tail thwapping the chair. "Your husband wouldn't mind?"

"Hah, no, much the reverse." He's really grinning now, showing white fangs while his tail swishes. "I'd love to introduce you to Percy. You'd be a lovely treat to surprise him with later, just the distraction he'll need after having that tooth worked on, but, moreover, we'd just appreciate the company. It's not every day we get to play host to a cute young coyote."

My ears splay, but from pleasure this time rather than anxiety. "I can't deny I'd love not to have to leave yet," I admit, but the words are probably unnecessary in light of my eagerly wagging tail and happily grinning muzzle. I don't know what's more exciting, that Gordon himself wants to spend more time with me, whether intimately or otherwise, or that he intends to introduce me to his husband. I'm sure 'introduce' in this context means more than just shaking hands. The thought of getting frisky with not one but two dad foxes makes me feel hornier than ever. "You know, coming here, I've been amazed at how beautiful your home is just in itself,"—I wave a hand generally to encompass the vineyards and the lake and the mountains beyond—"almost feels like I've landed in Middle Earth or Narnia or some other such fantasy novel setting, but meeting you here...that's been truly magical. So, yeah, I'd love to stay and hang out with you longer."

Gordon strolls over to sit on the edge of the table, chuckling. "Careful what you offer, we might not let you leave."

As I polish off another glass of wine my eyes inevitably drift again to his groin. "And I look forward to meeting your husband too."

"Oh, I guarantee he's going to like you." The fox smirks. "In fact, I'm sure he'd love to help me spitroast you later this evening. I haven't missed noticing you've got a cute rump, after all, and no doubt you're feeling pretty worked up by now. But, all things in good time. We can fix a nice dinner, pour some more wine, and get to know you better. We've got a back deck on our house with an outdoor table we eat at on evenings when the weather's nice—just don't get the chance to play host very often."

"That sounds lovely," I say, although again, my wagging tail and enthused grin are probably answer enough. "It'd certainly be nice to relax on the deck and share some conversation over a good drink. Much better than what my hotel or the restaurant there can offer."

Gordon reaches down to absently twirl a finger around his sheath. "Most restaurant dinners probably don't end with the chef bending you over the deck railing and fucking you while you watch a stunning sunset."

"No, but most wine-tastings don't end with you sucking off the wine merchant, or eating his ass," I observe, setting aside another glass. I've now gone through most of the wines. "Really though, thank you. This is going to be the highlight of my holiday."

"No problem." He glances at his wristwatch. "Percy should be home soon. If you want we can go ahead and wander down to the house; I'll get out some more wine and some *hors d'oeuvres,* and we can relax and chat till he gets here. Besides," he grins, "I get a sense you're feeling a bit cramped in those clothes. And, I've always preferred relaxing in the nude, myself. What'd you say we go down there and get more comfortable?"

"That sounds just marvellous," I gush. As I get to my feet and help Gordon gather up the empty wine glasses, I can't control the frenzied wag of my tail, or hide my enthusiasm. I'd come here thinking this would be just one other touristy experience, fun but unremarkable, but it's proved a whole lot more. First, I got to suck off a deliciously charming fox, now I'm invited to hang out with him and his husband in their idyllic home; how better can it get?

As we walk past the wine racks my eyes wander from the glossy bottles to Gordon's ass, and a thought suddenly occurs to me. I remember once reading that young Americans can get work visas for employment in New Zealand vineyards fairly easily. Gordon said Villa Serafina is a family run business, but that doesn't necessarily mean they don't hire vineyard workers sometimes, does it?

"Hey, Gordon," I bark. "Question for you…"

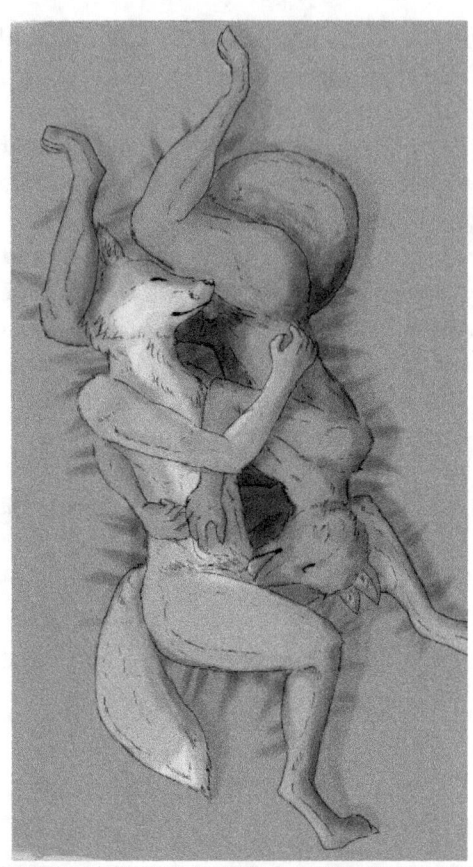

WHEN THE NEEDS ARE DENIED
MikasiWolf

MikasiWolf welcomes you to his parlor, wondering how you made it past the façade that fronts his headquarters. A wolf in reality, he also masquerades as other species in alternative realms called Stories, utilizing the powers of Worldbuilding and Characterization. Foxes aren't the only tricksters in this realm. To fund his quest of Wordcraft, Mikasi sometimes poses as a human Design Engineer to pay the bills. Species employment laws have yet to favor Furkind. He currently hides in the astral planes, which can only be accessed by two encryption keys, most commonly known as Username and Password.

   https://twitter.com/MikasiWolf
   http://www.furaffinity.net/user/mikasiwolf

As a fox, I just can't get enough of it.

You know what? Fuck that. *No one* can get enough sex. Anyone who says otherwise is a lying weasel or a snitching ferret. And, that includes those two species as well. It doesn't matter if you're dog or bear, wolf or hare, everyone feels the instinct at some point in their life. Or, should I say, every point in their life.

Since I turned 18, I've been hooking up with guys and girls every other week. They don't call it the freedom of adulthood for nothing. It started off as an experiment to see which end of the scale I turned to, along with the more tangible and, well, pleasurable benefits. By the end of Year Two of my sexual journey, I came to but one conclusion: I was neither straight nor gay. A most happy dilemma it was.

Then, I started seeing this guy I met at the Air Show. I was always one for technology, especially the kind that goes boom and whoosh, so I'd been going ever since I moved to this city. It's among the best choices I've made; I don't think my parents would've liked finding what I got up to each and every night, and I can't exactly have anyone sleep over at a place that wasn't mine. Even if we went at it all quiet-like, I've no doubt my parents would have a fit if they heard and smelt something that resembled whatever they did to have me and my bros. Dad probably wouldn't mind too much; my ma caught him a couple of times with some vixen or other. But my ma; she called the shots in the house. My parents were good, but they can be a pain when it came to giving orders and all that. I went to all the schools and courses they told me to, and even got a job that they found somewhat acceptable for one of the vulpine. We foxes prided ourselves on having good jobs and education, however one might define it. I must, however, say that knowledge in the streets is just as important as that in the sheets. Not knowledge I could use first-hand at my day job in Engineering, though I'm sure I would have made a great sex toy designer. Oh, the sights I've seen.

But, back to the Air Show. I was examining an unmanned drone built by some company or other. Something about the sleek curves along with its most phallic design had me wondering what it would be like to have it at my disposal, forget the 2.5 million dollar price tag. Figuratively, I mean. They don't have paper tags on things that expensive. Granted, I was also wondering about the engine propulsion that went into this thing, and how smooth and comfortable it would be to ride on.

The thing about foxes is that we tend to have a stronger scent than most other species. Not that we stink, though many speciesists would say otherwise. Because of that, most other species could easily notice every little scent we give off. And, in the case of the Fox Caressing the Phallic Drone, the scent of my arousal.

Unlike the other visitors and exhibitors, Sasha noticed me. He was representing the company whose drone I was getting all wet over, and being a sable meant that he was used to picking out the finer smells beneath the stronger overlying scents. He told me more about the drone's features such as range and payload along with how well it would give ground-based troops a run for their money. He then told me we could talk more about it later when he was off his shift.

We then got to know each other better. You'll excuse me if it just happened, but I find it was as good an introduction to someone as any. Dad always said that one should find someone of similar interests to spend your time and life with, and I can't quite say I'd disagreed with him. Sasha sure knew a pent-up guy when he smelled one, and, though I offered to show him a good time, all we did was feel each other up. Some of the empty booths of the exhibition hall were perfect for such endeavors, though not so suitable for any hard action, if you get my meaning. We left separately after that, dripping and satisfied, and, with his musk tingling in my nostrils, I knew I'd found the one for me.

I returned to the Air Show the next couple of days and met up with Sasha each time. He was surprised I turned up again after all that, but from his peaked ears and bright eyes, it was clear he appreciated the sentiment. When he was sure I wasn't just hooking up with him for an easy source of one-on-one action, we started going out. And that, as they say, was that.

We had a good thing going. Both of us were about the same age and from engineering backgrounds, so we understood the life; such as how some inane last-minute documentation could make the difference between going back on time or a lost weekend. He liked reading up on military technology; I liked doing that alongside playing Call of Duty. He liked going to the range to pop some rounds; I liked going there and pretending I'm playing Call of Duty. That got me in trouble a few times with the range owner, but there were plenty of laughs between Sasha and I. It was almost like we were made for each other.

As for our more personal encounters, Sasha enjoyed sex as much as the next guy. A great match, don't you think? The thing was, he wasn't as zealous about it as I was. Not that he didn't like it or perform poorly on one side of the equation; he was as enthusiastic a bottom as he was a top. He could even give and receive head like no equal. But, it was his frequency of it that got to me.

We had been together for about a year, then. Sasha had moved into my rental apartment six months before. Early in the relationship, he'd commented how sex must be taken in moderation, and how it depletes one's energy, mood, and all that. That would have been a warning sign to someone of my sensibilities were it not for the fact that I understood it as well-meaning advice a loved one would give. Someone like him would give. He never really denied it to me for the first few months we were together, either, and I wasn't naive enough to believe it was due to a submissive nature. Sasha wasn't a yes-man; he said what he meant, and disagreed with things he felt weren't right and fair. He could be equally persuasive at work or in the street, and once, my sable even stood up to a bear taking up two seats in the bus we'd taken for a night out, and I was sure it would finally be curtains for him. But, lo and behold, the bear chose to stand, letting another couple sit. I kept looking and sniffing over my shoulder all the way back, just in case the bear was sucking it up just to get even with us in an alley somewhere. Smaller species such as us both were far more likely to become victims according to countless government statistics.

But the one person Sasha couldn't sway was me. Maybe we were far too alike, or maybe I felt I was always right, but our arguments, be it over what groceries to buy or movie to watch, always ended in compromise. Except the question of sex.

Sasha never liked having sex during weekdays and even Sundays at times. He said he needed to conserve his energy so that he doesn't feel like he'd been wasted on booze. He said his boss had already threatened to fire him if he came to work looking like shit, and he couldn't possibly tell his boss what he'd been up to the night before. Even in the 21st century, there were people who couldn't get round the fact that sex was a natural part of life and recreation. So, I compromised, holding back my urges such that I was asking him to play every two or three days instead of one. Cunning, ain't I?

Sasha relented half of the time, but I could see he wasn't quite into it after that. He went through the motions whenever we went at it. Several times, when I was topping him, I finished only to find that he had dozed off. He didn't even get to cum. About seven times after that, we started quarreling, till he told me he could always leave if I didn't like it. So, I let it be.

If I was crafty, he could be even more so. From then on, he took to coming back late with the excuse that he had had work to do. I'd read all the smut available online and from mail-order catalogues, so initially I thought he was sucking off the boss or something. But Sasha denied it whenever I asked. He wasn't one to lie, and, given that every relationship was built on trust, like what we both had, I let it be. Besides, he always commented on getting a house of our own one day, and I couldn't fault him for all that overtime put towards it.

Things were such that I rarely saw him anymore. He would return just after midnight and go for a quick shower before going to bed. He didn't smell like he'd been fucking anyone, boss or otherwise, so I figured he'd been telling the truth about that. Part of me wanted to make it up to him for all that hard work he'd been doing, but he was always real tired at that time, same as I, so I kept myself in check. In the morning, I would see him briefly in the kitchen, where we had a quick bite before he left with a nuzzle against my cheek. Then, off we went to the office, where insane bosses and pointless documentation awaited.

I respected Sasha's wishes, I really did. But, always an uncomfortable tension in my loins kept me on the edge such that I couldn't even get to sleep. And yet, Sasha tempted me by lying oh-so-close every night, and only his wishes kept me from jumping him in the middle of the night, gasping and panting to a satisfying release. Jacking off barely helped; the lone scent of my musk reminded me what my sable was denying me and always left me feeling frustrated and sour afterward. I wanted to hold him, breathe in his scent, and even taste him if I was so inclined.

By the third month without a warm body above or beneath me, I made my decision. I had to find it elsewhere. Not that I was dumping my sable or anything like that. Despite his lack of enthusiasm with regards to higher pleasures, he didn't deserve this. It wasn't the first time I'd been in a relationship. Granted, my previous and first relationship lasting longer than three consecutive nights went on for a full month, only for my then-boyfriend Randy to bail on me one night. I later found out that he had needed a place to crash while he was waiting on his house renovations to complete. Tragic, but true. The fact that Sasha and I had hit it off from the start with so many things in common made me appreciate him all the more. I just needed to find someone who didn't mind getting to know good old foxy better, even if it were just for one night. Or day. It didn't make a difference, unless I had to run back to work straight after. Even if I went straight to the office showers, some colleagues might catch a whiff of what I'd been up to and get the whole department talking. I'd heard of cabbies and delivery guys who cruised around with their Grindr app on and score several times in the space of the day, though they had a flexibility with their schedule I didn't have.

But the problem with one-night-stands were that they

worked best when you weren't committed to anyone. Sasha had never said he wanted our relationship to be closed, but just who actually says that out loud? *Hey, Cliffy. Can we have a closed relationship? No fucking around behind each other's back, 'kay?* You get the picture. If I were to go back to my usual hangouts and cruise round the way I had, there was always the chance that word of my deeds would spread. Sasha and I weren't recluses; we had friends and acquaintances just like any other guys, and who's to say someone we knew won't inform on the other?

I needed a more foolproof plan, somewhere where discretion was key, and also where a guy having a night out was commonplace. To the east side of the city lay the red-light district, known locally as "The Night Market." That was a holdover from colonial days when prostitution was illegal. During then, patrons had to use code words in their conversation for fear of being arrested by undercover cops. It was perfectly fine to tell someone you're heading over to the Market rather than The Palace of Treasures.

A part of me felt this was cheating, but way I saw it, Sasha had it coming. It wasn't like I was leaving him for whoever I would be fucking at the Night Market, and it's criminal of him to deny me what every man needed. Hell, what every organism needed. Even amoebae see the need to split or multiply or whatever their manner of self-fucking is called. That said, I could easily get what I came for there and make my way back long before Sasha returned. The two of us would remain together, happy and satisfied with life.

The moment I finished work the next day, I got my stuff in order. Enough cash for the ride home, with a couple hundred more for the services of an impressionable stud. Loose-fitting casual clothes, so that onlookers don't assume they know where I'm headed. Driver's ID, in case someone needed to identify my badly-beaten self. I've had many an experience with bouncers before, and they rarely ever play nice. Even the mice don't mess around. Public transport was out of the question. Chances are, someone I knew might see where I was headed. I called a cab, and, while I waited, I strolled up and down the street, sniffing around for anyone who might be watching from the sides and alleys. I took a last look down both ends of the street as my cab arrived, giving directions quickly as I sat in the back.

I looked behind as the cab rolled onward, heaving a sigh of relief when it was clear no one was following me. It would be a real bitch if Sasha had hired a private eye to keep tabs on me, but I was probably thinking too much into it. There was a faint scent of the past two customers coming from the back seats, some rodent or other. Some cab drivers sprayed descentifier in their car every now and then, especially the canids, and this was no different.

The cab driver, a tawny-colored coyote with graying fur looked into the rear view mirror at me. He grinned knowingly as I returned the gaze.

"Aye, the first time's the most jittery of all." The coyote nodded. "Then, it starts getting easier."

"What do you mean?" I asked. I fought to stay calm, because curse it—we canines could smell fear. The directions I'd given didn't lead directly into the Night Market itself. It would be a fine thing to say, "Head to the red-light district," and face the hard silent stare of the driver who was to bring me there. I'd instead given directions to the streets adjacent to the area, which was famous for its fruit stalls and eateries.

"Son, I've been in this biz long enough to know what's what!" laughed the driver. I've always been creeped out by the way wolves and coyotes laughed. It sounded a lot like a staccato of barks, interspersed with an underlying howl beneath it. "Everyone thinks they got it covered, taking the long way to the Night Market. Always alighting two to three streets away, looking over their shoulders when they do. Some even tell me they're there to enjoy the food!"

"I'm not—" I began, but the coyote waved my comment aside. We'd left the residential district where I lived, and I almost couldn't recognize the roads we were taking. The bus route to my office was in the exact opposite direction to wherever we were heading. I recalled my colleagues at work speaking of the things that used to happen in the East Side, such as gang wars and crackheads lining the alleys. It was supposed to be all cleaned up now, but the stories of my youth still had weight on my apprehension. Like many red-light districts across the world, the streets that made up the Night Market was supposed to be officially gazetted for that very purpose, though the government didn't exactly make it known. It would be quite the scandal for a minister to admit that the government agreed to such a demarcation.

"I'm not judging you, son. There are so many reasons to seek the pleasures of another. Would you really fault anyone for that? If the big guy above didn't want us fucking, he wouldn't have given us the stuff to."

I wasn't religious or anything like that, but I couldn't quite disagree with him. "Listen, Mr. err…"

"You can call me Kasi. Or Cabbie. Whichever you prefer." The driver nodded at me.

"Right. Well, Kasi, you're right. Everyone wants to have a good one every now and then. I'm no different." I eyed Kasi in the rear-view mirror, trying to gauge if he was homophobic or not. Then, I figured, Hell, even if he was, he'd be hard-pressed to beat me down at his age. "But, my boyfriend, he doesn't understand how it feels to not get any. He even tries avoiding me to get out of it. Not that it's my right to impose on him, but…"

"I do understand. It's one of the more common reasons for it to happen," Kasi replied. I didn't have to ask if he meant my cheating rather than Sasha's avoiding me. "But, folks aren't all born alike, otherwise the world would be boring as hell. The fact that you two're still together—I'm guessing this isn't a short-term thing—means that your differences probably complement one another. It's fine if you go have your fix or whatever you call it somewhere else, but you have to remember that when other people gets involved, that's when you start seeing the faults and flaws in one another." The coyote gave a sigh. "Flaws that would otherwise be accepted as part of the person. Whores know better than to get attached, but they're professionals. The same can't always be said for their clients, and Old Kasi's been there. And here's your stop."

I was so engrossed in Kasi's verbiage, I hadn't noticed the streets around us. I could now see that we were right outside a most colorfully-lit street, illuminated with neon and all those newfangled digital lighting contraptions. Pink lighting predominated much of the streetscape. Then, I realized Kasi decided to drop me off at my actual intended destination, directions be damned.

"This isn't the place I asked for," I protested.

"Save it, son. If you step out now, the ride's on me," replied Kasi. For the first time, he turned around and regarded his passenger. "Just remember what I've said and consider it square."

Huh, some preacher this guy was. But, I could always save on cash. I muttered my thanks and exited, the thud of the door behind me louder than I intended. Kasi drove away, and I lifted my muzzle to catch the sights and sounds.

It turned out that, despite trying to maintain some semblance of unobtrusiveness by being a good sixty metres from a side road, the entrance to the district advertised its wares glaringly enough. A flashing lit bulb sign alternated from a right-pointing arrow to the word "Enter." Two foxes, one fennec, and one grey sidled up to me, but I did my best to ignore their words and paws, deciding to head deeper into the Market for a choicer look. I stepped through the lightly illuminated alleyway, sidestepping working girls and boys alike, including a couple of dazed-looking patrons. I wrinkled my nose at the stench of sex coming off one of them. Weasel, ferret, and skunk, tinged with the underlying scent of rodent. A most enjoyable and pungent foursome, if I had to hazard a guess.

Then, I stepped into the main square, where the sights and sounds of the Night Market assailed me. More neon signs crafted in a myriad of species outlines showed themselves, all voluptuous and dainty legs. I could identify those of cats and horses fairly easily, but generic canine and mustelid outlines could refer to any number of subspecies. Loud booming music could be heard from multiple joints, all meandering into an unintelligible noise. The smell of roasting meat and steamed vegetables emanated from several eateries, which had me wondering who actually came here to eat. I guessed even working boys and girls had meal breaks. There were so many establishments to visit, so many tastes to savor, and I didn't know which one to go to. Someone gripped my tail lightly, and I spun in surprise, my brush slipping out of my accoster's grip. It was yet another fox, a red just like me.

"New here? Show me a good time?" giggled the fox. I stared agape at her, eyes travelling from her head to toes. She really cut a good figure, which my eyes and sheath very much appreciated, with manageable but not overly large breasts visible through the light fabric scarf she draped across her person. I figured patrons would normally go for those of a similar species. There was something to be said for species familiarity, much like how rats would rather hang out with other rats, and wildcats would rather hang out with other smaller cats. Her scent, accentuated by a perfume resembling that of a vixen on heat tempted me to hire her right there and then, but years of shopping for entirely different merchandise told me to take a look around first.

"No, thanks," I stuttered. The vixen gave a mock pout. "Not that you aren't pretty or anything, but err…"

"Ah, it's okay." The fox flapped her paw in playful dismissal. "Come to try another flavor besides fox, eh? Just what are you looking for? Maybe I can help." She gave loud smack on her left rump. "I'm Virgo, by the way."

Crap, I'd not thought any further than that. The plan was to play it by ear and make a decision based on where the fancy took me. But, if I was going to have to pay, I might as well have gotten my money's worth. From my understanding, working boys and girls weren't generally priced according to species, but popularity. That said, some species would have been more popular than others for whatever preferences patrons may have had. I wanted a good time that rivaled the best of my experiences, but, try as I might, I couldn't recall any encounter that stood out. There was the badger lady, there was the skunk guy; there was even this she-bear that near squashed the life out of me when she rode cowgirl. Then, there was this sable…

Sable. Sasha wasn't the most skilled of bedmates, but he sure was energetic, even enthusiastic when we'd first met. He would leave me panting, be it when he was bouncing on my shaft, each squelch and slurp a testament to his vigor. And when he topped, he would grip my tail and yank my foxy self towards him, sinking his needlelike fangs into my ass, a virtue of musteline flexibility. It made me hard—I meant harder—just thinking about it.

But, the truth was that he no longer did all that for me. I would just have to find someone to do the same.

Virgo's smile lit up when I told her what I needed.

The waiting areas of brothels were quiet affairs, contrary to the din outside. Virgo explained that the sound from the loud-speakers outside were to get potential customers in the mood. Once they were inside, people generally wanted a quiet time to themselves. They could always turn on the digital radios in their room if needed. She bid me to wait in a waiting area while she went to see if my request was ready. The vixen had already explained that, despite the Night Market catering to all orienta-tions, my requested combination of gender and species wasn't common. It was just fortunate she knew about a boy that had gone into the biz a couple months back. I had a scotch on Virgo from the bar while I waited, lapping lightly through the mouthpiece of my glass. I guessed she would probably earn a commission from her referral, but at that point of time, I didn't mind as long as I got what I wanted.

The waiting room was empty, save me, and I would have seen it as a sign of the brothel's unpopularity were it not for the faint sounds of thumping and moaning my ears could pick out through the ceilings and walls. Soundproofing wasn't perfect, especially for us sharp-eared species, and the sounds of enjoy-ment were already making me painfully hard. Despite the horny clientele that would have sat here before, the waiting room didn't stink of musk and arousal with the underlying scent of pine suggesting descentifier being dispensed regularly. The room also had the usual reading materials one would find in a dentist's or physician's, but also included posters of the girls or guys that worked there dressed in nothing except their pelts and smiles. Aside from advertising, it must also help with the mood of the patrons. I couldn't see any sable males, however, so the management either hadn't decided on getting a full photo shot of him, or he wasn't a full-timer. Or, maybe Virgo was having me on with two enormous bouncers appearing soon enough with a statement that I owed them $200 for the scotch. I've heard of stories of such scams happening in establishments that appeared to offer sex but didn't, and it didn't help that it was my first time getting into this situation. I kept my eyes on the door and tongue to the scotch, just in case I had to get out fast. This wouldn't be the first time that had happened, not counting that college trip to Amsterdam.

Virgo was as good as her word, however, and a bear madame in a dress lumbered up to me. From her size, she could very well be two bouncers on her own. She barely gave off much of a scent, suggesting she might have long retired from active work. She kept her fur well-trimmed, however, accentuating her curves for God knows why.

"Yo, dear. Your boy's ready for you. Just head up the stairs and turn right. He's in Room 4. Virgo said you'll be booking a full-night service?" The bear smiled with her arms crossed.

"That's right." I made for the stairs, but the madame casually stepped in front of me. It took a moment for me to get the hint.

"Sorry, how much?" I fished my wallet out of my jeans. It was easy to forget sex wasn't always free.

"Four hundred. The scotch's on the house." The madame pocketed the cash somewhere in her shoulder scarf. "Go on, have fun!" She covered her muzzle in what had to be a diminutive giggle, but made her look like an abashed bear.

I needed no telling twice, scaling the stairs two at a time.

Call me desperate, but I don't believe anyone had ever been in my position. The second floor was a U-shaped corridor with rooms spaced throughout it. Here, the sounds of moans and groans were louder, with the faint hint of musks whiffing beneath the doors. Each door was numbered, much like a hotel or old-fashioned apartment building, but I was past caring about details. I padded over to Room 4, shaft positively bursting through my jeans.

I stood at the door as I composed myself. There was a mix of scents here. Dog, ferret, a type of civet, and even a horse. I couldn't imagine how the sable could manage such a customer, but one can't always choose their customers in this gig.

I could still back out now. Sasha was waiting for me at home, and the madame had already been paid, so there wouldn't be any bad feelings if I left. The boy inside would even be glad for the break, and I wouldn't have to feel guilty about cheating on my sable. Sasha's the only one who's stuck with me for more than a month, and loyalty like that's got to count for something.

But then, I told myself that loyalty was a two-way street. Though Sasha hadn't been disloyal by cheating, or anything like that, the fact that he didn't give me what I needed meant I had every right to take matters into my own paws. If he expected me to go without sex for the rest of my life, well, then he'd better find someone else. And, with that affirmation, I turned the doorknob and entered, pushing the door shut behind me.

The first thing I noticed was that the room was lit by candles, giving off a soft ambience. Scented, too, if my nose was anything to go by. The second thing I noticed was the sable lying back on the bed, his white underfur trailing from his neck to his groin, accentuated by the dark umber around it. A perfect picture of musteline beauty.

The third thing I realized was that the sable on the bed was Sasha, the sable I returned to each and every day, now naked and posed for what he'd denied me all this while.

The two of us stared at one another, the sable sitting upright when he saw and smelt who his next customer was.

"You!" I snarled, voice half-dying into a choke.

"You?" Sasha parroted, more surprised than anything else.

"What the fuck do you mean by that? You lied to me this whole time!" I was now yelling, wanting very much to step forward and shake that sneaky little mustelid till his fangs clattered.

To his credit, Sasha didn't flinch. "Like Hell I was. I told you, I've got work to do. This is it. Besides, you're the one that's cheating now." The sable got to his feet, and I tried and failed to avoid looking at his sheath. Damn.

"What—you—" I sputtered, furious that he had the nerve to use whatever I was doing as a defense. "You know what I meant! If you've been whoring yourself out, I've got a right to know!"

"But, would you want to?" Sasha challenged, and I paused at his intensity. The two of us were so very much alike, even our own arguments deflected each other like sparring partners. "If you'd known the reason why I'm exhausted and not in the mood each time I come home, would you have stopped me from working, just so you could have more sex with me? I'm here not because I enjoy it, but because I work towards a better future for us. Do you really want to live in a run-down apartment in a questionable neighborhood all your life, only to have some lowlife rob or kill you on the way back? But yet, I moved in with you so that you wouldn't be alone. I never stopped loving you, Cliffy."

My emotions were rather conflicted by now, and I couldn't decide whether to run, stay, or sock my sable a good one. "You could still have given me some of yourself!" I wanted to yell, but it came out as a pained whine. The fact that this was my sable, the only person who didn't stay with me just for one night of fun or free lodging made this incredibly hard to bear. "Do you know how hard is it to keep it all pent up, just so I don't cheat on you?"

Sasha opened and closed his muzzle, and for once, it looked like he was at a loss for words. But, my sable never was.

"I know that, Cliffy. It's just that it's tiring after a night like tonight, you know? I've had four clients come through already—"

"I know." I tapped my sniffling nose.

"—and you understand how competitive this business is. Some clients like to feel like the boy toy they're fucking is having a good time as well, and a few even insist on seeing me cum. One needs to have enthusiasm and stamina in this profession, and I'm sorry if I held off things with you so that I can keep going. Reviews from customers go a lot towards the madame deciding if I'm worth signing on full-time. I'm still technically on contract, so most of the clients I get are those who have special requests."

I nodded, remembering Sasha wasn't featured in the posters downstairs unlike the others that worked here. Part of me was convinced that if he'd told me what he did for extra cash, I would have understood, but the truth was, I might never have. We'd all been brought up by the society we lived in, taught that sex was taboo, and the people involved in the trade even more so. The fact, however, remained that I was now here, and neither Sasha nor I could go back to the illusion we had before. We were no longer a happy couple living together that came straight back to where they lived after a hard day's work just to enjoy each other's company. We were a couple who discovered one was cheating on the other, believing they had no other choice.

Sasha cleared his throat. "Have you paid Madame Bari yet? I can see about getting you a refund."

For a moment, I considered telling the sable he could shove my hard-earned cash up his ass if he needed it so much. Then, I realized that perhaps he really did need it that much, such that he let complete strangers shove whatever they wanted up it, subject to their own whims and fancies, their lusts and their kinks. I never asked Sasha how much he earned in his day job, but a friend of mine who worked in a similar field mentioned it was more than I did. And yet, if my sable still had to work here so many nights per week...

"I don't want it," I replied. Sasha made to protest, but I

waved it aside. "I want you to do whatever I've paid for."

Sasha's eyes narrowed. "Is that what you see me as? A fuck toy?" His voice rose to a screech.

"No!" I stepped forward, and Sasha stepped back, falling back onto the bed as he did. He tried getting back up, his paws outstretched to keep me back. My paws were longer than his, however, and I took hold of his shoulders.

"You've been doing all this for us, I get it," I said. Sasha made to pull my paws off, soft amber eyes looking away from me. "But, I don't get to see you anymore these days. I know I've been an oversexed asshole and have probably been getting on your nerves for the past year. But, I very much want to share this with you again—something I've missed for a very long time."

"I doubt it. Just look at where you are now," Sasha snapped. "If you really wanted to be with me, you wouldn't have come here. There's any number of species you could have your way with."

"Why did you think I asked for a male sable?" I asked. Sasha stopped trying to break free and finally looked back into my eyes.

I went all out, hugging my sable close, and he gasped, his paws slowly circling around the top of my back uncertainly as he always had. My sable may be short, but that never stopped him from reaching higher. I couldn't take it anymore, and tears finally burst free as I whined, my sable stroking up and down my back, making hushing noises as he did. I cried for the times we'd missed together and my betrayal of such a wonderful mate. Sasha fought back his tears at first; he'd always been the more resolute of the two. Then, his tears came. Tears of anguish that he'd led me to act this way, seeking something he should have been there for. There exists a saying that it takes two paws to clap, but it also took two to fuck, the underlying conundrum that only recently existed between us. But, it didn't have to. Even if I had only one more night with the one I misjudged, I would be a most happy fox.

Then, Sasha steered me towards the bed, and it was my

turn to fall back against it, my sable falling right atop me. Well-practiced paws unfastened my fly as I tensed. The sable then hooked his paws under my shirt, taking it off in a smooth motion without the chin of my muzzle catching onto it as it usually does. He'd had plenty of practice.

It'd been a while, but no one ever forgets how to go through the motions. I started to kick off my pants, only to have it brought all the way down by outgoing sable paws. My sheath sprung free of my briefs, the red of my arousal bobbing as it did.

Sasha leaned close to me, his breath a warm tickling in my lifted ears. "What would you like tonight, dear?"

I held my breath, ears skewing as realization set in. Normally, the two of us would feel each other up, much the same way we had when we first met, and let things go naturally from there. Neither of us saw the need to ask for any particular kink or preference, eventually finding what the other desired or accepted. But, for the first time ever, Sasha was asking me for a choice, and I could finally request anything I wanted. Just like so many others who'd come through this room.

But to me, Sasha was no whore. Even if we couldn't change the past, I could decide how to treat him. He was my light and my mate, one of the few constants in my life.

"Whatever you want," I said, and the look of surprise on his muzzle said I'd made the right choice.

Sasha raked his claws through my belly fur, running furrows through it. Like any canid, my feet kicked in a rotating motion, my tongue out and lolling. A smile dancing on my sable's lips, he drew his claws down to my sac where my thumping ceased to an almost pained whine.

Then, his paws sought to flip me over with my chest resting against the bed, my body tensing as I wondered if he was doing what I thought he was doing. Then, he positioned himself over my rump, his knees spread alongside my hips, and I realized he was. The scent of vigor washed over me, and I realized he was more excited than he'd been for a long time.

The sable held my brush to one side, and I shivered as he

lubed up my hole with something cold, most likely the high-grade stuff the establishment provides. Then, I felt that almost familiar pressure upon my ass, first a gentle prod, then a firm push. I shuddered when I felt his cock push through, groaning as much as whining as it filled me. Sasha rubbed my ears as he held it there, massaging lightly as he let his breath waft against my cheek ruffs.

"I can stop if you ask me to," he whispered. At first, I thought he was taunting me, the moment he got the chance for full control. Then, I realized he really was checking if I was fine. It'd been a while since he'd penetrated me like that, and one's own digits didn't do it justice. My breath was coming in quick gasps as I forced myself to relax.

"No!" I replied, hasher than I intended. I could almost feel Sasha's dick twitch in his surprise. "Do whatever you have planned. I'll be fine."

Sasha gave a smile—I could see it in the mirror placed across from the bed—and began a slow but regular rhythm, stretching and pulling at my insides, each move scratching at that itch I held so long inside. I gripped the bedsheets and buried my muzzle beneath my chest, letting the sensations soak and wash away at me. The sound of soft smacks filled my ears, and the initial pressure I had felt had now dulled away into a gradual presence, reminding me I was no longer alone in my ministrations. I almost couldn't believe this was happening, and I reached back, feeling for Sasha lest it turned out to be a dream. Sasha gripped my paw back, then relocated his from my sides to my shoulders, controlling every move he made, working in symphony with the other parts of his body. His hips thrusted while his paws held my shoulders, massaging and controlling the momentum of his thrusts the way I liked it.

Pressed to the bed, my shaft was rubbed to the point of bursting. Normally, the mattress at home gave me a painful burn if I tried that, but the one here were soft, with silky bedsheets that practically glided over my shaft. My pants started becoming ragged, the tension in my groin multiplied by that warm tightness in my ass. And then I came, yipping louder than

I remember.

Sasha bent forward at the last moment, his fangs sinking into my butt. I yipped again at the sudden pain, a burst of warmth coating my bellyfur beneath me. Sasha screeched in an almost feral peal with several hard twitches in my ass followed by an outpouring of warmth.

I groaned as I sank into the bed, a warm flush washing over me. Sasha slumped on top of me, another blanket of warmth I gladly accepted. His head reached only my upper back, but still I felt his pants tickling my ears. Our backs rose and fell with our exertion, and I was glad we finally had our time together.

"I so missed this," I muttered. I rolled onto my side, Sasha rolling along so that we ended up facing each other.

"Was it just sex you missed?" Sasha commented drily. I would normally get all relaxed and sleepy after all that, but my sable always kept his wits about him.

"That too, but mostly you." I hugged his head against me. Sasha didn't resist, rubbing his muzzle into my fluffy chest. "I hardly see you at home anymore. I understand if you're tired after working here, but when you don't tell me what's happening, well...I thought there was something else going on. Like maybe you were, err..."

"Fucking someone else?" Sasha asked. I remained silent. "You were right, but I never gave my heart to them. My clients, their wants and desires; it's all part of the job for me. A few thought they could find love wherever they put their money, but they don't realize how much of a dream that is. Madame Bari banned a few customers for harassing a few of the girls and boys. Not only is it bad for business, but working girls and boys deserve to be free of commitments once they clock out. You are my only love, Cliffy. That, I assure you."

"Do you still intend to work here?" I asked. I felt Sasha tense, so I stroked his ears. "I won't be offended if you do, it just feels strange that my boyfriend's fucking other people while we act like everything's fine. And, you always come back so tired."

"Nothing's changed between us. But, one should always

aim to improve their quality of life," Sasha replied. "Even if we don't get mugged in all the years we stay in your neighborhood, the lease on the apartment building isn't going to be forever. It's on a planned redevelopment area, so the government could always buy out the landlord that owns the building. Our current savings won't be able to get us another apartment in a good neighborhood. This job pays far better than my day job, but I can't work full time, otherwise any jobs I apply for in the future would want to know what I've been doing all those years I'm not in engineering. So, yes, I'll still be here till we've got enough money to move."

I hummed in acknowledgment, and Sasha, relieved that I was not going to go all ballistic on him, lay his head back against my chest. Then, I wondered about something.

"How popular are red foxes in this industry?" I asked.

Sasha glared up at me. "Are you trying to get one back at me?"

"No, dear!" I hastily denied. "I just figured that if you're working here to get us a better future, I should be doing my part. Pardon me if I say this, but you don't seem all that enthusiastic in sex as I am. If I were to, say, work here in place of you part-time, do you promise to take a break at home? I can't have my sable doing something he hates for a fox who refuses to carry the burden, too. You look like you could use a break anyway."

Sasha stared intently back at me, and I, him. This was a challenge: to further confirm if I was just pursuing my own selfish desires, but deep inside, my sable knew I cared for him as much as he did.

"On one condition," said Sasha. "To answer your question, foxes are popular bedmates, especially with those domineering canine types. Dogs, wolves, and coyotes always want to play the alpha; nobody knows why. But, I've built up my network of clients throughout the last few months, and a newcomer like you will take some time to have the same success as I do. For the next few weeks, I'll work my shifts as normal, and I'm sure I can get you an immediate position with Madame Bari. Once you get more established, I can cut down my working nights from four to two, and you'll only work two days per night on the same shift as I. This way, we can keep an eye on each other despite being in different rooms, and be able to spend time together on our days off. And, once we get enough money to move elsewhere, we quit. Is that a deal?"

I didn't fully agree, because if I worked four days, we could get that house he always wanted faster. But, when people don't spend enough time with each other, bad things happen. Like how things that day came close to becoming.

Either of us might not like everything about what the other proposed, but the foundation of every relationship was understanding. And, for the both of us, it was also compromising. We would have to work for the better part of a year with this arrangement, but I believed we could make this work.

I breathed deep the scent of my sable beside me, and he did the same, and that was all I needed to get through this.

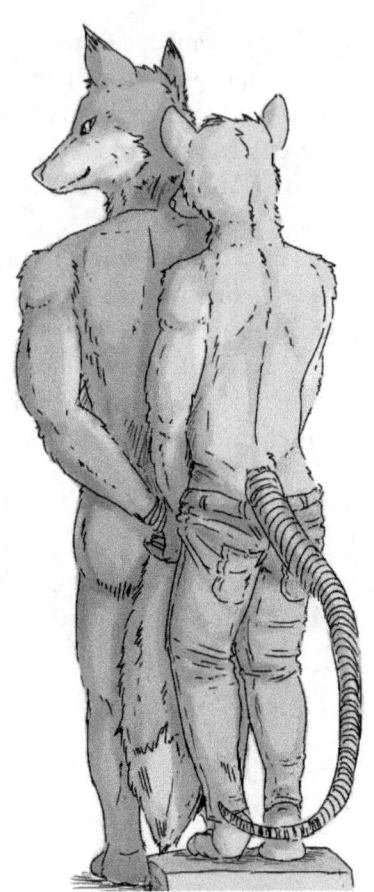

ORIENTATION
TJ Minde

TJ is a rat – I mean fox, totally a fox; red fur and all of that – that moved to Ohio almost ten years ago. After scurrying – I mean pouncing, in a foxy way! – into the fandom, he picked up the pen. TJ is incredible grateful for the community of artists, writers and friend he found; they helped him discover something that he cares about – writing. TJ enjoys squeaking – yipping! Totally meant yipping – with others about the worlds and character's they've created. TJ's other works may be found in Roar, Fang, and other anthologies both in and out of the fandom. For thoughts, comments and replies – and other very foxy things! - in small chunks, he can be found on Twitter @TJMinde. Do you think he's a fox yet?

The black fur on my knuckles rose as I gripped the strap of my messenger bag tighter and walked through the front door of the hotel. I looked around the lobby, then at the small, plain business card in my paw. I was thirty minutes late. Gazing around the room, everything looked and smelled normal; small reception desk off to the side and big comfy chairs not far away. But, there was a small, simple sign with one word and an arrow: "Orientation." My tail curled around my ankle and I followed the directions. *I hope I don't look foolish,* I thought to myself.

As I rounded the corner, a lion with a bored expression across his muzzle, leaning back in his chair, lounged behind a table. When our eyes met, he sat up. "Hey there. I'm Pride. You here for Orientation?"

I felt my ears warm in a blush. "Uh, yeah. I was worried I didn't go to the right place." A nervous chuckle escaped me.

The lion smiled. "It's okay. Just like any other lecture. Just not as boring. But, I doubt a good looking dude like you needs much of the info here. Probably *foxy* enough, right?" He winked. "I just need to see your ID for a moment." He held out a tan paw.

Did he just flirt with me? How do I respond? I blinked before fumbling for my wallet. *And, what did he mean by 'foxy enough'?* I handed the card to him. He looked from the fox in the picture, then to me and back, then handed it along with a clip board to me.

"I need you to fill this out." The page was filled with fine print.

I stared at it for a moment. "What's this?"

Pride crossed his arms. "Legal documentation saying you're here on your own volition, understand 'no' means 'no,' and contains a very strict NDA."

"NDA?" My tail curled around my leg.

He nodded. "Due to the nature of the event, we take privacy very seriously. If you want, feel free to read through it."

"O-okay," I stuttered.

"There are some extra seats over there." Pride pointed

across the room. "Take your time."

I headed over to the cushy chair the lion pointed me to as I read over the contract. It was deep. Lots of legal jargon, but there was an extra page with footnotes in laymen's terms that cleared up most of my questions. Still, it was heavy. I spent twenty minutes reading of the few pages there were before I printed, then scribbled my name near the bottom.

When I made my way back to the table, Pride smiled again. "Just need to take one last peek at your ID," he said as he took the clipboard. After looking at my name on the card and the name on the page, he handed the plastic rectangle back. "Thanks, Bash."

I tilted he head. "Bash? My name's—"

"Ah ah." Pride raised a finger, cutting me off with another smile. "It's nicknames only, here. Part of the privacy bit. I only look at your ID long enough to ensure you're you and your signature is legal."

"Okay." My tail curled tighter around my leg and my ears fell. "Why Bash?"

The lion chuckled. "Look at you: you're so nervous and bashful. It's adorable, and it fits." He slid a nametag across the table to me with my new nickname already written on it in bright blue marker. I kept my head down as I removed the plastic-y paper from the back and stuck it over my breast.

"Bash?" said the lion in a gentle tone.

It took me a moment, but I met his gaze.

"No one here will hurt you or judge you. Just remember, 'no' means 'no.' People will respect your boundaries. I promise." He looked hopeful.

"Yeah." I nodded. "I'm just…" I rubbed my arm, pulling at the orange fur near my elbow. "I'm nervous. Not used to…" I waved my arms around my head. "This feeling. Like, I'm walking into a very…unique place, and I have no idea what that's like. I mean, I only just started to ask if I'm—" My voice caught in my throat.

The lion waited patiently with his paws laced in front of him as I struggled with the word.

I can do this. I paused and took a breath. "Gay."

Pride gave me a look of sympathy and I nodded. "Well, this is a good place to explore." He pointed his thumb over his shoulder. "Go on in. And, try to enjoy yourself."

"Thanks. I will." I gave the lion a small wave before walking past the table and into the meeting room.

As the door closed behind me, everyone looked at me. "Hello there, uh…" said a ferret from the front of the room, squinting through his glasses. "Bash. You must be special if Pride let you in so late after the lecture." The rest of the room chuckled, and I wanted to hide in my jacket. "Hey, hey. Be nice," he said to the rest of the room. "I'm Prof. I lead the presentation. Have a seat." I nodded, grabbing the first open chair near me. "Very good. Now, as I was saying, that was the more passive portion of the lecture. We'll pause here for those who need a break or care to step out. No harm either way."

An older badger near the front and a few women in the back stepped out. As the people moved about, I took in the view; interestingly enough, the room looked more like a large lecture hall. Sorta. It didn't have the incline to the seating area I was used to, but it still had the rows and rows of chairs. Still, there looked to be about fifteen to twenty folks scattered around the room. Canids, mustelids, rodents. It didn't look like there was a lot of variation on age either. Most of the attendees looked to be college students in their twenties, like me. Though, there were a few older people milling about.

On the stage, Prof stood to the side of the room near a podium, looking at papers. *Probably lecture notes,* I assumed. By the back corner was a large duffle bag, and in the center of the presentation area was a tall metal frame, about a body and a half tall with a chair just beside it.

Not sure what to expect, I pulled out my notebook. *It's a lecture, isn't it? Might as well try to take notes.*

While waiting for the presentation to resume, I scribbled away at the page. Not writing anything down, just doodling here and there. My tail was curled around my hip, and the white tip flicked from with every other mark of the pen on paper.

After a few minutes, one of the two women returned and gave Prof a thumb up.

"Okay. Seems like we're all back, so let's continue." He clapped his chocolate paws together. "I'm going to assume that you've all at least watched porn and understand the basic mechanics of sex." The room let out a nervous chuckle. "I also hope you realize porn is a shitty instructor, but nevertheless, I'm going to skip past the basics of 'tab A into slot B' and go a deeper into the nuances of intimacy. The first subject I want to talk about is role playing." Fewer people chuckled this time, but enough did. "I know, I know. It sounds silly. But, if you're able to get into the right headspace and hold it, it can be a lot of fun for both people."

With a small nod of my head, I started my notes as he spoke.

"Now, at the same time, communication with your partner is important. Knowing their limits and what they're comfortable with is important." As Prof looked around the room, a few attendees nodded along.

"For this next section of the demonstration, I'm going to ask one of my aides to join me. Swish?" he called in a stern, loud voice. "Come here."

A door in the back of the conference room opened up, and another red fox like me sauntered into the room. And I mean *sauntered*. His arms swung relaxed at his side and his hips swished with every step making his tail, held high and proud, sway. Seeing how he moved and carry himself, he was obviously gay.

That must be what Pride meant. He's so confident in himself. I started making notes, looking from the other fox to the page as I wrote.

While he made his way to the font, the ferret continued, "Parts of the lecture will be generally applicable for those of either sex. However, we're obviously focusing on the male form, so your mileage may vary." Swish trotted up the few steps of the small stage and spun around, with a smile across his muzzle and his arms at his side. And, even though he stopped in front of a chair, his tail still—well—swished in a slight wag. He wore jeans and a plain leather vest with no shirt. The more interesting things were the bracers of what looked to be rope around either wrist. One stopped mid-forearm, while the other went almost to the elbow.

The ferret walked behind Swish, sliding a paw along the aide's back. I noticed the fox's red tail flicked as the white fur of the tip brushed against Prof's arm. *That was intimate.*

"Swish, for the class' benefit, are you aware of what's about to happen?" Again, his voice was commanding.

He nodded. "Oh yes, sir."

"Very good. And, what are your rules?" The ferret paced behind Swish with his own arms behind his back.

"No speaking out of turn unless it's to use a safe word. And, moans and the like do not count."

"Very good," Prof said, patting the top of the fox's head, making his tail wag faster, "and what are the safe words?"

"'Yellow' and 'red,' sir."

Prof addressed the crowd. "Anyone guess why those might be the words used?"

A black paw from the back went up.

"Midnight?" said the ferret, acknowledging the wolf with dark black fur.

He lowered his paw and looked to the floor as his ears fell. "B-b-because he might say something more...normal...when you're doing what you're about to do?"

The ferret smiled. "Very good. He may want me to stop, but unless he uses the safe word, I'm in control of the scene." Prof looked over his shoulder at the fox. "Take off the vest and prepare the rope, Swish."

It is *rope,* I thought.

Without a word, the fox draped the vest across the back of the chair. He stood there, shirtless, for a moment, with a grin across his muzzle, spine erect and tail up.

How is he so sure of himself?

Then, he began to unbind his wrists, starting with the long-er of the two pieces.

As Swish worked, the ferret continued, "Now, before we start, there is another rule of play I'd like to touch on: SSC." He counted each off on a digit. "Play safe, play sane, play consensually.

"It might sound straightforward, but let me explain each to cover all the bases. Playing safe really does mean safety first. For example…" Prof paused, walking behind the fox, "when we play with rope, we have a set EMT-grade safety sheers nearby," he said, pulled the scissors from the fox's back pocket. "So, if he doesn't feel good or right, or if we need to stop right away, we can do so. Communication is key."

As he spoke, my paw worked fast, taking notes as he went.

"Playing sanely is similar to playing safely, but focused on the mentality of the participants. Don't go places that will upset your partner, and know your boundaries. I know Swish's limits and past and know how far I can go, and I stay within those boundaries. If you don't, you're being an asshole. And, that's not sexy, that's abuse. Again, communication is key."

"Here, sir." The fox handed Prof the first rope then started working on the second.

The ferret took it with a nod, folding it in half again and again as he paced the stage looking at us. "Finally, playing consensually is making sure that your partner is willing to do the things you are looking for them to do. Or, willing to let you do what you want. Again, Swish is aware of what may happen and is okay with that. As you all heard."

When the fox finished untying the second rope, the ferret turned to him. "Drape that over the chair." With a smile across his muzzle, Swish did as he was asked. "Good. Now, come here."

It didn't take long for the fox to comply, tail wagging as he stood there.

"Tail down and turn around." Prof commanded.

Swish did as he was told, but it looked like it troubled him to keep it low.

He's so expressive with it. Should all gay foxes be like that? I made another note.

"Now, the first thing I'm going to show is a rope harness. I'm going to start with the middle of the rope, also called the bight, in the middle of his back."

I started a new section of notes, writing down "bite" while I watched the ferret work. He moved the rope around Swish, explaining each pass. Each step was slow and methodical, taking his time to wrap the fox. When the rope was pulled across each of Swish's nipples, the fox bit his lip with a soft grunt. After the second time, Prof addressed the fox directly. "You like that?"

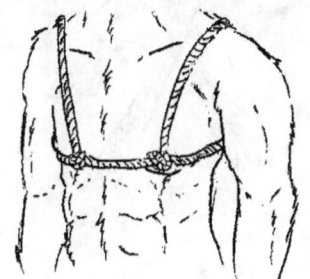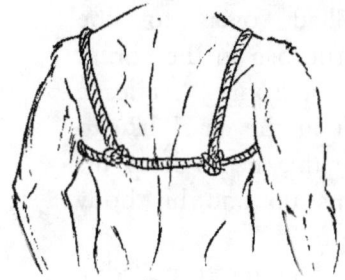

Figure 1

"Yes, sir," Swish moaned.

Seeing the look of pleasure in his eye made me squirm in my seat. *He really enjoys that.*

"Very good." Prof kissed the fox on the side of the muzzle. "Almost done."

Again, Swish nodded. After a few more tugs of the rope, Prof tied off the ends, securing the harness in place.

"Now, with this tied, there are a few things you can do," said the ferret. "These lines going over his shoulders can be nice handlebars." He wrapped his paws around the ropes and pulled the fox closer to him. "Then again, someone likes to be pulled around, don't you?"

Swish shuddered. "Yes sir."

Prof let him go. "Turn around and hold your arms forward, fists close together but not touching." He then turned his head to the audience. "I'm going to bind his wrists with a simple two column tie." As he picked up the shorter rope, the fox turned towards him and complied with the instructions. A few twists of the rope later, the fox's paws were in front of him, with a thick column of rope around his wrists.

"The type of rope we're using allows his wrists to bear a little weight. But, we aren't going to suspend him from them." Prof walked over to the duffle bag in the corner of the room. "At least, not in the air. I like to use this tie to keep his arms up and his body exposed."

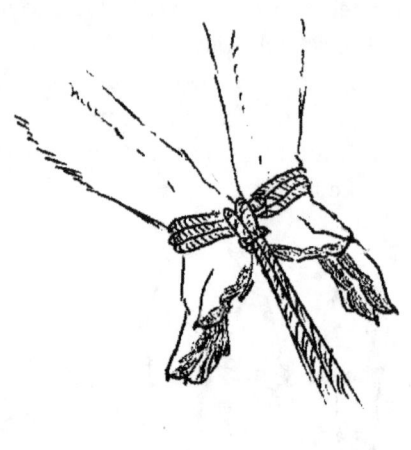

Figure 2

The ferret pulled a few metallic objects from his bag. "I have a few different tools for that purpose. These are nice starts." In one paw were two metal S's, and the other held a short rope with two metal rings on either end. "I have this sturdy stand here just for this purpose." He hooked one S over the central bar and fed one of the circles through the other end.

Prof curled a finger to the bound fox. "Come here, Swish."

Doing as he was told, the fox held up his arms to the ferret.

Prof hooked one end of the second S between his wrists and the other through the larger metal ring, leaving his arms up as he mentioned, and his chest exposed.

"Now, from this position, there are a few things we can do. If we want to be light, we could tickle his sides or belly." The ferret demonstrated, making the fox squirm at his touch, though Prof quickly stopped. "We can also bring in some pain, if that's your thing. This is a great position for floggers and whips." Swish let out a soft yip as the ferret smacked him on the rear.

Figure 3

I winced a little in sympathy, though the fox's tail still wagged. Pain wasn't my thing, and I wasn't sure if I wanted to watch someone else go through that. Then again, I wasn't expecting to see someone bound like this either.

"But," Prof continued as he stepped closer to his aide, "what I enjoy doing more is bringing out toys." The ferret moved back to the bag and, instead of pulling something from it, picked the whole thing up and set it beside the fox.

"Depending on the way I have Swish tied up, it's sometimes fun to make him squirm with electricity. Playing with conductive rope can bring tingles and shocks to unexpected places."

Swish's tail continued to wag, though his ears fell and he let out a whimper. *I can't tell if he likes that or not.*

"However, for the sake of time, I have three toys we'll be playing with instead. Though, before we can do that, someone here is a little overdressed." As Prof moved behind the fox, his paws went right for the button of his pants. With a smooth motion, they were opened and more fur could be seen.

He's not wearing any underwear. I squirmed in my seat as I felt myself reacting. *But, I can't get hard here. That would be weird, right?*

Before I could answer myself, the fox's pants were on the floor. His knees were together, and his tail curled between his legs as he attempted to hide the swelling red shaft that was beginning to emerge from his sheath. The scent of his arousal filled the room.

I guess not... I squirmed in my seat as my groin responded in kind.

"Now, that's better," said the ferret as he removed the pants from the floor and began to step around the fox. A look of surprise crossed Swish's muzzle as he was pulled by the back of his harness around.

And the view from the back was just as good. His red-orange fur was peppered with black strands along the center of his back that spread around his tail and rump.

"Swish, tail up, or it gets secured up," commanded the ferret.

With another yip, Swish's tail rose, exposing his taut rear to us. And, I felt my own shaft swell at the sight.

*Having someone at your command, doing what you say. Wow...*I crossed one leg over the other, trying to keep my own arousal down and placed my notebook in my lap.

"Good boy," Prof said as he squeezed the fox's rump with a paw before moving back to the duffle bag. "The first toy I want to show is closer to a standard butt plug." He held up a rubber-looking bulb with a wide base and holes running along the length. "I like using this at the start of play; it's a nice small stretch to start out and is an easy way to prep your sub." He pulled out a small tube from the bag. "We, of course, start with lube. And, I know how this fox likes to be stretched, so I'm going to start by just putting enough on the toy to get it in." The ferret flipped the cap up and poured the clear liquid on the toy.

"Now, I don't recommend this, new, first-time toy-users. Normally, I'd suggest warming yourself up with digits. But, some foxes are special cases," Prof said with a wink to Swish.

Some foxes? Am I not fox enough?

Before I could think on that any more, my thoughts were distracted as the ferret pressed the tip of the plug under the fox's tail and pressed it in. As it stretched him out, Swish began to pull away. Then, a second later, he pushed back on it, sliding it in to place.

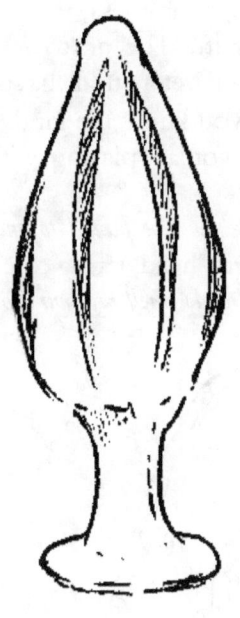

"How's that, Swish?" Prof said into the fox's ear. If it weren't for my hearing, I would have missed the question. Swish's muzzle moved, but almost no sound came out. "So everyone can hear, dear."

"Nice. Comforting. It's part of our ritual that gives me ideas of what's next." He bit his lip and let out a soft moan.

And as I heard that moan, my dick twitched in yearning. I've seen porn, as Prof said, but I'd never seen a person pleasure another like that beyond a computer screen. And, unlike porn, I didn't question how real that sounded.

Prof smiled over his shoulder to us. "One of my favorite things about this toy is how versatile it is. Not only does it stretch a person, but those gaps you saw allow extra lube to pass through." The ferret walked back over to the container he set down and pulled out a screw cap with a long, thick tube kinked at a ninety degree angle. Removing the original cap from the lube, Prof twisted the new lid on and turned it upside down. "This plug has a little hole at the base that allows more lube to enter with the toy in place." Prof bit at Swish's neck as he slid one end of the tube under the

Figure 4

fox's tail.

As the ferret squeezed the bottle, clear liquid ran down the tube and into Swish, and the fox let out a moan. This time, I moved my white tail tip over my groin to hide my growing bulge.

"Keep that in place," Prof said into the fox's ear as he removed the tube from under his tail. Swish squirmed as a few drops of the liquid dripped onto the floor.

Without a second glance at the fox or the mess, the ferret moved back to the bag and stood over it. "The next toy I'm going to show you is a vibrator. Now, I bet you all have an image in your mind of a canine shaft—you know the kind: the pop-up or banner ads online show a woman playing with a thick, red cock."

We've all seen those ads, I thought. *I know I've pawed to enough videos of guys playing with them too.* I shook my head, trying to clear that image from my mind. *Stop it. I can already smell my own arousal mixing with his. Don't need to make it worse.*

Prof pulled something out, but it didn't look like any dildo I'd seen in porn— gay or straight. It was more L-shaped, with curves and ridges along the longer end.

"This is a vibrator intended for men. Once in place, it will rub Swish in *all* the

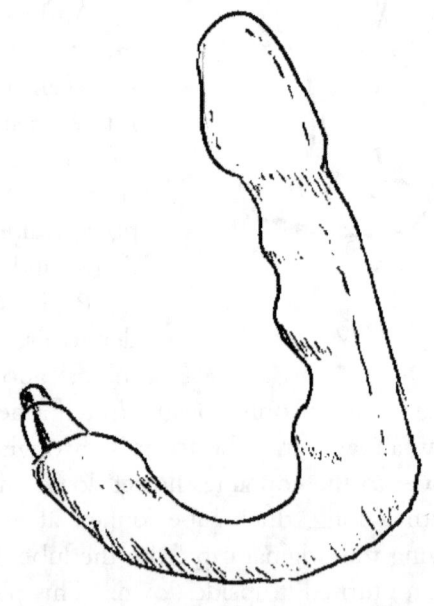

Figure 5

right places." Prof looked over to the fox. "Isn't that right?"

Swish visibly squirmed in anticipation. "Yes, sir," he said over his shoulder.

The ferret stepped towards his bound assistant. "You think you've been good enough to deserve this?"

"I think so, sir. Please?"

Prof reached under the fox's tail and removed the plug with a small yip from Swish, setting it on a nearby tray. After slicking the toy up, he readied the device in place. The fox's desire for the toy was clear. When he tried to press back onto it, Prof pulled it away, keeping it in place and making Swish pull against his binds.

"Oh, please, sir. Can I have it?"

The ferret stood, removing the toy from his rear and wagging it like a finger. "Did I ask you a question that time?"

Swish's ears fell. "No sir."

"You're being a bad fox."

"Yes, sir. I'm sorry." This time Swish's head and tail lowered as well. But, the smell of arousal was still strong in the air.

"Did I tell you to lower your tail?" Prof asked.

The fox responded right away, raising the fluffy appendage high, with the white tip near his own neck.

"Well, since you apologized and responded right away, I think you can have this." He brought the toy down between Swish's cheeks, with the short base towards the floor and pushed in it.

"Oh, sir," Swish trilled. "Thank you." The fox pulled away a little from the toy then pressed back again. Up and down, taking more and more each time.

Holding the toy in place, Prof grabbed on to the strap of the harness again. "Turn around," he said, before taking steps to the side, moving the fox to face the audience.

And I shouldn't have been surprised. Really. I mean, I knew what I was watching. Yet, when I saw Swish's rigid cock hanging there, my jaw still fell open. It would fit nice in the paw or muzzle. Well, I assumed as much, anyway.

Prof looked over the fox's shoulder to address the room. "Now that we have this in place, I can show one of my favorite things about this toy." He kept his paw behind Swish for another moment before the fox began to squirm and moan. "This vibrator works two different spots: the prostate inside him, and the perineum—right behind his balls. With this turned on, it's essentially working his most pleasurable spot in two ways at once."

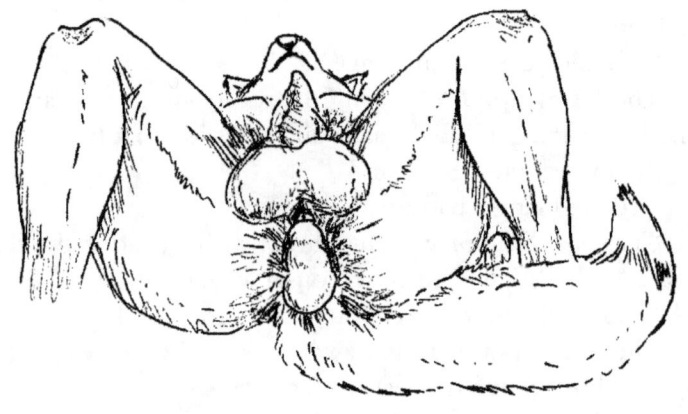

Figure 6

The ferret stepped away from Swish again. "Something else that can be fun is just let him stand there, teasing him along."

The fox whimpered and squirmed. His shaft throbbed and swelled in need, and pre oozed from his tip. And, as Swish stood there, my length pressed harder against my jeans.

"He can get off like that, and it's fun to watch, in my opinion. It's tough for most, but that fox can do it." Prof crossed his arm and watched with a smile as Swish moaned and his cock throbbed in need.

Holy hell, that's hot. But...I know I couldn't finish hands free. Every time I've played with myself, I needed my paws to finish. Maybe I'm not fox enough. My ears fell.

"At the same time," Prof continued, pulling me back into the moment, "depending on how he's been—if he followed instructions or not—I might bring out something to help him along." Again, Prof reached into his bag of goodies and pulled out a shorter cylindrical tube. "'Strokers' or 'masturbators' are nice little—or not so little—toys that you can use solo or with a partner. They can be molded to look and/or feel like a person, man or woman. Or just be as simple as this." He poured lube into the toy and slid it around the inside before adding more into his paw. He then walked back behind Swish.

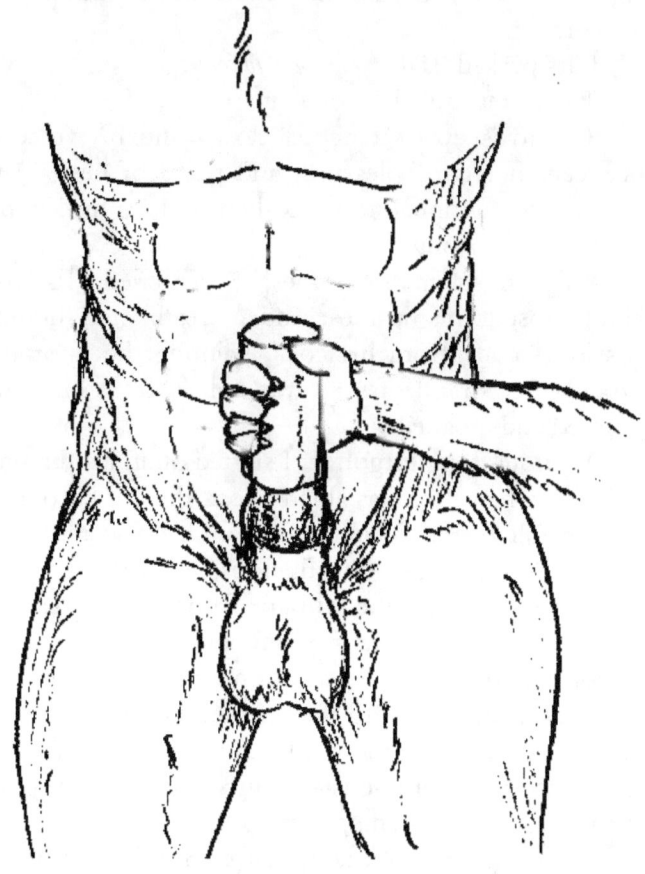

Figure 7

He wrapped his slicken paw around the fox's shaft and eased his way along Swish's length. "Now, sure, I can keep this up and use my paw. But, sometimes, I get eager to see him finish. And, I want to keep him safe, of course." He moved the stroker to the lubed up paw and slid it over the fox's shaft. Up and down the ferret slid it, covering half of the fox cock with the toy at all times, keeping a steady rhythm.

Right away, Swish's breath caught in his throat and he squirmed more. This time, the fox tried to press into the toy and paw between his legs.

"How you feeling?" Prof asked.

"Close sir. Can I finish?" There was a whimper of need in his voice.

Ears perked. *Is he really going to come?*

The ferret smiled. "You may."

The fox's eyes wrenched closed and his voice alternated between moans of pleasures and pants of need. And, all the while, Prof continued to work the toy along his length, coaxing Swish further along.

"Ah, oh, sir, here it comes," Swish cried. His arms tensed, and he rose to his tip-toes. And, a breath later, the first shot of passion sprang from his cock, painting the floor under him. Strand after strand of seed was milked from him Swish as he grunted and moaned.

My notes long forgotten, I started on in lustful interest.

And when Prof was able to coax the last bit out of him, he rose to full height, licking seed from his paw and reached for a towel. "Now, there's one final lesson to this part: aftercare." The ferret removed the vibrator from Swish's rear, placed the chair behind the spent fox and pulled his arms down. "It's important, after the scene is done, to care for your partner." Prof guided the fox into the seat and began to untie his wrists. "Especially after his release, he might be wobbly, or dizzy. My goal is to make sure he is safe and cared for. I'm going to pull the rope gently, loosening as we go."

Once the fox's wrists were free, Prof stood him up again. "For the harness, I'm going to work in a similar fashion.

Though, instead of having him seated, I'm going to keep his body in contact with mine at all times in at least two places, continuing to check in with him. I can use my paw, chest, groin or leg as a few examples."

When Prof began rattling off the points of contact, I remembered my notes and wrote down what he was saying.

When I looked back, the ferret was again taking his time working the rope off the fox. Step after step, Prof continued to whisper in Swish's ear. The fox had a relaxed grin across his muzzle, nodding or shaking his head as appropriate. Once the final bit of rope hit the floor, Prof led Swish to the chair again.

"I am going to step out for a moment to grab him some water. This would be an excellent time for our final break. As before, if you don't want to stay around for third portion, you may leave. And for those, we thank you for coming." Before anyone else could respond, the ferret walked to the back of the room where a water cooler stood. Swish, in response, sat in the chair, rolling his head from side to side.

I tried to not focus on the naked fox and instead tried to write down what was said about aftercare. *Third part? When I was told about the lecture, they only mentioned the first two parts. Should I stay? Or not?*

While this internal debate ensued, I sat there. And once my erection went down enough—though not my general arousal—I stared at my notes. Something that I could focus on to distract myself from, well, *myself.* And, from the others in the room.

As I scribbled around the margins of the page, my mind wandered on. *This entire presentation has been interesting. I mean, it was...hot watching Prof work Swish. Seeing two guys that aren't on a screen doing stuff was...fun. And different. Something I don't really ever expect to see again. Let alone with a group like this.* My tail curled back around my hip as I uncrossed my legs, and my ears lowered. *Not that I'm complaining about being with a group. But Swish looked to ready and willing. Though...is that what being a gay fox is about? Being ready for sex whenever? And, aren't most gay foxes, uh, takers in the bedroom? Someone that can get off without touching them-*

selves? I haven't thought too much about that. If that doesn't interest me, am I broken? Am I not gay enough?

I was so lost in my thought, it wasn't until Prof clapped his paws together again that I realized there were only about four or five of us left.

"Before we start the final part, let's bring in a few other TAs," said the ferret. And, as if on command, the door in the back and the side opened. Pride walked in, as did about half a dozen other guys of all shapes and sizes. Mostly canids, but there was a buck and cougar along with the lion I knew. Big, muscular, short and tall. One aide was dressed in full leather and had a riding crop, while another had more rope around him than Swish did. All of them moved with a confident gait. As the men made their way down, Prof continued. "So, the rules, as the contract stated, are simple: 'no' means 'no,' and respect boundaries. I trust the TAs to know their limits and respect yours. I do expect you to act accordingly. Now, when you're ready, feel free to come up and talk with the aide you would like to work with."

All the TAs stood in front of the stage, side by side. I looked from guy to guy, and when I made it to the lion, he was looking right back at me with a small grin.

Right away, the wolf from the back—Midnight—stood and marched right up to another fox in the front. After hushed whispers, the two walked out the back door; the wolf led the fox along. A beat later, another fox from the audience stood and walked up to Pride. The two exchanged soft words before the fox then moved to the buck. All they had to do was lock eyes before the tall, strong deer picked up the much smaller fox, making him giggle.

As the two passed in front of Pride, the lion looked to me again. *What was that? Hope? Expectation?*

Little by little, the others in the room made their way to the front and exchanged words with one or two of the TAs—one guy actually walked off with two of them at once. But, each time someone approached the lion, they would have words then move on.

When I noticed I was the last one there, I gathered my things. The remaining TAs watched me as I made my way to them. But as I got closer, they stepped back, putting Pride ahead of them.

"Does this mean I'm with you?" I asked the lion.

Pride smiled wider. "If you want, Bash, but you don't have to. Any of the other guys would be more than happy to assist in your education."

My ears lowered. "Well, it seems like you know what you're doing. And, we've already talked a bit." I rubbed my arm as a nervous habit. "Care to teach me?"

"I'd be happy to." The lion wrapped his arm around my shoulder and lead me the way everyone else went. I felt his tail slink back and forth with the tip touching mine as it went.

I tried to remember Swish's walk and told myself to keep my tail up, but it only made it about half way. My nerves were so on edge; I still felt my shoulders sag under the weight of the lion. "So, uh, where are we going?" I asked as he led us down room-lined hall.

He pulled a keycard from his pocket. "Just back here." A few steps later, he pressed the card against the electronic lock and it chimed. Pride pushed the door open. "After you."

With a nod of my head, I walked in. It was a standard room for any hotel: bed, desk, chair, mini-fridge. I set my bag on the desk as the door closed behind me. Turning back to the lion, I crossed my arms, looking at the wall and not at him. "H-how are you going to uh, assist in the education?"

Pride walked to me and set his paw to my check ruff. "However you want, Bash," The lion purred.

I took a step back. "W-what?"

A look of surprise fell over the lion's muzzle. "Don't you understand what the third part of orientation is?"

I shook my head. "All I was told is I could learn how to be…gay. I heard there would be a lecture and demonstration, but no one would go into detail. I figured they show me how to, well, walk gay or talk gay." I sat down on the bed. "I mean, look at Swish. Everyone could tell he was flaming. He had to walk down. He was confident. And, he can come hands free. I don't know how to act gay, look gay. I don't know anything about fashion." My head hung low. "Maybe I'm not gay enough."

"Oh my," sighed the lion. "I see the issue now. I thought you knew what you were getting into when you got here late." From the corner of my eye, I saw he started to move closer, then stopped. "Do you mind if I sit next to you?" I shook my head and Pride sat beside me.

"So, let me try to explain. This program—if you will—*is* about being gay and teaching you about it, too. The first part is a lecture. It's more about how to be gay socially. The second, as you saw, is more about how things can happen behind closed doors. That's the demonstration you heard about and saw. And, the idea behind the third part is hands on practice. If there is anything you wanted to try out, say from the demonstration, I could lead you through it.

"However, your comfort is way more important. If you don't want to do anything, we don't have to."

"So the stereotype of all gay guys being promiscuous is true? Just looking for the next lay?"

Pride shrugged. "Some do. But, there's nothing that says you have to. Hell, some straight guys just chase tail. I mean, I know a monogamous gay couple that has been in a relationship with only each other since high school."

"But Swish—"

Pride cut me off. "—is a flaming homosexual." The lion laughed. "But, that's just who he is. And, just because you're a fox and the queer community has strong stereotypes about species doesn't mean that has to be you too. Let me sum up the first part of Prof's lecture that you missed: being gay is more about being yourself. You want to shake your ass while you walk, do it. You want to kick ass in the boxing ring, do it." He poked me in the chest. "Do whatever feels right here. If that means dressing up for every occasion, cool. If you want to wait until you like a guy to fool around, then wait."

"You won't be disappointed if we don't do anything?" I

asked.

The lion shrugged. "Eh. I look forward to getting off at these events, but there will be others. Really, your comfort is way more important. I can just take care of myself later."

I nodded, thinking about his words, and my heart began to beat faster. "Well," I paused unsure how to continue.

I kept my gaze forward, but I felt the bed shift as the lion perked up. "Hm?"

"Uh, watching Swish did get me worked up. And, I've never seen a feline hard outside of porn. Would you, uh, maybe mind pawing with me?" I scratched the fur behind my head as the scent of my own arousal became stronger again.

The lion got up and moved to the chair, smiling all the while. "Shall I start?" he asked as he unbuttoned his pants and lowered his fly.

WHAT I DO FOR LOVE
Patrick Lambert

Hi, I'm Patrick "Damn Foxes" Lambert! Mexican crocodile and horror and erotica writer, outsmarted by a fluffy tail to write about a fox biting off more than he can chew. Foxes knows no boundaries.

Even with his headphones on, Ryan heard the door slamming at the other side of the hallway. The fennec took them off of his huge, pointy ears and waited, feeling in his hands the steady vibrations from the big and expensive device, which followed the rhythm of the latest "Makeup and Vanity Set" release. Completely still, he looked like his feral counterpart did when he felt a threat incoming.

His next tattoo design could wait. Ryan put the headphones down and left his room, walking into the lit hallway that always blinded him after several hours trapped in the dark. Almost right in front of him, the white, closed door said he shouldn't open it. But, since the fennec couldn't talk with inanimate objects, he opened it anyways.

"Get out, Ryan," the muffled claim played instantly in a monotonous tone that make it sound as the automatic answer it already was.

Unlike his room, Keith's chamber had a more appealing and charming look—which said a lot, considering how messy Keith had it. It was actually a nerd temple: the shelves and bookcases had boxes filled to the brim with comics—the name and issues written on them with black marker; the very few books he had were Omnibus editions and non-fiction related to the comic industry; and scattered over all the furniture, he had busts and articulated figures of his favorite characters. He kept order when it came to his comics, but his clothes and notes roamed around the floor and desk respectively as if they had lives of their own, and not because the lion lying face-down on the bed was extremely lazy.

"As if that has worked before." And, in reply, he caught the pillow Keith threw at him. "What happened this time?"

"Fuck off! I'm not in the mood…" Even with his maw shoved on the bed, his voice sounded loud and clear for Ryan.

"Yeah, sure. Start explaining how Blink Coyote met his assistant, and we'll see if you're not in the mood." He made his way to the bed, trying not to step over the dirty clothes. "You need to clean up this place."

"That's not even canon."

"It's not what the author said," Ryan sharply replied, already on the bed edge with his hands together over his legs and a trickster smile waiting for the lion.

"A Twitter comment doesn't make it canon!" Keith roared with the passion of an offended fan.

"But it gets you out of bed."

There was a brief moment when the lion appeared completely disconnected from reality—a look that pushed the fennec to laugh.

"Fuck you."

Not only were their rooms different, they looked like opposite poles too. While the lion showed his vibrant fur tones—especially his thick and silky red mane—the fennec did the same with his dark-dyed fur, the outlines of his ears and his chest keeping their natural white. Big and muscled versus small and thin, their differences even bigger once the lion sat beside the fennec; colorful clothes versus a coat and pants dark as night.

"What happened?" Ryan finally asked before the silence turned into something awkward, hiding his worry under a fake curiosity.

Keith glanced from the corner of the eye and sighed one…two times before he spoke again, weary and hopeless.

"What did not happen?" and, given the emphasis he gave to each word, Ryan assumed how bad it was. "I talked with dad in the morning, and he insisted on fixing things with Erica before it's too late; the editor-in-chief said my reportage isn't complete; I had to cover up Joshua again because he fucked up his sources." He threw back into the bed and pushed the pillow against his face to muffle his roar. "The worst part is that the editor now has me in his sight because of fucking Joshua."

"Why do you keep helping him?" Of course, he didn't want to ask that—he already knew the answer and recited it with him in his mind.

"His father is an investor. What am I supposed to do?" The pillow flew through the air and fell close to the edge of th ebed. Keith's claws found their way to the fluffy fox tail that worked as a perfect substitute to a ball of yarn.

"Tell him to fuck off and let him fix his own mistakes? You can't be his babysitter forever!"

"And risk myself getting into troubles because of it?"

"Or, show you have a pair and that you're not afraid of standing up for yourself!"

"It's easy for you to say that because you don't—" Keith stopped in the middle of his outburst, and his anger turned into a regretful face in an instant. The tail escaped from his grasp when Keith stood up to look down at him. Even with his size and the cheerful look of his huge ears, he still managed to hold an angry and scary look.

"Say it: it's because I don't have a fancy title like you." There was something in his low, deep growl that always frightened the lion. It sounded like the monster that lived under every basement's stairs.

"That's not what I meant." But, his apologize wasn't enough to erase the anger from the fennec's expression. "It's not like the tattoo shop. You don't compete over your position, your partners are honest about everything…" Keith stood from the bed, and his face turned to the closest bookcase where a box was slightly out of his position. "It's not like the office."

"But you can't let everyone do this to you. What's going to happen when you really get into troubles for it? Would Joshua stand up for you? And, what about Erica?" The sound of her name felt like a stab that pierced through his heart. "Are you really gonna wait to tell her it's really over because you're scared of what your father said?"

"Ryan, this is not the moment."

"Then, when?" Even Ryan's tail raised by the unrequested passion that his words acquired, a sort of needy attitude that contrasted deeply with his usual playful and cheeky behavior. "Every time I try to help you, you do the same: lock the door, cry alone, then pretend nothing bad happened. We can't continue like this!"

"…We?"

Without raising his head, Keith looked at Ryan, puzzled by

the connotation of his words. Ryan took a step back, already feeling his cheeks burning red under his fur.

"Sorry…you know we're friends, and I worry a lot about you." But, the indifference with which the lion looked at the floor now brought the regret to him. "I don't like seeing you like this. You shouldn't carry this alone."

His puzzling slowly faded into a smile. The lion stood up and approached the uneven box in the bookcase, looking carefully at the comics sealed in their plastic bags, one after the other, in perfect order.

"Thanks, Ryan," he started again, seconds away from the awkward silence both feared so much. "Trust me. I admire who you are—how strong and brave you act. That's what you should expect from a lion." One finger pushed the box back in place, the dragging sound noisier thanks to the fragile tension between them. "I'm just trying to be like that at my own pace. And, I'll thank you if you let me do it that way."

Nothing more to add. Another brief attempt to help him that ended in the same way: with him walking out of the room and Keith locking himself in for the next couple of hours. Of course, he knew Keith had all the right to do things at his own pace, but there was a difference between doing something slowly and not doing anything at all, one difference that the lion hadn't noticed.

Ryan wouldn't let him go alone through that. Keith needed help; a kind of help that he wouldn't reject—not because he didn't want it. He needed an invisible hand pulling the strings in the right direction for him, and only a creature from fantasy would have the power to do such a thing. Luckily, Ryan knew exactly where to find such a thing.

Ryan knew stuff. Stuff about the arcane. Stuff about the occult. Stuff that only those of a true open mind knew. Because one needed an open mind to see and bear what lies beyond the veil between this world and the other. The knowledge given to a closed mind always led to madness.

The fennec had an open mind, of course. It was expected

for him to know stuff that defied reality. Spells, sigils, and wards, elements of fantasy stories that protected him in the real world. In his body, he carried keys to other worlds; in the little notebook hidden in one of the many pockets of his coat, Words of Power written in his blood, so he and only he, released their effects when his sharp tongue conjured them. He knew the occult, and where to go if one wanted to find its many doors.

Wards and barriers hidden anyone from the mortal eye, but not from other magic users. They knew what to look for. They knew how a barrier looked, how the magic smelled. But even the mortals had their own magic, and Ryan quickly learned that plain sight was the best hiding spot: look like an occultist. Mortals wouldn't pay attention to a freak, and not even the finest nose would find magic where there wasn't. That's how he hid every day. That's how he reached the Grindhouse.

An underground club at night, a deserted place at day—that was the best way to describe the warehouse turned into a nightclub for those looking for a wild night. Rumors said, among those that enchanted their bodies with pills and syringes, that something powerful could be heard below them, like the grumbles of a hungry beast. Of course, no one paid attention to those words.

Ryan knocked three times at the heavy metal door. The ground had dozens of cigarette butts scattered without any order. At the other side of the narrow door viewer, a panda searched for whoever called and chuckled once he looked down at the fennec under the viewer's level.

"Sorry, Ryan. I always forget to look down."

"I can pull out your eyes so you don't need to worry about looking anymore!"

The heavy sliding door ground in pain as the rusty rollers pushed it behind the concrete wall. Kaz, the fat panda, still dressed with his usual rider outfit from his youth, beckoned Ryan to enter with a bowing, halfway joking, halfway respectful, only to be greeted by a fox tail all over his face.

"Did you finish?" Ryan asked him as they walked through

the concrete hallway leading to the main chamber.

"It's not my cleanest job, but no one should notice it. Have you tried it before?"

"It's not the first time I've summoned a demon." Ryan raised both shoulders, ignoring the grim tone in which the panda talked.

"That's not what I asked. I'm asking if you have done it through this method."

"I'd have to do it eventually." He halted his walk at the sight of the panda's belly, who glared down at him. "What?"

"This is not a game."

"I know," snapped the fennec. His agile attempt to evade the panda was countered by Kaz's size. With an angry huff, he backed up to look at the massive beast. "Fine: it's dangerous, I know! But, I want to remind you—"

"Three generations of wizards doesn't prove anything," Kaz calmly interrupted. "No matter how good you are, there are things that not even a fox can't outsmart."

"There's where you're wrong." With arms-crossed, he frowned and gave Kaz the most arrogant smile he could imagine. "And, that's why I can slow time while you summon a bunch of weak familiars."

Kaz's lips trembled, and Ryan regretted his words for a moment after hearing something similar to a sob. He would have gone if Kaz didn't beckon him to keep going.

Instead of following into the main chamber, Ryan and Kaz went through the blue metal door with a sign saying "Staff only." In front of them appeared a set of stone stairs going down into the darkness. The panda advanced first, followed close by the fennec.

Pipes came out of the walls and went back in, dripping dirty water on the steps and over the grey wall. Exposed veins of a wounded abomination were trapped within the concrete; its growls translated into the hammering sound made by the blood that traveled throughout the rusty pipes. Ryan's big ears twitched as he went deeper into the belly of the beast, unconscious of his huge tail hidden between his legs—his black fur waving by its quiet and sleepy breath. Despite having no lightbulbs, light surrounded the duo and followed them until they reached the last step and entered into a seemingly infinite chamber without any visible walls in the darkness that preyed over them. Two or three bodies away, a ray of light fell over a set of six full-body mirrors, positioned to make a hexagon, with only one mirror out of place that worked as a door to get inside the hexagonal chamber.

"Safe travel," said Kaz, and he left Ryan to cover alone the remaining distance.

Ryan gathered strength with a deep breath. That was the closest one could be to the Other Side. One wrong step, and nothing would save him from the endless fall into the Void. He had been there before enough times to remember where to step; and yet, a cold shiver ran down his back and bristled his fluffy tail.

One paw after the other. Never look down. Ignore the change of directions, where up became down and forward turned into backward. It was not an illusion, was real; but was a reality that you shouldn't look at. Those were the unspoken rules.

The mirror closed on its own once he entered the hexagonal chamber, where he faced an infinite number of reflections, one followed by the other, all moving with a brief delay, like a domino chain. He sighed, and his reflections sighed with him; every fox in that mirror looked scarier than the previous one.

Ryan made a small cut in the center of his right palm using his fangs, too small to taste the single blood drop that came out, but enough to call them. Or call it. He put his hand against the mirror, and so did his reflections. A warm feeling immediately surrounded it, and he felt a force sucking it into the glassy surface.

"My name is Ryan Toledo, heir of Alexander Toledo, seeker of the Primal Truth. See through my blood and look for my desires." As he spoke, the tattoos hidden under his black fur glowed in crimson red, an arcane circuit from which his powers came from. "Come to me, unnamed demon. Answer to my call

131

you who can follow my commands. I am ready to make a deal."

A breeze fluttered his fur. One by one, his reflections shattered and fell into the void. The infinite reduced to finite by the sheer power of the beings who defied logic. His plea accepted, he had nowhere else to run. In his reflection, he saw his expression distorted by the fear that crept over him, a freezing sensation inside his body that came from the hand connected to the mirror.

A million.

A hundred thousand.

A ten thousand.

A thousand.

One hundred.

Ten.

One.

The last reflection that stood before him held his hand and smiled back at him, a wide, sickening smile filled of broken and bloody fangs. The fennec at the other side of the mirror slowly grew in side, pulling Ryan's arm with him and forced him to stay on his toes. It ripped apart the leather clothes until those fell off his body turned in rags. Furless spots appeared in its unnaturally large legs and arms. Its chest swelled, and a hump formed in his back. Ryan tried to pull his hand away from i, and only succeeded when its back burst open and the husk that once was his reflection fell on the ground.

A dragging sound played behind him, and someone pulled Ryan out of the hexagonal mirror prison. He ended up face to face with Kaz, whose disturbed face brought his paws back to the ground, back to the reality he could accept as possible. He wasn't in a pitch-dark infinite chamber, but in a storage room with piles of boxes and broken furniture. The moist smell made him wrinkle his nose, and it gave him a sudden urge to leave the place as soon as possible.

"Ryan! Ryan! What happened?"

The fennec wanted to answer, but no words came out. His maw was dry, and his stomach grumbled. His legs trembled under his weight. He felt…exhausted, and in need of fresh air.

The first thing he did was get out of the warehouse. Not even the stairs showed the previous decay from when he descended. But, he knew something else had changed, and not for the good. Scared wasn't the word to describe how he had felt. An emptiness in his chest, an uneasy feeling left by the exposure to the unnatural dimension of madness and debauchery.

The fresh air felt like burning poison melting his throat. Sunlight too low and horns too loud, nothing had logic in that world anymore. He wanted—no, he needed to go back and lock himself in the mirrors again, back to the comfort of the unnatural and maddening realm of the Other Side.

"You said you could control it," Kaz, panting after running stairs down, complained from the threshold, visible angry with him.

"I did," ensured Ryan, although his reply lacked the actual need to clarify things and felt more like an automatic thought to evade a trouble.

"Then, why did you stay three hours inside?"

The question felt like a punch that took his breath away. Ryan waited for Kaz to say it was a joke, but his face remained the same, a mix between anger and worry. The fennec stuttered in disbelief, but the setting sun and the traffic explained the changes in the ambience.

"I knew you weren't ready! I shouldn't have let you! Idiot! Idiot! Id-!" Kaz started to hit himself in the forehead with his palm, but stopped to reconsider it. "Wait a minute, why am I hitting myself? I should hit you!"

This said he proceeded to smash Ryan in the head, forcing him to defend from the flurry of hits with his arms up.

"Never stare back at the Other Side! You know the rules!"

"I know! I know!" Ryan tried to apologize—words that were ignored by the furious panda.

Having cornered him against the wall, Kaz stopped, taking a moment to breathe and relax, even when he didn't feel like it. Ryan knew that he had done something wrong, but, holding to the pride of any wizard, refused to accept his mistakes. He did the things right; no matter the mistakes committed, he came back unscathed.

"No, you don't," Kaz finally said, apparently more serene, at least in his voice. "No matter how tempting it could be, never watch how a demon bends reality."

"The desire to understand how they—" Ryan started, and quickly got interrupted by the heavy panda's finger pushing his shoulder.

"Don't act like a brat!" Kaz roared. "Why would I want you to repeat the rules if you can't follow them? You ran with luck in there! But, what if you couldn't look away? The reflections caught you, right? Right?!" Ryan jumped in his place by the sudden outburst from the normally cheerful Kaz and couldn't do more but nod. "You could have spent years trapped there— an entire life...hell, maybe even more."

Another pause, another breath. Kaz looked remarkably more relaxed, but at the same time he kept a lugubrious air, as if he had foresaw an inevitable fate that was worse than the eternal captivity between worlds.

"You were lucky he accepted your deal."

And those were his last words. He went back into the warehouse, and that was the last Ryan knew about him.

When he was back at home, Keith's door was still closed, and the fennec supposed his mood hadn't gotten any better, so he dragged his paws into his own chamber and fell over the bed like a trunk. The summoning ritual proved an exhausting feat that had him about to faint a couple of times on the way back. Before Morpheus claimed him, the little vulpine got rid of his clothes, all of them—among his naughty kinks, sleeping naked was one of the softest he had. If Keith had entered his room, he would have been greeted with an unprotected fox rump waiting for him...one of his favorite fantasies, and the one he was thinking about before his body finally gave up.

A loud bang woke him up after what he felt was less than a minute of sleep, followed by the heavy steps at the living room. Keith had arrived, of course, and he was mad. Ryan jumped out of the bed and dressed from the waist down, failing a couple of times for how tired he still was. Of course, he prepared himself for the common speech about him being too worried and to leave him alone. But, when he went out to the living room, his surprise was great, seeing the eager and kind of excited expression the lion welcomed him with.

"What's going on? Shouldn't you be at work?" His tail wagged from side to side, and his ears pointed towards the feline, whose vibe made him believe it was a dream.

"Not anymore. I got fired."

Ryan felt as if everything he learned so far in his life disappeared from his mind and tried to put the five letters in a different order like some kind of puzzle that would unlock his knowledge. Shaking his head proved a more effective and faster way to do so.

"Wait a minute, what do you mean by 'fired'?" There was another definition and use for that word, Ryan was sure of it, and Keith was using that unknown definition...

"Yeah, they fired me." He wasn't. "I told you, the moment I said something to that asshole, he would call his father to kick me out of there. Well, guess what? He did!" he waved both arms in the air and walked between the old sofa and the tasteless center table, seemingly angry. "I told him in front of everyone to solve his own problems and to fuck off! Half an hour later, the editor-in-chief told me that my work hasn't been good enough in the past few weeks and fired me! I knew that would happen."

The lion was angry. Ryan couldn't remember the last time he had looked like that, with claws out and fangs pressed against each other. And, he felt responsible for it, knowing how much Keith cared for that job. A knot in his throat forbade any words to came out, leaving the fennec alone and powerless without any idea of what to say or how to fix what he had done. After all, he had insisted so much that Keith stand up for himself.

"I'm sorry, Keith." That was the only thing his body allowed him to say, probably because it wanted to keep all the remaining strength to endure the anger and fury of the lion who would blame him for everything, for following his advice and being an awful friend; he rubbed and messed the fur of his left arm, like a scolded child.

"Sorry for what? No, no! I'm angry with myself!" The words dazzled the already confused fennec, whose expression managed to make the lion chuckle. "I should have done this before! I shouldn't have let them abuse of me like that! But, I couldn't because I convinced myself that I was being the better man, acting maturely, evading conflict, trying to fix everything through dialogue, when in reality I was just being a fucking coward!

"That's right, a coward!" he repeated, probably believing Ryan didn't get the word's meaning again. "I was running away from troubles because it seemed easier to lock myself in my room and wait for things to magically solve themselves on their own. You…shit, I can't believe I'm gonna say this, but you were right…" Halting his march, Keith looked up at Ryan and gifted him a sincere and pure smile. "Thank you. "I don't know why I didn't listen you before. I haven't felt like this in years."

Ears flattened, head tilted, the look given by Ryan was quite adorable, enough to drastically reduce the anger and excitement from the lion, who covered the distance between the two with a couple of strides.

"You should have seen his face. It was worth losing my job."

"You're taking it very well," Ryan pointed out.

"I know, right? I feel…reborn! I don't know what it is, but I feel powerful." He shook both fists in front of him. "I don't want to lower my head before anyone ever again. I won't." One hand messed with the antennas Ryan had for ears, and which still tried to make sense of the conversation. "Thanks for supporting me all this time, buddy. I couldn't have done this without you. Knowing that you would be here for me…Thanks. Tell you what, let's get something to drink, ok? It's on me."

And he ran into his room, happy and excited as he had

never been. And, for that moment, to have the joy of seeing that warm smile in his loved lion, Ryan thought he had done the right thing.

They drank and ate for hours. Keith spared no expenses in satisfying his thirst and hunger and showed no concern for the wasted money that he would badly need in the days to come. No, he wanted to celebrate, and Ryan was invited to the never-ending supply of food and beer that came to their table. And, no matter how many bites and sips he took, the fennec wanted more.

Their feast continued back at home, after sharing shameful stories that neither of them had told before and enjoying the rebirth of their friendship seen through another's eyes. The alcohol kept coming, and, only then, in a familiar place with a familiar friend, Ryan started to feel its effects—talking became a difficult task, the simplest of words had their syllables mixed; several gestures that might have looked embarrassing were the common way to show friendship; hands moving down the chest and arms, followed by unintelligible speeches about the stupid clothes standing in the middle...

Then, a kiss. A slow, deep, and passionate kiss given by the lion, whose silky mane offered no resistance to the fennec's finger that traveled through it, carefully pulling it from the root in the same fashion of lovers fought the eagerness of the first encounter. Lead by the lion, Ryan laid in the sofa without breaking their kiss apart, the link between the two males something that he wanted for years to experience. A warm and wet kiss that let him taste the lips he had craved for so long.

The size difference made pretty easy for Keith to seize his friend, who gave no resistance against it; in fact, that aggressive posture with hands squeezing at his wrists and the loud huffs hitting his face turned his initial bliss into desire. Ryan's heart pumped faster against his chest, driven mad with nothing but a kiss, and, dear God, what a kiss! Sharing his own breath, in and out, was beyond glorious!

One quick move and Ryan found himself with his chest

exposed after the golden claws ripped apart the white t-shirt he had worn during the day. And, only when he pulled up from the couch did Ryan noticed the look in Keith's expression: passion, yes, but the selfish type of passion that never cared about their lover's pleasure. If his lips hadn't have closed around one nipple, Ryan could have stopped him. Instead, he moaned. Keith knew very well where to touch and bite; how to please him so damn well.

That thought made him snap. It was odd for a male, whose sexual experiences had never gone beyond a female, to feel that comfortable about making out with another male. No matter how much alcohol he had drunk, that was the passion one could only achieve being at his five senses or by...

Ryan rolled away from him; the lion's fangs scraped the surface of his chest because of the sudden move. He jumped back to his paws and backed away from the couch, where his roommate looked at him with an uncanny naivety.

"What happened? I thought this was what you wanted," he said, trying to get Ryan back into his embrace.

But, his presence wouldn't intimidate him, no matter how tall or powerful it was; the dread found itself trapped in a little room of his mind, only giving its existence away for the constant screams that told Ryan to follow the most basic survival instincts.

"Your name; I know it." Ryan stood his ground, showing no signs of fear that could feed the disgusting beast he was talking to.

"Do you? You wouldn't be afraid to call me by my name, then?"

The bliss and naivety on Keith's face disappeared in an instant, turning into the sinister smile of a male who had no regrets for the things he had done. Ryan knew the only safe place was his room, where he had what he needed to send that monster back into its maddening side of the universe. But, the world turned on it axis as he did, and Ryan found himself facing the lion again. However, he had changed: the unnerving aura around him distorted light itself, blackening everything around his body as if his touch could suck anything into the Other Side, like a sentient black hole looking to destroy anything close to it.

"What's the matter, buddy? I thought this is what you wanted." As the lion talked, his voice changed too, turning into the high-pitched tone of a voice changer.

"What do you mean by that? I'd never ask for such a thing!"

"You didn't? Or, maybe you simply didn't understand how the rules work. You asked me to see your desires, and I looked not the ones you believed, but those that you hide even from you. Were that dumb to actually believe you had no selfishness in your heart? That your friendship was pure and honest? But, you knew that you wanted him to be more than just a friend, and you truly expected that your help would change that, even when he felt no interest in males. Well, I can give you that, if that's what you're looking for. A brave lion loving you for the rest of his life."

Ryan hesitated hearing those last words, but regained his senses knowing it was nothing but a trick; demons knew exactly what the mortals wanted to hear and would do anything to trick them into their games. But, he was smarter—a clever fox, after all, wouldn't fall for such childish games, no matter how tempting they were.

He was wrong. With a simple touch, Keith melted his clothes away as if they were dust. His white and golden fur shone despite the dark nature of the lion, and his member throbbed out of the sheath, completely hard. He looked so...handsome, even better that his dreams; he might not have been that strong, but his poise and the impeccable look of the trimmed and brushed fur made him even more attractive that he already was. That pure sight stirred Ryan's groin and sped up his already agitated heart.

"Isn't this what you want?" he was back at his usual voice, only this time with a husky tone that bristled the fur at his nape. "Isn't me what you want?" Keith approached slowly, the predator seeing his wounded prey. His body couldn't react, the bond between them strong enough to retain control over him… "I can make him love you. I can make him want you. All I want is a puppet."

"A…puppet?" No…he wasn't moving for the demon's control; not even his pride could deny that he wanted him.

"That's right, nothing but a puppet. A little boy to do the errands I can't do without a physical body," Keith took Ryan by the chin, his touch electrifying. "I promise I won't hurt him. Just give me that, and all this can be yours."

Just like Keith did with his own clothes, Ryan felt his own turning into something close to the fine sand of the beach. Exposed as he had never been, and ashamed by his own erection, which he quickly hid with his tail, the fennec looked away to evade the desire in the lion's eyes—a desire that wasn't truly his, Ryan repeated to himself.

"You know he won't change. You have known him for long enough to know it," remarked the lion, his hands slowly making his way down Ryan's body, drawing groves through the fur on his sides. "He's weak and a coward, too soft to take the reins of his own life. You wouldn't have called me if you believed he had the slightest chance to be brave."

"He won't be himself," Ryan muttered, fighting his desire to do the same the demon was doing to him, to feel his warm and soft fur. His face was at the right height to shove it into the fluffy chest that looked like the softest pillow in the world.

"Of course he will. Time will soften his heart, and he will see you with love and devotion." One playful hand found Ryan's swelled sheath, and a squeeze made the fennec whimper. "But, if you don't agree, we can end this deal, and you can go back and hope for the day he finally decide to grow up. I think you have enough patience for that."

But, he hadn't. He knew, and shamefully accepted, that he hadn't. And, while the offered deal could be dangerous, the bond between them gave him the power to stop the demon if needed. He only had to prove himself stronger; and he would, for him…for Keith…

A nod of his head was enough. The lion pushed him back,

and Ryan saw his surroundings fading from the living room to the messy lion's bedroom, where he fell over the unmade soft bed; Keith's musk covered the sheets, a familiar smell that made him feel he was in a safe place.

Before he had a chance to look back at him, a warm and humid feeling at his rump startled him. The lion's muzzle was between his cheeks, licking up and down at his tight entrance with an increasing hunger. Whether the lion was a natural at it or the demon had certain influence over his pleasure, Ryan didn't know; he could only think in the torrent of feelings that ran throughout his body as his lover prepared him with one lick after the other. Two feline hands grope at his thighs, keeping his legs up as he enjoyed the delicate body that laid on the bed, the fox that had been wanting him for a long time. Soft but firm, masculine and dominant—those were the right words to describe the lion's touch.

The lion's tongue found no resistance as he started to push in. Ryan shivered in pleasure and did nothing to quiet his high-pitched moans. Everything started to disappear from his mind, and he focused entirely on Keith, on his lover, repeating over and over again that it was him. It was him. It was. And, the more he repeated it, the more he convinced his mind—along with the intense pleasure that he hadn't felt before. His twitching cock leaked constantly, asking for some attention, already fully erect and dangerously close to the point where it hurt to stay like that. He felt the two hands spreading his cheeks nicely to get that tongue deep, and an instant warmth started to grow inside him for a moment, only to vanish when he pulled out his tongue.

That continued for a time that Ryan couldn't specify. He only knew it stopped when the tongue moved from his insides to his entire dripping length, giving a good lick at the tip as if it was a lollipop. Then, his lips closed around the width, and inch after inch went into Keith's wet muzzle, received by the skilled tongue that showed off a new set of movements to please the fox. He tried so hard not to rip the sheets, even when his claws were already out and poking through the blue cloth. Keith took it all to the knot with such diligence—and being careful with his teeth—that Ryan forgot it was Keith's first time with a male. In and out, he bobbled his head to stimulate every inch of the vulpine member, licking every drip of pre as soon as it came out.

It became harder to focus, even in the pleasure. He couldn't find the exact words to describe the sensation, something close to a security net softening his fall or quicksand sucking him down. A soft squeeze with his lips and then the tightness of his throat, licks from side to side, and the slurping sound he made—all of it started to drive the poor fennec mad, who was now humping at Keith's muzzle, wanting to facefuck that beautiful lion and feed him a delicious load of his seed. But, of course, the king of the jungle's will weighed more, and Ryan was more than happy to let him do whatever he wanted to him.

What followed had no logical explanation; not that any of it had one. One by one, the sensations overlapped, like the takes of a movie played at the same time. Where the lion touched him, Ryan felt the same caress over and over again; the rimjob Keith just gave him started again, from beginning to end; his lips squeezed the thick shaft one time after another. Reliving every sensation, that's how he reached his first orgasm, whimpering loudly as he fed the lion his load. For an instant, more than a movie, he considered all of that like the infinite reflections of two mirrors facing each other. But of course, that sounded dumb.

The lion stood in front of him when Ryan opened his eyes. The smirk Keith gave him sent a shiver across his spine. But, seized by the intense and infinite pleasure, he couldn't do anything else but watch and enjoy the feline member slowly making his way inside his loosened up hole. The warmth sensation came back and grew stronger with every inch he took, a delightful burn that extended throughout his body like fire. Ryan wrapped his legs around the lion's body and pulled him closer, arching his back away from the bed in response to his own eagerness; the pleasure was indescribable, and it repeated immediately as the lion started to thrust, going all the way in and pulling almost all out. Ryan closed his eyes once again, and gave up...

He opened his eyes when a warm breath blew his long whiskers. Keith had leaned over him, instantly melting him with his red eyes fixed at him. He had the look of an anxiously excited lover, trying to make love to him but ending up fucking him rough and passionately. Ryan held him closer, chaining his arms over the lion's neck, a gesture that Keith quickly mimicked. His strong embrace once again made the fox feel in heaven—a place he wasn't looking to leave anytime soon.

"How does this feel, my dear?" Keith asked in a whisper. But, Ryan didn't see his mouth moving. He could only see his eyes.

"It's...it's fantastic..." he managed to reply between moans. Keith's thrusts became faster at every second; the pleasure grew unbearable.

"Would you like me to stop?"

"No! No!" he whimpered, still fixated on those red bloody eyes. Harder, faster—he could already feel the lion's climax building up through the hard throbs from his cock.

"Would you like me to keep going?"

"Yes, please! Don't stop...make me yours," his peripheral vision blackened, and it slowly faded to the center, where the red eyes were shining like rubies.

"Make you mine. Yes, my love, you will be mine for all eternity."

Ryan wanted to taste his lips, to feel his body once again, but all of his strength left him, seeing those beautiful red eyes. Filled with bliss and pleasure, he completely ignored the darkness surrounding him, incapable of seeing anything else that wasn't those fiery eyes. Getting closer to his climax, the magic circuits tattooed on his body glowed and became visible as straight white lines under his black fur, but Ryan couldn't see that—neither could he see those same circuits appearing on the lion's body, starting from his nape, where it was all connected. No, he only focused on the pleasure, on the lion making love to him, and on his beautiful red eyes.

And, when the lion reached his climax, he wished for that to last forever.

The six mirrors fell apart at the same time without making a single noise until the shard crashed to the ground. In the middle of it, the fennec stood proudly, with the cheeky smile of a child that just got away with mischief. And, Kaz? He could only sigh. The ritual had lasted less than five minutes, but at the border between reality and the Other Side, time was a shapeless concept that obeyed the will of the strongest.

"What did you do to him?" He had seen enough to not be afraid of the being that stood at some feet away of him.

Ryan looked at the panda, who already had his circuit activated, a trio of lines running across his right arm.

"Kaz, right? You don't want to do that, pal. You have no chance against an inherited circuit—unless you want to be smited by the accumulated magic of three generations."

Kaz said nothing in reply. He also had no pride left, not like Ryan or many other magic users that were too stubborn to admit when a foe was stronger. The white lines disappeared from his arm, and he adopted a more relaxed pose.

"That's better. Now, you don't need to worry about your friend. I gave him what he wanted, and he'll enjoy it for all eternity." The fennec strode over the mirror shards, acting more like the cartoon character that tried to not make any sound. "The problem with you mortals is that you don't understand the implications of 'want.' A powerful word, don't you think? You believe that 'want' implies a conscious desire that you accept, when it actually refers to the desires hidden under the shame and selfishness. And, no one likes to admit they're being selfish, right? You think you can trick a demon by acting like the better one and showing off your morals and ethics that had no actual power over someone like me. But, you already knew that, am I right? I have seen those eyes in the void before. You already know how it works."

Kaz contemplated the fox's words for as long as he could sustain his red eyes. He wanted to say something else, plead for the friend lost in the void…

"He knew in what he was getting into. If he failed, the blame is on him." He knew, sadly, that the demon was right.

"You said it, pal." The fennec gifted him a warm smile, and, for a moment, he convinced Kaz that it was Ryan who smiled. Of course, that was impossible. "No one else is to blame but him. But, that's the problem with mirrors." he shrugged and smirked, looking back at the shards. "Tricky tools. Anyway!" His loud clap startled the panda who, for a moment, thought about defending himself. "I like you. You're a smart guy. You might be useful later. Find me when you want to make a deal. But, not yet. I still have my part of a deal to finish."

"What are you gonna do?" Kaz questioned the fennec when he jumped to the third step of the stairs.

He didn't look back, but the offended posture he took, with his hands at his hips and his loud huff, made Kaz regret asking that.

"Your friend was very ambiguous with the 'want' thing. Apparently, I need to help a coward grow a pair." Slowly shaking his head and clacking his tongue, he remarked the disgust such petition made him feel. "Oh boy, what you mortals do for love."

DIARY OF A SLUTTY FOX
Ferric

The Author has had a lot of experience with foxes, even having one of his own to love and cherish...and who comes over to eat all his food all the time. From that collective knowledge he's assembled the 100% true and accurate observation of fact that...foxes are sluts. Much time and research has been put into this eventual conclusion, but it was a labor of love...so to say. So he's decided to share his findings with the world in this 100% true story (based on true events in the mind of The Author). The Author has been writing furry stories for more than seven years now, with a few even including foxes, although he's just recently made the effort to get more of them published on places other than Sofurry and FA.

August 31st

It starts tomorrow! September Slut-off is back again! Man, I've been waiting for this ever since the end of the last school year. I've won all but one of them, and I know this one's in the bag as well. I've already got people texting me and asking when they can blow their load in me. Like, dozens! I had to make them wait, though, and the wait is killing me too! I pulled out a toy for the first time in ages and gave that a good ride yesterday just to make sure I was still in shape. A day without a cock in my rump is no day for a fox! But, that'll change tomorrow. I already have a long and ever-growing list, with a few I'm rather looking forwards to, and a few I'm going to do my best to avoid. At least, try to avoid until I become desperate at the end of the month...I like to think I have standards and such, but in the end, a cock is a cock, after all.

A competition between a few close friends to see who can get the most loads in a month...I'm surprised this isn't a more common thing amongst friends, to be honest. We have all the stereotypical sluttiest species involved in this one, from foxes such as yours truly, to bunnies like Arthur, and huskies like Justin...had an otter in the group too, but he transferred to another school last year. Still on the hunt for a good snow mew or cheetah for a feline competitor...

Rules are the same this month as they were the last time. However you can get a load out of someone counts as one point. Anal, oral, pawjobs...bare or safe sex doesn't matter. It's not how you get it done, it's just the end result that matters. Only three loads per person per month count towards the total, though. Thank Arthur and his 'Master' for that rule, damn cheater. Photographic proof is preferred, but not mandatory. It goes to break any ties though...heh, ties...

We have a spreadsheet set up to post everything online, from your partner's species, to dates, to pics...everything you could need to know about what we've done. I post every line with pride myself, chest fluffed out and rippling in the breeze. The higher the numbers, and the bigger the cocks, the better! This time, I'm going to see if I can break my own record and get even more than last time. 71 loads in a month is totally doable!

September 1st

Today, I went all out and really swung for the fences. I was rather pent up myself as I'd been holding back as well, knowing that it'd drive me crazy and keep me going on game day. And, boy, did it ever. Started off with a pair of wolves, good friends, look almost like brothers which is pretty hot, and I got a nice spit roast out of them. Two loads down. Then, had an elk and his mate come take turns on my ass leading to two filled condoms—one displayed on each ass cheek proudly for the camera in the end. A zebra gave me a twofur, one on each end. Stroked off a puma in the bathroom real quick. Barely had time to ride a chipmunk before his next class, and I almost didn't get his load. Didn't get a picture of that, though, but I'll still record it as a load for me. And then a few hybrids, folf and...God if I know what the Hell that other thing was. But, he had a nice cock and came buckets over my back and tail! What else could a fox ask for?

Ten loads down in one day, and I think I overdid it just a bit. I am a little tender in places, and my knees and legs hurt just a bit, but, so far, it's been a successful run. A good start to a hopefully record-breaking slut-off! I'd write more, but I've got another load or two to squeeze in still. Off to meet a panther and his cock!

September 6th

I haven't had the chance to write anything down in a few days. Every last free moment was dedicated to squeezing yet another load in. Thirty, can you believe it? I hit thirty already! It hasn't been easy though, and I've missed a good bit of school work to do it. Not to mention that I'm starting to run out of back-up condoms. What kind of college student doesn't carry a few around with them? I can't bang everyone raw, after all. I get tested for stuff every three months, but I highly doubt most of the others do it so frequently, if at all. I love the feeling of cum dripping down my taint as much as every other fox, but, at the same time, I don't want that fun to end due to something dumb either. So, rubbers it is!

I'm proud of myself at the very least for all my hard work. I'm gonna have to slow down a bit, though. My body is finally fighting back with a few strong aches and pains. Places hurt that I didn't even know were used for sex. It's worth it for such a good start, though!

Let's see, what are the highlights...? Oh, that double penetration of a cougar and fox both in my rump was a wild ride, although they fit almost embarrassingly easily together, and neither one of them was what I'd call small. In fact, a few people commented on how...open I was, and some couldn't even cum because of it. A day or two of some strong muzzle and paw work will let that tighten back up, though. I already know a few people who wouldn't mind something non-anal related. It's just so much fun to bend over and let someone go at it that I forget there are other fun things to do as well.

Speaking of, that gloryhole idea was a great success, although I had to be a little sneaky to grab some 'proof' without anyone's consent. I'm sure they didn't mind, though. They just had their cock sucked by a Masterful fox, after all. I think I'm entitled to a picture of my cum coated tongue with their spent cock close by for my hard work. I was a little worried about what might show up as I've never quite done a glory hole before, no matter that most of the people were screened beforehand by the guy setting it up, but nothing showed up that caused me any concern...at least, not from the look and taste of things.

I originally wanted to just take a huge movie of the whole night and then cut it into pictures or clips later, but my stupid phone began to run out of space not even halfway through. I did my best to grab some pictures of the others. It was hard trying to time when they were ready to blow and making sure I had my phone on and ready to go at that moment in time, but I think I was crafty enough to make it happen. Still, seven loads in a few hours? I'll take it!

Other than that, I pretty much worked through my backlog of needy friends. Everyone had at least one round, with some getting two or even three already. People I haven't talked to since last Slut-off were more than eager to catch up and chat, acting like old friends before and after adding their names to my list. Psh, I just want their loads! I don't have time to talk. A fox can't talk with a cock in his mouth, right? Then, why should he need to? Besides, if I talked to everyone after they fucked me I'd never get to make it to everyone who needed me. I'm quite the...popular fox, I must say. Even some of the teachers have heard of me and my exploits, with one getting to see them firsthand! Can't say anything about that though—I promised I wouldn't, not even in my journal.

The week one update is coming out soon as well. I'm eager to see how Arthur and Justin are doing. I think Justin is still busy with school and volleyball and stuff, but Arthur, I have to watch out for...That bunny could get up to no good rather quick. Then again, that only helps my drive to keep on pushing myself further and harder!

September 9th

So, things have slowed down a bit as I've finally had to go to class and catch up on some work. I've still found time for plenty of action, but, at the same time, I have a good lead over Arthur and especially Justin. That left me able to take it easy for a bit, picking up a load or two a day at a slow but con-sistent pace. Everyone else's schedules seem to be picking up too, and I don't mean just the Slut-off contestants, but just everyone around campus. Not to mention, the number of ditchers has left me frustrated. Three in the past two days have said they were gonna do stuff, then didn't show! What dicks! And, not in the good way!

It's all part of the game though, and I know it well by this point. I've even started to check the hook-up app on my phone more regularly with my backlog of friends taken care of. I've spotted some new Freshman faces this year, along with a few old reliables that are still hunting on there. But, I haven't gone all out quite yet in finding partners. This is my chance to keep things easy and casual as my rump and jaw heal up for another burst of activity coming soon. My roommate is leaving for the weekend, so I plan turn my room into a non-stop fuck fest over the next few days. Time to invest in those odor eliminators and scented candles before he comes back...maybe even a plastic sheet to throw over his bed and stuff too...

Not to be a downer, but Jake managed to find me again a few days ago as well. I did my best to try and avoid him for as long as I could, but he knows how to find me. He knows my profile pages, my usual hang out and naughty areas around campus, and he knows who he needs to talk to so he can get to me.

He's...Well, he's still Jake, for sure. He just...makes me cringe every time I think of him. He's not exactly good looking. He's not exactly very...publicly presentable. He's awkward and annoying enough to make me think he never left his parent's basement until he went off to college. And beyond all that, he just won't leave me the fuck alone! I was desperate the last and only time we hooked up, and I just needed another load to win the current competition at that point. But afterwards, I just felt...dirty and bad, and not in the good way!

He was and still is...creepy. He's that kind of guy that you know doesn't get much action, and he wants to romanticize every last moment of an interaction. I wasn't there for sweet talk and love. I was there for pure, primal sex! And, he wasn't even any good at that really. Small cocked, awkward, and he had no idea what he was doing. It killed the mood pretty quick for me, and I was happy when he finally managed to get off and I could think of an excuse to go. That encounter was bad enough, but with his multiple texts and near stalkerish tendencies afterwards about how amazing every-thing was...It left me trying to distance myself from him in the following weeks. I ignored him as much as I could, and, eventually, he stopped sending me messages...only to start up each and every time I begin to go into slut-off mode.

His hygiene is still in question, and I can usually smell him before I see him, thankfully. That helps me avoid him most times, but, this time, I finally got cornered and had to say 'hi' to him outright. I told him I was busy and had to go, but that I'd be in touch soon...Let's hope that gets him off my case for a bit...although I somehow doubt it.

September 13th

Man, what a weekend! Fuck if I can barely walk after the workouts I got! And the best part is, when my roommate came back Sunday night, he had no idea...or, at least, he didn't seem to know anyway. He even commented on how nice it smelled around the place, thanks to all the scent neutralizers and flowery candles I'd been burning all weekend. Added a little romance to things as well...ha!

But damn, I don't even remember all of what went on to be honest. Thankfully, I have the pictures and videos, because it was just one load after another...constantly ramming in, dripping cum, huge cocks...filled condoms laying everywhere, Sunday afternoon...mmph. Enough to get me excited again just thinking about it. I think I accounted for everyone, but, at the same time, some loads might have slipped through the cracks...when they weren't busy slipping through my crack! Heh, that's a joke, I'm funny. Anyway, where to start...mmph...horses, cheetahs, a full-on wolf pack...and that was only the beginning! Let's just say, I'm really glad I did invest in that plastic covering for my roommate's stuff...A few people got a little more excited than I was ready for and shot over my head with their first shots.

Over fifty loads now! Fifty-one is my new total, and, damn, does it feel good! I mean, any number of loads feels good, but the more the merrier. I look forwards to seeing the numbers when I get the full report in the next few days. I love seeing just how far ahead I am. At this rate, I'm going to hit a hundred, I can feel it!

September 17th

Another few slow days as I recover from my weekend party. I'm still doing my best to keep one or two loads going per day, and with my phone app buzzing all the time, that is almost too easy to do. I'm a good-looking fox, and I have quite a few nice pictures up on my profile. I can't go a few hours without someone sending me a wink or a message, although half of them are kind of under my league. I'm not that desperate to suck and fuck anything that moves...yet. I've still got plenty of prime meat to go after and get my three-load maximum from. But, who knows? Maybe I'll have to settle for a few of the lower-class partners one day. These competitions do get intense! Eh, I'd rather not think about it to be honest...Jake's name and body come to mind when I do...But, a fox's gotta do what a fox's gotta do!

I did finally get to do something I've wanted to for a while, though. I found someone willing to let me give them a pawjob underneath their desk during one of my classes. And, not the huge auditorium classes—one of my small high school like classroom classes. It was a decently good-looking deer with just a little chub, but a decent enough cock to get the job done. Long and thin, much like deer are known for, but plenty to grab a hold of and stroke as quick as I could.

We had to prepare a bit when we first got into the room. We took one row of desks and gently angled them in towards one another, decreasing the space between them as they went further back into the room until the last two seats were just about touching. Those were the two seats we took, and, with a little clever backpack and notebook placement, we were able to hide most of the action. He flipped his notebook sideways so the front hung off the front of his desk, and, with that cover, my paw was able to slide underneath and slowly grab a hold of his groin without looking too suspicious.

We pulled it off pretty well. I'd say. He managed to keep his moans down, and I managed to keep my motions to just a few flicks of my wrist. It was pretty hot. I'm not gonna lie. I was hard as a rock while I was doing it, all while trying to hold my twitching ears and tail steady from the fear of being caught. Scent...well...a few of the people around us knew what we were doing, for sure. But, then again, I told everyone I knew to sit by us, so they all weren't too surprised with what I was up to. Some even offered to be next!

Anyway, I managed to get him off with a little hard work. I was even able to sneak a picture of his cum dripping down my clenched paw underneath his desk. Then, with a sly little grin, I slid my paw back and quickly licked off the evidence. That almost got me busted as everyone around me quickly turned to watch me do it, silently cheering for me to make the sexy show even sexier. Thankfully, the professor only paused for a second before we all turned our attention back to him as innocently as we could.

Man, I love having the attention to myself though, and I love proving stereotypes right! I dunno, there's just something super fun about meeting and then exceeding someone's expectations of what a fox can be. I don't half-ass anything, especially when it has to do with my own ass. If society thinks I'm slutty, then by fucking God, I'm going to be the biggest slut there is. September Slut-off victory here I come!

September 20th
I saw Jake again today, and this time I had no good

156

excuse to get out of it. I'd managed to sneak away from his advances and his attention almost all month, and I was feeling pretty good about it. But, he knows I'm in the contest, and he really wants to help. He even offered his room up and told me that he could give me at least two if not three loads. Results come out for week three tomorrow, the final check-up before the dash to the finish line, and I was feeling a little nervous after talking to Arthur and hearing all the stuff him and his Master had planned. Maybe it was just meant to psyche me out, but still...it was a risk I wasn't willing to take.

So, I went through with it and finally said yes to get Jake off my back. Ugh God, I'm glad I just had to bend over and let him go at it. I didn't have to look at him, I didn't have to watch him...I just had to wag my tail and moan. That was enough for him, although it took even longer than either one of us would've liked. I swore that he would tire out before he could cum, and, as I felt him slowly weakening, I finally began to push back a bit, driving myself onto his shaft and saving the day with a few tighter squeezes of my rump around him.

I still only got one load and a picture of a full condom from him, and I rather quickly rushed on home to take a shower afterwards, struggling to get the scent of him and whatever cologne he tried to use to mask his nasty scent out of my nostrils. I'm so glad he didn't ask for any oral. I don't think my muzzle would survive getting that close to him and his junk. God forbid if he wanted to make out or something...Ick!

Switching topics to something much more fun, I

might have found someone to bring into the Slut-off next time! I think I finally found an elusive snow leopard that might be game to try his luck in this competition. I still have to talk to him a bit, but he seems cool. Met him at a threesome with this big rhino I kinda half-know, and he even gave me a load of his own after the rhino was spent. How sweet of him to add to the total, right? His name's Andy, and I think he could help take some of the loads away from Arthur as well, as he knows Arthur's Master. I'm sensing a few things I could use to my advantage here....Sneaky fox senses tingling!

September 22nd

My grades are suffering. Remember that part about me being able to slow down and focus on school for a bit? Yeah...well...cocks have a funny way of stealing my focus rather quickly. I missed an important assignment that was due for one of my major classes. Like, not even half-assed something to turn in. Like, completely gave zero effort into trying. I'm not too proud of it, but...I'm still in the lead in the slut-off totals! Seventy-one for me, and sixty-five for the rabbit. I knew I could make 71, and I still have a few days to go to bring that total up even higher. A sacrifice worth taking? Eh, let's hope so...that means a lot more work I have to do in order to catch up and get a somewhat decent grade later. My GPA isn't stellar to start with, really, but damn if my libido doesn't get in the way more often than not. College is for experimentation and such, right? Who has time for this learning stuff when I've got some real life experiences to get out of the way!

Speaking of life experiences...I almost had one I really didn't want to experience...At least, not by anyone I didn't already know. I have a favorite public bathroom I like to do my business in since my roommate isn't exactly...well...cool with random gay sex going on in our small dorm room all the time...or ever. The bathroom is one of those locking unisex ones, almost like a family bathroom, if you will. It's in a building in the middle of campus that almost no one uses, so it's perfect for a quick hookup location. It's almost been my second dorm room this month, and my scent is still strong each time I walk inside. Not to mention the strands of red and white fox fur all around the place that even the cleaning staff can't seem to get rid of.

So, me and a bull were going at it, rather hard I must say, with the big guy grunting up a storm as he held onto my hips and viciously pounded away. Somehow, all that noise didn't make it out into the hallway, and one of the three people that actually use that building decided they had to take a potty break. Well, with all the heavy slapping going on, I didn't hear any knock on the door. Only when it opened up with a rather loud squeaking noise did I know something was up. I could've sworn that I'd locked the door like always, but with a big and sexy bull ready to get down to business, well...Things like that have a way of slipping my mind, I suppose.

As that little flash of white hallway lighting shot in, I felt the bull behind me do his best to spread himself out and make himself bigger. His rear and back were facing the door as I was bent over the toilet, mostly hidden from the door's line of sight myself by his large frame. Before I could even turn my head to look, I felt his paw quickly grasp onto my tail and pull it into a tight clamped ball, hiding the last bit of me from whoever was at the door.

"Hey, knock first!" he shouted back with as loud and angry of a snarl as a bull could manage. It was quite intimidating as it even left me shaking a good bit underneath him. I didn't see anything, but from how fast the door shut after that shout, I don't think the other person saw much either. I heard a sudden squeak before a few loud footsteps began to echo out in the distance.

I was a little worried about the intruder to be honest, but the bull kicked right back into bucking when the door closed once again. That quickly took my mind off the situation. He wasn't as shocked as I was, and the interruption didn't interfere with his erection as it still pulsed freely inside of me. He even came a moment later as if nothing had happened, getting his picture before cleaning up quickly and casually. We slid out of the bathroom together, although I was almost hidden in the bull's shadow as I walked through that door right behind him. To my slight surprise and relief, there was no one there to meet us or even see us stroll down the hall and out of the building together. I think I'll take a few days off from that bathroom, just in case they have someone watching it. I have other places I can go, after all...

Jake contacted me again too. That damn clingy bear won't leave me alone! But, I gave him the slip and avoided most of his messages. I told him I'm too busy to hang out later too. Hopefully that works...although once again, I doubt it.

160

September 25th

Alright, the last big push! I don't know if I'll find time to write again before the big day as I have a good bit planned, and plan to do a LOT of hunting to make up for all my friends I maxed out on already. I did manage to finally get some work done, though. I turned in a make-up assignment to my prof for skipping that major one and at least got some points, so I'll take it. I feel like I caught up with most other classes too, but that work has let Arthur catch up to me in the load count. I know he has big plans, and his Master knows more people than I can ever hope to, but I'm still confident that I can push on through and win.

The one thing that could possibly hold me back is other foxes. I'm a good-looking guy for sure, but there are a few others around campus that are finally getting into the game at this point in the semester. With so many options for tops around, it's hard to crave the same, rather common fox over and over again, even if we are the best fucks around. But still, it's only three loads I'm asking for—they should be able to stomach that, at least, no matter how common a fox hole is. The other foxes can have the ones I've already gotten three loads out of if they want, but they need to stay away from any fresh faces! They're mine!

The worst part is that we all kind of know each other, and a few of the regulars on the app are friends of mine. We've done...things together. We've done a few shows for people and parties, and even acted like brothers or twins for a few people who are into that sort of thing. Most of them are cool guys. They know my game, though, and

I can only promise some of them away with future access to the cocks I need now. Some of them take delight in stealing away the new people from me, though, taking pride in outwitting and out-maneuvering me to get to the best cuts of meat. It's all in fun, but...so help me, if they make me lose this contest...I'm looking at you, Steven! I know where you sleep at night!

Jake won't leave me alone either. He keeps telling me that he owes me two more loads, and...eh...I want to say no, but...every load is going to count. If I have some spare time, and he's free.... The thought makes me shiver, but....

September 29th

So...much...action...It hurts just thinking about it. I thought I'd be fine for a small group of horses since I'd been doing super extra duty all month. But, horses are still horses, and damn...it feels like I went a few rounds as their punching bag and not just their cock sock. It hurts to breathe sometimes as they *really* know how to hit deep, and they're not shy in doing so. Hopefully that wasn't a fatal mis-take to take all of them on in one big group. I still have two days to go...and fuck, Jake is calling me again. I don't have anything better planned...This is the first open time I've had in the past few days. Last week, Arthur was only six loads behind, and I know he likes to go big at the end...ugh, fuck! I think I have time for a quick dicking and another shower if Jake has an open place...I've just gotta keep telling myself that it's all for the contest...It's all for the glory! Not every moment can be per-fect...Sometimes, you've gotta get down and...ewww...dirty...

November 2nd

FUCK YEAH! Fuck yeah, and owww...That about sums up my day yesterday and today. I slept in on November 1st as I was going hard up until midnight on the 30th, hopping from room to room and sending text updates to the otter trying to keep track of all three of us. I'm sure all of our nights were crazy, but all that hard work paid off! At least for me, anyway, and maybe the otter, as he probably had a few good wanks at the pictures flooding in. I'd done it! The Sluttiest Species Award is once again in its proper place...probably shoved up a fox's butt like everything else. If it was inside mine at the moment, then I don't think I could even feel it though...that's how bad things have gotten back there.

Eighty-nine loads for me in one month...in one of the shorter months, even. Almost three per day, although spikes and depressions in the rate certainly came and went. I swear that I can still feel each and every one, though. Ah, God...it's hard to sit down and write. Hell, it's hard to lie down and write...it's hard to exist and write. I know it's not something you'd hear me say often, but I think I'm good on sex for a little bit. I'll probably take a few days off, just to rest and recover. Even thinking about sex right now makes me hurt in places that I'd rather not.

I had to give in to Jake...twice...in order to get the title. But, you know what? At that point, I didn't really care. I was in pure load mode, and he was just another guy giving me another one. But, at the same time, he did leave me feeling a bit strange. After our second session, I felt him trying to be cute and cuddly once he finished up. He nuzzled his nose into the back of my neck as his paws slowly slid over my chest and fur, trying to keep himself inside of me as long as possible. It was then that he whispered, "I love you," into my ear with a little rumble in his throat afterwards.

It wasn't the first time that I've been told that. Not even the first time this month. Sometimes, it was just part of the rush of feelings during sex, and it squirted out of people. I usually didn't mind. Hell, sometimes I'd even say I love them back just to get them moaning and thrusting even harder. Getting into the right headspace is rather important during sex for most people, so I'm not above telling them what they want to hear in order to make it happen. But, when Jake said it to me, it caught me off guard. It wasn't just the fact that I couldn't see myself ever actually loving him, or even lying to him about it. It left me feeling so funny because deep down inside, I knew that he really meant it.

Say what you want about me, but I don't think I'm boyfriend material. To settle down with one guy and really *love* them...I just don't get it. There's so much fun to be had out there that I can't imagine trying to be with just one guy. But, love is a strange thing. As I said, I've heard the word before, but the *meaning* of it...the meaning in Jake's voice...that, I can't say I've honestly heard before. That's why he follows me around and almost stalks me and puts so much effort into finding me and trying to get with me. He doesn't do it for fun or the desire for sex. He does it because he loves me. And...I don't know what to do with that.

On one hand, I like it. The attention it brings is awesome, and to see someone so dedicated to you is rather impressive. On the other hand, I don't really get it...but at the same time...I want it. Why does Jake keep trying to get at me when he knows I won't? Does love really have that power? That drive? That sort of connection associated? I've had plenty of sex in my time, and it's the best thing I could think of doing, but, at the same time, I don't really feel attached to anyone beyond it. I'm attached because they're good at sex, but not because...well...love. Or am I, and I just don't realize it? How many people would I enjoy hanging out with even if there was no sex involved? Very few, if any I think...and that part kind of struck me when I heard Jake speak those words...

Eh, anyway, sappy part over! Back to the fun stuff. Arthur came in second with eighty-six loads, and Justin came in last with only twenty-five. I kinda feel bad for Justin. He's far too busy and too focused on his school and volleyball work to do well. Maybe we'll have to find another husky...haha. Nah, I love Justin, no matter how busy he is. Who knows? Maybe during one of these things he'll surprise us all and finally claim the sluttiest species title himself...

Nevertheless, I got the title now, and I will wear it proudly with my chest puffed up and my fluffy tail raised high! February Fuck-fest is right around the corner, though, and I can't wait too long before beginning my training for that. But, before I do, I seriously have some school work to catch up on...and a few long-spent friends I need to get reacquainted with. I told them not to go three rounds so early, but you just can't stop some people from wanting more.

Hmmm, is that what love is? Wanting to reunite with friends? I mean, it's for sex and everything, but...I do want to see them as well...I think....gah, I dunno. That damn panda and the lack of cum left in my balls has left me all confused! Eh, I'll figure it out eventually. Just gonna take some time to think about it...some time and a few more Advil...if I can reach the medicine cabinet without collapsing in pain.

UNEXPECTED GIFTS
Jelliqal Belle

Mrrrr? Jelliqal looks up in annoyance at being interrupted from licking her pet arctic fox, Inusan. He moans because she stopped and tries to entice her to resume, but he is held firmly by violet shibari ropes. A resident of Atlanta, this zebra-striped cat girl loves to see her fox with a sheen of sweat on his hot bod. When Jelliqal is not teasing her pet, she is writing fur fiction, mysteries, press releases, and whatever else is needed at the time. Jelliqal Belle is the writing facilitator for Furry Weekend Atlanta. Her other fur stories can be read in ROAR 8 *and* Dissident Signals *(FurPlanet) or* WerewolvesVersus. *@Jelliqal on Twitter or JelliQal on Telegram. Now excuse me, but she has a fox to finish.*

Some days, five o'clock could not arrive soon enough, especially on the Friday before a long holiday. Always seemed that everything came to a head about 3 pm, like all the bad stuff for the days off had to get compressed into the last few hours before you got to go home.

I had to fire one of the accounting clerks for inappropriate behavior in the storage room with a cute otter intern. Hated doing that right before the holiday, but legal witnessed the act, so what are you to do? And now, accounting was complaining they would be short-handed for doing the year end books. Thank goodness I was home for a few days. I could write the summary for the annual report and prepare for the upcoming board meeting in peace.

I was finishing my second glass of Prosecco when I heard the garage door open. I poured another and waited for her to come in, saving the spreadsheet I had been working on. She taught in a Title III school on the other side of town, true to her nanny goat's nurturing nature. She usually got home earlier, but, that day, she had helped deliver Angel Tree gifts to needy families.

She was a much nicer person than I was. She had a big heart—guess that is why she fell for this broken fox who is always hungry for more, always looking for an advantage and worrying about how others are going to trick me. Just waiting to be ambushed from behind like I often was when I was a kit. I heard the door close and waited for the smell for pizza which never came. Curious, I got up and went into the kitchen.

Her eyebrow arched with something approaching disapproval upon seeing me still in my CEO uniform of a pencil skirt, jacket set, and blouse. I was so over today that I was even still wearing my pantyhose. I opened my mouth to vent about the day I had when she pressed a finger gently to my muzzle.

"Shh, not a word." She took the wine glass out of my hand and set it on the counter. She leaned over and kissed me with unexpected passion. Her thick goat tongue slid deep inside my canine mouth.

Oh, this is sizing up nicely, I thought. I was panting when

she pulled away.

"Go get out of those clothes and into something more appropriate."

I thought of a hundred things that might be more appropriate when she added, "I am thinking the purple and black one."

As I went to change, I considered her choice. The 'purple and black one' was a long gown with a deep cleavage in the front and virtually no back, held together by black lacing along the sides. The sateen gown had a slit along the center back starting at the tail base. Easy for tails to stick out, and, if I am lucky, for other things to go in. It is so hard to get into and out of, I do not think we have used it but once or twice. I heard her walking in and out of the garage as I changed. My curiosity made me a little wet.

The way she looked at me when I came out—oh, made me feel beautiful, wanted, desired, sexy. Not like the abandoned pup I still was on the inside. She strode across the room, her hooves clicking crisply on the tiled floor. She had changed into her leopard silky top and golden spandex leggings. The top accentuated her ample capricanae bosom. She grabbed me by the hair in the back of my head and directed me where she wanted. She licked from the nape of my neck up to my ear, then gave my lobe a little nibble that sent a shiver through me. She ran one hand down along my side and stopped. "These won't do. Vixen, go to the sofa and lean over."

I had put on the black thong crotchless panties I usually wore. I was confused. I leaned over the sofa. I wonder if she was going to pull out the paddle. We had not done that in a while. She did not like to hurt me, but, sometimes, after a bad day, I found it a nice stress relief. I looked straight ahead, not watching her, but listening to try to guess what treat she had for me. The curiosity was eating me alive—that was part of the delicious fun.

She placed a number of things on the counter behind me before flipping up my gown such that it was almost over my head. With two hands, she slid my panties off me, gently caressing my legs as she moved. As she stood, she ran her fingertips along the inside of my legs. I breathed in a happy sigh, a gasp for more. I quivered with anticipation as she ran her nails over my cheeks. More please, I mentally begged. My lips quivered, both sets. I struggled for control. My vulpine tail wanted to flap about in excitement. That would have displeased my mistress.

"I see you are a little wet, but I think it will not be enough." She ran two fingers covered in cold lube along my folds, sliding in and out just a bit, then more along to my anus. She took a small plug with more lube and slid it in and out, and in and out, and popped it fully in. I arched my back in delightful reaction. This was new. I started to look over my shoulder at her. I wanted to kiss her. I needed to kiss her.

She gently pressed me back down. "Not done yet." She slid in one egg into me, then another. After a moment, I could feel them vibrate within me. *Ah ah aah* the plug swelled up in my *oh my ooh*. Then, they slowed down, then sped back up . I quivered. I panted. I waited for more *oh* please more.

"Good," she purred as she pulled my gown back down, then took off her latex glove. "I see you like the new toys. They are bluetooth, connected to each other and my phone. I have different program choices. Set between low pleasure and edgy, for now. Don't want you spent too soon."

She picked up a blindfold and a latex hood from the counter. "Pick one."

I indicated the blindfold.

"Good choice. The hood it is."

I tried not to smirk. I knew this game well. I liked the ability to focus just on me that I got in the hood. I get to be selfish and just feel, not be responsible for anyone else. *Ah aah* the vibrators activated *aah* again. And then back down. I panted and felt a bit light headed.

"Do you trust me?" she asked, watching me carefully.

She was the only person alive I trusted without reserve. "Yes, completely."

Apparently, she saw what she was seeking in my amber eyes. She nodded, satisfied. She clipped on my collar and a leash. "Follow me." She gave a little tug.

Unexpectedly, she led me to the garage. I felt exposed with no panties. Vulnerable in a way I am unaccustomed to. I shivered all over in the cool air. I was outside, exposed, my scent rich in the air. I was thrilled and frightened about this new twist. She opened the back of the van. To my surprise, she had folded down the seats and set up an air mattress. "You need me, you kick three times." She strapped my legs together at the knee and ankle, then secured my hands to the back of each seat. After checking if I was comfortable, she slipped the hood on.

I don't know how long she drove. I think I might have dozed off now and then, but the eggs and anal plug kept me edgy. I twisted on the mattress, trying to get more, trying to get less. I was breathless and hungry. It was still night when we stopped. I could smell her arousal.

She climbed in the back of the van, pressing against me. I breathed hard in expectation. She pulled the hood off and kissed me deeply. "For this week, you are all mine. I am not sharing. I am a horny goat, my little fox. No computer, no cell, no TV, just you and me. And, I am going to take my sweet time."

I gave her a foxy grin. "Yes, mistress," I murmured. She unstrapped me and helped me slide off the mattress. I gasped at the cold ground. I looked around at the snow on the mountains reflected by the moonlight. I smiled. My tail wagged madly, shooting alpine air between my legs. A week—I could focus on her, on us, without the guilt that I wasn't doing some project or other for the office. Best gift ever.

BLACK AS MIDNIGHT, RED AS BLOOD
Miles Reaver

Miles Reaver is a white wolf, obsessed with coffee who likes to howl and enjoys making others awoo. He likes to write stories about crime and coffee, as he believes there is no good crime without good coffee.

The city swept in darkness cooled off in the rain. The gray brick buildings became a shade darker than normal, and the streets lay absent of life after the clock turned ten. They didn't like the rain in the city—not like they did out in the country, free of the chemicals washing over the citizens and getting into their fur.

Michael sat at the back of the café and scrolled through his iPad, reading the news about the environment. He didn't like the rain touching his white fur. It became matted down and ended up looking like a bad rag. Michael covered the rest of his fur with a pair of blue jeans and red flannel shirt. He owned a large trench coat, which was now draped over the vacant chair next to him, left to dry.

It was a slow night for the bear. He drank his second vanilla latte of the night and wasted hours of his free time in the corner street Starbucks. He had no clients in the evening, no schedules to keep. Nothing at all but free time.

Bored of the environment news, he switched tabs on the website to Crime. There were many stories, and all had the same ending: murder. Michael didn't work for the police, but it felt exciting imagining himself as a top dog detective solving the real crimes of this city. For now, he was just a P.I, and it paid just enough for a one-bedroom apartment and a vanilla latte a week.

Michael caught a familiar news story. It was about an unknown murderer still at large. Bodies had been piling up all around the outskirts of the city, and now, there was a new murder. The bear reread the last lines of the story. The crime scene wasn't far from where the bear was sitting, then. Michael frowned and scratched the top of his head with his paw. An eerie thought to think about. The murderer's identity and motive were unknown, but their MO was always the same. The victim's throats were cut, and the bodies were found in some kind of sexual position.

Michael shuddered. It was a bad way to go. He twisted his muzzle from side to side and grunted. The grunt turned into a sigh when Michael grabbed his Starbucks cup and found a lack of weight to it. There it went—all joy gone.

The bear didn't want to leave. Though the rain had stopped an hour ago, he lacked any means to entertain himself. Michael leaned back in his chair and straightened his back. His eyes shifted towards the barista, a young wolverine in his early twenties. He wore a green employee shirt and brown pants. His paws were flat on the countertop, unmoving. A smile crawled across his muzzle, like he was about to drool at any moment.

He was mind controlled by the fox sitting at the counter. At least, Michael thought it was a fox.

The fox sat on the bar stool at the middle of the counter. His fur was black as midnight, with the upper part of his muzzle colored a bright red and reaching across his head. He wore plain blue daisy dukes with the white stems still hanging from the edges of where they'd been cut. His stomach was exposed. The crop top with a skull and bones logo looked slightly loose on the fox and reached only to his chest.

The fox screamed gay, and, if that wasn't an indication of it, the rainbow belt around the fox's slim waist was.

Michael's eyes stayed glued to the fox and the way he made the barista drool. The fox held his cup delicately with one paw while the other flew around, making gestures.

Michael flicked his ears in their direction and leaned closer to hear them.

"...and it's absolutely awful," said the fox with a heavy southern drawl. "They keep me awake all night. I need my beauty sleep—it's good for my fur." The fox used his free paw and dragged if from his muzzle, down to his neck. The edges of his claws tugging at his shirt, pulling it down by the neck.

The barista all but adjusted his pants. He had no idea the fox was toying with him.

Michael grinned to himself. Foxes were as much trouble as vixens, it seemed; they liked to play games.

Then, the fox caught Michael's eye. He turned to look the bear in the eyes, noticing Michael's grin. The fox studied Michael for a moment, then flashed him a grin and looked at the wolverine again.

There was a wag to the fox's tail. "If only there was *someone* who could help little ol' me," he purred. "Why, I think I'd do *anything* to repay them."

The fox was trying, and that was Michael's cue. The fox was attempting to drag the bear into it, and it was working.

Michael slid his iPad back into his bag. He picked up his trench coat and took his time making it to the bar. The bear kept his gaze fixed onto the checkered flooring, his stride casual and patient. He walked past the fox, then put his bag and coat onto the bar as he positioned himself to the fox's left.

Michael gave the wolverine a sharp look. The bear gestured with his muzzle towards the end of the bar. The wolverine got the signal and excused himself before heading somewhere in the back. Michael and the fox shared a brief silence, waiting for each other to start a conversation. Michael noticed the fox's subtle glances backwards and the playful twists to his tail.

Michael cleared his throat and dragged his paw across the wooden bar. "I, uh, heard you've got a little problem. Noisy neighbors?" he said. "I might be able to help." He played the game just like the fox wanted him to.

"Oh?" The fox turned his head slightly towards the bear, but kept his gaze forward. "Ain't it rude to listen in?" The fox pressed his maw together as it grew into a smile.

"Sure," said Michael. "I'm bad like that." The bear leaned onto the bar with his left elbow.

"I wonder just how bad." The fox turned in his seat and faced the bear. Michael picked up a sweet scent being this close. It was strong enough to be noticed. Michael found himself pushing his head closer. He wanted more of the fox's scent in his nose. He wanted the scent on himself.

"Why don't you find out?" Michel whispered. "I did say I could help."

The fox purred and readjusted himself on the bar stool. He arched his back and let his eyes wander up and down Michael's body. The bear was a standard cut of his species. He had a fatter stomach and short shoulders, but he was tall and neatly combed.

"And just how would the big and bad bear do that?" asked the fox. "Packing heat?" He smiled at Michael. Part of Michael waited for this opportunity. He loved to show off. "Maybe," the bear answered and let the words hang there for just long enough. "I'm a detective, a P.I." Michael reached into his coat and then took out his wallet, opening it to show his license. The fox's ears perked and his eyes widened. He reached towards the bear's wallet, but stopped himself from touching. Michael let the fox admire the eye logo on his card for a moment.

"Oh, my," the fox purred and smiled. "A real detective."

The bear chuckled. "So, what do you say? Am I good enough to help with the neighbors?"

"Neighbors," the fox echoed and licked his muzzle. "Oh, you'll do just fine, hon."

Michael waited outside as the fox gathered his things, and, a moment later, the two walked down Rinko Avenue. The fox introduced himself as Taylor and insisted that the bear held his arm. The streets lay abandoned, and whoever did pass them didn't look closely at the two guys holding paws. Not far from the corner Starbucks stood a series of yellow apartment buildings that had seen better days. It was a one-to-two-room complex that was cheap on rent, but heavy on loud neighbors and marijuana smoke.

Inside, the dark gray hallway was dimly lit and smelled of heavily-used foot wraps. Michael let Taylor lead the way there. They headed upstairs, maneuvered through the narrow hallways, and moved past locked up bicycles and trash bags left in front of doors. The two ascended to the third floor, then went to the end of the hall. Taylor unlocked apartment 3C and walked in, letting Michael close the door.

The apartment was bigger than Michael expected. The kitchen was a fridge, oven, and a series of counters in the corner of the right-side wall. The rest was the living room and bedroom combo. A blue couch was pushed to the right-side wall by the windows and faced a small TV placed on the shelf.

The double bed was a pull-down built into the wall. It was neatly made and covered with a pink cover. Michael observed the way the weak light let the corners of the room remain dark. The apartment smelled heavily of fox, but there was something else in the air—something poisonous. Michael could see the colorless bleach stains around the tiles where the kitchen was. A small train led all the way to the foot of the bed.

"Here we are." Taylor stood in the middle of the room, paws hidden behind his back, legs crossed.

Michael put his bag and trench coat on the kitchen counter and shoved his paws into his pockets. He looked around the room and enjoyed its silence.

"Do you have a 'plan,' you called it, for my problem?" Taylor shifted his weight.

"Fight fire with fire." Michael's eyes dropped across Taylor's frame. He snapped his jaw together, sucking in air through his fangs. Michael liked the way the pants were tight on the fox. "This is a pretty bad part of town, you know," Michael went on. "Got to be careful when you're playing with fire."

Taylor chuckled and stepped closer to the bear. The fox kept his paws behind his back and then brought them in front of him and placed them on Michael's chest.

"Oh, I know," said Taylor, "but I feel much safer now that you're here." He looked up to match Michael's gaze and licked his muzzle. "How could I ever repay you?"

Michael smirked, letting his paw squeeze around Taylor's hip, then dragged the paw upwards to feel the fox's fur on Michael's paw pads.

"I'm sure you can think of something." Michael used his right paw and pressed it against Taylor's flat stomach. He pushed it downwards, slipping his fingers into the fox's jeans. Taylor wasn't wearing any underwear.

Michael watched Taylor suck in his stomach, gasping slowly before moving his hips forwards and backwards. The fox followed Michael's paw with his eyes, watching himself getting groped. Michael could spot Taylor's wagging tail and flat ears. Following Taylor's gaze, Michael felt his paw being pushed against the jeans. He felt the wet tip push out of Taylor's sheath and touch his own paw pads.

Taylor squeezed the bear's shoulders. "Let's move to the bed." He grinned and guided Michael a few feet to the side, then turned him slightly and pushed him onto the bed. The bear splayed across the mattress, then rose to tug at the shirt tucked into his pants. Taylor helped Michael undo his belt, and in no time, Michael sat on the bed in his underwear and with a warmness growing around his sheath.

In front of the bear, Taylor kept his paws on his hips and slid them towards his groin. Michael could spot the way Taylor's cock slid out of its sheath and towards the right side. The fox ran his paws across it, then shifted his legs and showed a coy smile. He unbuttoned his daisy dukes, then lowered his zipper and tugged the flaps to the side.

Michael licked his muzzle and groped his own sheath. He could pick up the double scent of arousal filling the room.

Taylor's eyes caught Michael's paw. "Enjoying the show?" he asked.

Michael nodded. He just needed to see a little more. "Then, you'll definitely enjoy your reward."

The fox pulled at his jeans. He spread his legs so that they didn't fall down right away. The resistance was sexy. With the flaps of the jeans spread, the fox's cock popped up from the side. A wide, red cock pointed upwards at the fox's stomach. Michael could see, looking closely, the way the cock visibly pulsed and grew longer out of its fuzzy covering.

"Nice to see you so excited," Michael commented, a tent growing in his own boxers.

"Oh, hon, you have no idea." The fox grinned and bent over, sliding the jeans down the rest of the way.

Taylor's balls, like the rest of his body, were dark. Michael loved the way the fox reached down to his round orbs and gave them a squeeze and tug.

Michael patted the side of the bed next to him, ushering Taylor to join him. The fox, with his bouncing erection, climbed the foot of the bed and moved above Michael's erection. The bear placed his right paw on Taylor's thigh. He was eager to grab the fox's cock and push his own erection into him. But, the fox surprised him.

With a wide grin, Taylor moved further up the bear until his thick, long cock was an inch away from Michael's muzzle.

Taylor sat on the bear's chest. Michael's head darted back into the pillows. He smelled Taylor's musk and the pre that formed on the tip of the fox's cock.

"How about a little taste, papa bear?" whispered the fox.

Words got stuck in Michael's throat. He stared up at Taylor with his muzzle partially open.

"Papa bear?" Michael giggled.

The fox smiled solemnly. "I grew up on a farm." He dragged a finger across Michael's muzzle. "You remind me so much of home." Then, Taylor took hold of the bear's paws and placed them on his own chest, letting Michael feel his slim but warm frame.

It wasn't a yes or no question. The fox was ready now, and by rubbing Michael's head, between his ears, he was helping himself to the bear's muzzle. Taylor moved forward, pushed his tip towards Michael maw, and slid in.

Michael curved the lips of his muzzle below his fangs. His muzzle was wide, but the fox's cock was even wider. The bear opened wide and swallowed the cock.

Like Taylor's perfume, his cock tasted sweet and warm in Michael's muzzle. The bear's paws moved on their own. He groped Taylor's fuzzy chest and felt the fox breathe steady at first. Then, as Michael's muzzle locked around the cock and gave the first few sucks, the fox's heart rate quickened.

Michael growled playfully, and the rumble in his muzzle vibrated the tip of Taylor's cock. The fox got musky fast. The bear's paws slid down Taylor's body and held him on top of his chest, keeping him from thrusting.

Taylor huffed. "Such a tease." The fox struggled against the bear's grip and eventually gave in. Taylor straightened his back and opened his muzzle to huff and moan loudly. Michael knew he was getting to the fox. He moved his muzzle back and forth, sliding his tongue across Taylor's tip when his head pulled back.

At the edge of Michael's muzzle, the bear could feel Taylor's balls squeeze and relax. He was getting the fox closer to climax, and he didn't want that to happen just yet. Michael's own cock painfully pushed against the fabric of his boxers, begging for release.

Michael's maw squeezed Taylor's cock together and sucked a few more times before pulling his head back and letting the cock slip out of his muzzle.

"Satisfied?" Michael licked his muzzle. Taylor flicked his ears.

"Oh, hon." The fox reached to the tip of his cock and slid a finger across the urethra. He took a swab of pre-cum off that stretched like a spider web and placed the finger in his muzzle to suck. "I'm just getting started," he said, adjusting his weight. "Are you ready for the next part?"

Michael nodded. His paws moving from Taylor's thighs. They reached towards the back of the fox.

"Good," said Taylor. "Now turn over."

Michael's ears flicked. The fox surprised him for the second time. His cock twitched at the command, but his eyes blinked quickly.

The fox giggled, placing a paw in front of his black and red muzzle.

"Oh, darlin', you didn't think I was a bottom fox, did you?" He shifted his weight on top of the bear.

"Well, I—" Michael started, but Taylor laughed again. "Won't you at least try? It'll be fun. Promise." The fox licked his muzzle again and offered a smile.

Michael thought of arguments against it, but the more he could pick up Taylor's musk and see that wide cock dangle in front of him, the more that excited him. After all, how bad could it be?

"Alright," Michael agreed, "but I do you afterwards."

Taylor flicked his ears at the bear. "Oh, trust me. You'll be so dead afterwards, you won't know what hit you." He added a wink for effect and climbed off the bear.

Michael reached for his boxers and slid them down. He hissed as the boxers, stuck to the wet tip of his cock, tugged off. Michael couldn't help but stroke his shaft, if only to relieve the pressure in his cock. He watched Taylor bend over and rummage through a drawer. Michael watched Taylor's small tail-hole on display under his tail. Michael made a circle with his fingers and slid his cock through the grip, imagining how tight the petite fox was.

Taylor returned with a long device that looked like a pump and some rope.

The fox made a circling motion with his paw. "On all fours," he said. With a groan, Michael forced himself to release his cock and shift on top of the bed. He positioned himself on his knees, and then bent down to hold himself on his forearms. The bear faced the pillows. His cock dangled below him weightlessly. He couldn't see the fox, but he could hear him move around and then felt his touch.

Michael felt the wet tip of Taylor's cock press against the back of his thigh. Then, the fox took hold of the bears cock. He didn't stroke it like Michael thought the fox would. Instead, Taylor used Michael's pre-cum and spread it across the bear's cock, then pushed it downwards and into the pump.

It wasn't a regular masturbator. It felt tight inside, but it didn't feel like any particular species. The bottom of it fit tightly around the base of Michael's cock. The fox secured the pump with a strap around Michael's waist. The rope landed on the side of the bed, still wrapped up.

"There," said Taylor. "All nice and readied up."

"What is this thing?" Michael moved his hips and made his cock, along with the machine, swing around.

"You'll see soon enough." Michael could imagine the fox smiling. "Now then." And then he felt Taylor's tongue under his tail.

Michael gasped. His buttocks got spread by Taylor, and the wet prodding tongue slipped inside his tail hole. An inch is all it took to get Michael to moan. The pressure against the right spot was a new sensation. Taylor's tongue moved clockwise around the outside of the tail hole, and Michael buried his face into the pillows. He dug into the covers with his claws.

Michael drew in breath and then held it for a moment before exhaling between moans.

"Oh, fuck," Michael managed in a gasp. His cock no longer felt all the need for attention. This new feeling, like an itch that needed to be scratched, made him push his rear backwards into the fox's muzzle.

The bear felt Taylor's vibrating maw as the fox moaned. Then there was a series of wet squirts. Michael couldn't see, but he imagined Taylor stroking himself. The fox moved his muzzle left and right, as though he was heavily kissing the bear's tail hole.

Michael's buttocks got spread again as Taylor removed his tongue from there. The bear's tail hole muscle squeezed and relaxed. With Taylor gaping it open, the fox spit into Michael's entrance.

"Fuck," Michael caught his breath. He turned his head to look at the fox positioning himself behind the man. "Where did you learn that?"

Taylor growled playfully. "I grew up on a farm," said the fox. "Could hardly get hard unless I was up in some good ass." The fox teased the tip of his cock, then released it and let it fall onto Michael's buttocks.

The bear wanted to watch, to see Taylor enter him. Michael never thought he would have such thoughts, yet there he was.

Michael felt Taylors cock slide to the side and prod at his tail hole. The bed shifted, and the fox opened something with a small pop. Cold goo dripped onto Michael's tail hole. He shifted at the cold, but the sensation that followed was heated, like an itch needed to be scratched. The bear twitched his sphincter muscles, finding a gap that needed to be filled.

He felt Taylor's cock back in place, prodding into him. "You ready, papa bear?" asked the fox.

Michael grunted into the pillows and nodded. This was it. He was ready for it.

"Oh, I almost forgot." Taylor chuckled and reached below the bear's waist. The fox fiddled with the pump attached to Michael and twisted a knob.

A set of rings inside the pump gripped around Michael's cock and started to move up and down his length. The bear gasped. The pump was quick, and it wasn't vibrating—it was simulating a blowjob. He pushed his hips back. The milking of Michael's cock was moderately quick, running across his entire shaft. Michael could hear Taylor giggle behind him, clearly pleased. Then, a moment later, as the fox's paws tightened around Michael's hips, Taylor's cock slid into his tail hole.

This was a new feeling. Michael squeezed his sphincter muscles by instinct. It prevented the fox from getting in, but he didn't give up. Taylor tried again. The tip of his cock slid out of Michael and re-entered a second later. This time, it was Michael who gave in. The cock in his tail hole kept the pressure there and slid inside inch by inch. For Michael, it felt like the fox was pushing into his stomach. After a moment, Michael felt any resistance he had dropping, and Taylor's wide cock fit into him perfectly.

"Oh, sweetie," the fox moaned, adjusting his weight on the bed. "You're so wonderfully tight."

Michael knew he was. The wide cock made his tail hole burn as it adjusted to the length. It wasn't just the new feeling, but the bear thought of things he wouldn't at any other time. Michael wanted the fox to move, to keep on filling him up. He was curious to see what cum inside his tail hole would feel like.

The bear issued a deep growl. "Yes, fuck me, please." He said it out loud, and then buried his muzzle into the pillows. The fox moaned something in response and then moved. He pulled back, sliding his cock outwards, but not all the way. The relief of pressure in Michael's tail hole felt amazing. It hurt going in, but felt great going out. The mix of two was the perfect balance. Michael was glad they had lube.

The milking pump forced Michael's hips backwards, making him simulate humping. At the same time, he pushed back onto the fox's wide cock with hunger. Taylor's thrusting was fast but gentle. The fox increased his breathing, releasing a high-pitched moan. The sound of Taylor's cock filling Michael's tail hole got louder as the lube squished together.

"Harder," Michael gripped the bed sheets with his claws. "Come on, harder," he grunted, moving his hips in a rhythm with Taylor's. The fox lowered his paws onto Michael's thighs and pushed off them, slipping out.

"Lay on your belly," Taylor said, and helped the bear shift.

Either it was the position or the fact that Michael's weight pressed against the milking pump, but the blowjob simulation gripped at his cock tighter. It kept up a quick pace, putting pressure on the back stripe of his cock. Michael squirmed, thrusting his hips into the bed.

The fox picked up the discarded rope and tied Michael's wrists together.

"Just relax." Taylor offered a smile and stretched the rope around the bedposts to keep Michael's arms stretched and bound. Taylor's weight pressed onto him. The fox moved Michael's legs together such that they were straight and then tied around the knees. Once done, the fox then put his own knee on each side of Michael's thighs. It kept the bear from moving them apart. Michael's rear was tight in that position. The fox on top of the bear pressed down onto Michael, using his paws to move the buttocks apart. The fox slid his cock into the bear.

Michael grit his fangs and grunted into the pillows. There was something about being pressed onto the bed with weight on top of you that just felt amazing. The movement restrictions, the cock inside Michael going deeper. The fox's length felt endless, and that's when the real thing started. The bear could feel Taylor getting into position. The fox kept his paws on Michael's hips, but lifted himself up with his feet, spreading widely. Michael's legs got pinned together and then his hips as well. The fox pulled back, careful not to let the tip slide out of Michael's tail-hole and then pounded into the bear.

The first forceful thrust hurt Michael, but it was a good kind of pain that came with pleasure. He definitely wanted more of it. The bear gasped in quick succession, and the fox pounded away. The fox thrusted into him, pounding Michael's own hips into the bed. In return, Michael's hips moved the milking pump with his cock inside at an angle. The bear breathed heavily, evolving his moans into deep cries. His moved his hips to match Taylor's thrusting and then Michael's body shook. He filled the milking pump with his cum and kept coming.

With quick movements, the fox on top of him matched Michael's grunts. Taylor's grunts turned into high cries. With the help of his paws, the fox was able to pull himself into Michael faster. His balls slapped against Michael's rear, rapidly sliding in and out of him. Then, the fox on top of Michael trembled and wrapped his claws firmly around the bear's hips, sliding the paws under Michael. The fox squeezed and whined into Michel's ear. The bear felt Taylor buck into his tail hole. The fox held the pressure there for a moment, catching his breath.

This wasn't so bad, Michael saw. It felt pretty good. Now that the fun and orgasm were over, Michael felt embarrassed. To make such noises and say the things he said, especially now with Taylor still inside of him, made him glad no one had witnessed it.

But, the fox was right. Michael was dead tired, and his eyes were too heavy to keep awake. The milking pump connected to his cock was still on, and now hurt more than gave pleasure. It might have been the only thing keeping Michael from falling asleep.

The fox slid out of the bear, leaving behind a trail of cum that dripped onto the bear's rear. The room smelled of heavy musk and cum. Michael thought it was naughty, and yet exciting, with the way Taylor rubbed the tip of his cock into the bear's tail fur.

"How was that?" Taylor asked, standing somewhere behind Michael. "Not bad for your first time?"

Michael grumbled into the pillows. "Not bad," he echoed the fox. Then, Michael opened his eyes, remembering what they had decided at the beginning of their night. He struggled against his restraints, but unable to get loose.

"Hey," Michael called out to the fox. "It's my turn now, right?" The bear moved his head, but couldn't see behind him. There were giggles coming from somewhere behind Michael. He heard the rip of the velcro, followed by a few taps against a screen, and, finally, a camera shutter. Michael assumed Taylor was taking pictures with his iPad. Foxes—dirty and sneaky.

"Taylor?" Michael called out, but got no answer. Instead, the radio in the far corner of the room turned on—a local pop rock radio station. The volume increased until Michael couldn't hear Taylor moving around. Then, a moment later, the bear felt a weight press onto the bed and climb over his back.

"Oh hon," Taylor giggled over Michael. The bear felt something long, cold, and sharp press against his throat. "I did say you would be dead afterwards." With a free paw, Taylor wrapped a muzzle around Michael's maw. The bear struggled, but the fox easily overpowered him.

"Maybe not dead just yet." Taylor kissed Michael between his ears. The bear shivered, shifting his paws and feet. "We've still got all night." Taylor tied a rag around Michael's muzzle. The bear protested, half convincing himself that it was a joke. Though, the knife didn't move from his throat. Its sharp edge drew the first bits of blood when Michael lowered his head for a second.

Taylor brought his muzzle close to Michael's ear. "I always take before and after pictures. I like to remember everyone as they were." Taylor slid his tongue over Michael's cheek. The bear could smell the strong scent of coffee from Taylor's breath, mixed with his own bits of blood, dripping from his neck.

"Now," Taylor giggled. "let me show you how big and bad I can be, detective."

ARCTIC FOX
Sisco Polaris

So, I was in this bar and I slide up to this big, old, daddy, polar bear. He glances at me with a look that lets me know he can spot a fox on the prowl for some fur. I introduce myself and we start talking, turns out he's a writer, named Sisco Polaris. The bear has been at it for a good number of years. Apparently he has a few novels out, The Stable Boy *and* Dyeing to be With You, *he seemed proud of them since he mentioned them by name. I was suitably impressed and said I had never met a serious writer before. He laughed and said, "serious writers use the words cock and ass far less than I do". Seems the bear likes to write stories with a bit of an erotic element to them, which are the type of stories I like to read, when I'm not living them. So I gave him my best foxy, come hither, look and asked if he would like to live an erotic story instead of write one for a change. Turns out, the old bear lives up to his writing.*

A cunning plan that had been his downfall. As a fox, many would say there was some irony in that. However, as far as Max was concerned, irony could kiss his fluffy white ass. The plan had been perfectly fine: tell his parents he was heading back to college a day or two early to make sure he got there safe. In fact, he was to drive to his friend Kyle's flat and spend those days hanging out with no clothes and not moving far from the bed, mainly thanks to the ropes. Then, leave late and drive almost nonstop for forty-eight hours to get back to college just in time to catch his first lecture.

As a plan, it couldn't be faulted on its merits. However, it could certainly be faulted on all its damn faults. Firstly, there had been his mother, who had insisted he get a full breakfast before he went. That meant he didn't even leave until after midday, and he left with a stomach so full of eggs and bacon that the first thing he did when he got to Kyle's was set up camp in the bathroom. Ropes had to wait because there was nothing sexy about getting stuffed when you were already stuffed.

By the evening, he'd finally recovered from his mother's big special college boy breakfast. Ropes had been applied, and a nice and fun stuffing had been give multiple times. Things felt like they were going right—he had an ass full of cum and another day to look forward to. The second day had started well: a healthy breakfast heavy with vitamins D and C. Then, Kyle had strapped him into a sex swing and stepped out 'to grab some whipped cream for later.' Seven hours of dangling alone and fighting with his internal needs along with imagining the headlines and how his mother would feel when the police finally battered down the door to find her son dead in a sex swing, covered in his own excrement.

Kyle had returned eventually. The stupid asshole had gotten caught speeding, and, instead of just taking the ticket, he had hit on the cop. That had been a bad move. The cop had not been gay or even bi-curious. He was, in fact, extremely hetero-furious. Also, the stupid rhino still had enough alcohol in his bloodstream from the night before that he had failed a breath test. When he had finally returned, Max had lost any trace of his normal easy-going sense of humour. Maybe in the future, he would be able to look back and laugh. Right then, he was looking straight ahead and screaming into Kyle's face.

Things had gotten worse when Kyle had asked him to leave. Seven hours immobilised left his arms and legs so nearly dead that walking in a straight line had been a challenge. He had made it to his car, ignored the front seat, crawled into the back one, and fallen asleep. It was snowing and nearly afternoon the next day when he finally awoke. He was twelve hours behind schedule, and the snow slowed him down further.

The smart thing to have done would be to go home, beg his parents to pay for plane fare, make up some excuse. However, to do so would involve explaining where he had been for the last two days. His parents knew he was gay, he'd been out and proud since he was fourteen, and his parents were supportive. Supportive has its limitations, and 'hi, mom, I spent seven hours locked in a sex swing, I need to sleep' was so far beyond those limitations the limitations were a dot on the horizon.

So, Max had driven slowly as the snow had fallen not so slowly. The city was behind him and the mountains were in front of him and his plan started to look stupid. More than stupid; suicidal. He'd realised too late that he was the only car left on the road. The last signs of civilisation were miles behind him, his phone was showing no connection, and nobody knew he was even out there.

In his panic, he had kept driving until the snow was too deep and his car had just stopped. His phone still had no connection and his total food stocks were one flat half-drunk bottle of coke and half a bag of Cheetos. On the plus side, he had almost every item of clothing he owned in the trunk. His own fur was a nice bonus too. Thick, plush arctic fur designed to keep him warm in the coldest of winters.

Two hours later, he was wearing almost every item of clothing, shivering and making himself a promise. If there was an afterlife, the first thing he was going to do was find God and demand a fucking refund for his worthless fur. It was long, it took ages to fucking groom, and when push came to shove, it wasn't even good enough to keep him from freezing to death when supplemented by six t-shirts, four sweaters, and two hoodies. That God dude owed him some serious answers for this death. On the plus side, his mother wasn't going to find him dead on a sex swing.

He closed his eyes, pulled his bundle of clothes around him, and sent up a silent prayer that he would be recused. Max's eyes had barely closed when he was roused by the muffled thump of gloved knuckles on the window. Max's heart leapt into his mouth and he struggled to sit up and opened the door. The icy blast of air coming in the gap hurt his face. However, the sight of a red face poking out of a heavy hood was worth it.

"Hey, you seem to be in a bit of a situation, son." The voice was muffled by the scarf covering their muzzle and by the whistle of the wind. The fox couldn't really deny it. This was definitely a situation, and he was slap bang directly in the middle of it, four feet deep in snow. "You want to join me in my cab? Got a heater and some food."

"Th...thanks!" Max stammered as he climbed out of the car, slamming the door behind him a little harder than he needed to. It felt good, though—the damn box on wheels had betrayed him, at least in his mind. The other guy was already moving away, and Max could see the bright headlights of a truck just behind him. He couldn't believe the huge thing had pulled up behind him and he hadn't noticed, although the wind was high, and he had been wrapped up in his misery.

The truck was huge, and he had to practically haul himself up into the cab. Only, it wasn't just a cab. Behind the front seats was a small cabin where his saviour was currently pulling off his scarf. Max pulled the door shut after himself, and the warmth of the cab started to seep through his layers of his clothing.

"Make yerself at home, son," muttered the trucker as he pulled off his coat. Now that he could see the guy more clearly, Max knew his saviour was a squirrel, a red one. He looked in his late forties, maybe early fifties, his arms looked quite big, and he had a stomach that told of long hours on the road with a few too many snacks. "I'll give you the tour. That's the bed, stove, fridge, and back there is a small toilet and a shower. Though, I wouldn't recommend you taking one of those right now. Though, given how stupid you must be to be out here in a little box on your own, with, from what I could see, no food or water, or any way to get help, I suppose I wouldn't be too surprised if you took a shower and ran out into the snow butt nekkid."

The fox didn't know what to say. He couldn't exactly claim to be the most thoughtful person in the world. "Thanks for getting me out. I promise, no showers or running around butt naked."

"Aw, now I'm disappointed," chuckled the older man as he turned on the stove. "You want some soup? Oxtail—it'll warm you up from the inside too."

"Yes, thank you again." Max looked around the small cabin. It was cosy and neat. A small bed that doubled as a seat, and a tiny one-ring stove next to a small sink. At the back was a little door that the fox guessed led to the shower and toilet. "So, how come you got stuck out here too?"

"Ah, well I made a bit of an error in judgement," replied the guy as he stirred the soup slowly. The cabin filled up with the strong smell of beef. "There was a bit of a bonus offered to get this load to Dallas by Thursday, and I thought, 'Damned storm can't be that bad.' Then, it turned out…"

"The storm was that bad." They said it together, and Max couldn't help but laugh. He squirmed, a little uncomfortable in so much clothing. "You mind if I take off a few layers? I kinda put a lot on—no heater in my car."

"Naw, go for it," replied the trucker. "Name's Karl, by the way."

"Max," replied the fox as he pulled off the second of his hoodies and removed all his sweaters, then three of his t-shirts. He pulled off all but one pair of sweatpants. "There! Now I can bend."

"Bending is very important," agreed Karl as he poured the soup out into two mugs. "I imagine it comes in handy for you gay guys. Here you go."

Max's jaw dropped as he took the proffered mug. "How...did you..."

"Ah, well. I've travelled to every corner of this country and been on the road since I was your age. I have met hundreds of people. Thousands, in fact." The squirrel sat down on his bed and took a sip of his soup. "So, I've seen it all: straight, gay, trans, and everything in between. So, when I meet a guy, I know if he is gay."

The fox gulped and took a sip of his soup. It was hot and warm, it didn't taste bad—store-bought, obviously, but not that cheap. Max was very impressed. He had never thought of himself as someone who was particularly camp or twinky. His body was quite fit, but not overly so, and he was average height and weight for a fox. Not someone who might be easily spotted as gay. "Good soup."

"Thanks, I opened the can myself," chuckled the squirrel. With a wink, his eyes flicked down the fox's front. The rodent was smirking at him, and, for a moment, Max thought he had spilt soup on his shirt. His eyes dipped down and Max laughed.

"Travelled every road, met thousands of people, huh?" asked the fox as he stared down at his 'I heart cocks' T-shirt with a picture of a rainbow-coloured rooster as the O in cocks.

"Yes indeed, and something tells me that you, boy, like cocks," laughed the trucker, slapping his leg and then yipping a little as he spilt soup on himself. "Ah, damn it. Guess I deserved that."

"You did," chuckled the fox as he drank some more soup. "Still, this is a lot better than I thought today was going to end. Guess I got lucky."

"Yeah, according to the radio, the storm is going to be a couple of days. It might be a while before I can drive this rig out of here. So, at least I will have someone to keep me company. Afraid there's only one bed though," Karl said, leaning back in his seat.

"That's ok, I can just sleep up here in the cab. Anywhere is better than the icebox you found me in," Max replied. He glanced out of the window at the snow-covered road, and he could just about make out the roof of his car through the heavy snowflakes. He felt strangely at home, so he sat back in the chair and just looked out. "It's really coming down."

"Oh, yeah. If it keeps this up, you and me are going to be stuck here for a couple of days. Hope you weren't rushing to a hot date," replied the trucker, and Max couldn't help but laugh.

"The exact opposite," chuckled the fox, taking another sip of the warm soup. Somehow, the sight of snow made the warmth of the soup feel so much better.

"Sounds like there is a story there." A deaf person could have heard the hint in Karl's statement.

"A very embarrassing one," admitted the fox with a smile. It would take a lot more than a mug of hot soup and saving his life to get that story out of him.

"Ah, well, I have a few of those myself," Karl replied with a cheery voice. "Twenty years on the road and four years in the marines, I got a shit ton of them."

"You were in the marines?" The fox wasn't entirely shocked. The squirrel wasn't badly built, and he was clearly prepared for the blizzard. That spoke of some discipline.

"Twenty-third Marine Division, one tour in Iraq, the first Gulf War, part of Operation Desert Shield." Max's jaw dropped as the squirrel casually dropped a bomb. Of course, he now knew Karl had training in just exactly how to drop a bomb.

"Wow, did…did you, like, see action?" It wasn't subtle, but anything to divert away from telling the sex swing story.

"Yes," Karl replied, and in a voice that did not invite any further questions. "When I came back, I decided it wasn't a career for me. I joined up to train as an engineer. I was pretty good at it, then I found out there was good money to be made driving freight. So long as you don't mind long and lonely, hours. Or, the lack of personal hygiene facilities, most places, eating food that'll kill ya slowly and make you have to choose between gassing yourself or opening the window and freezing in a blizzard."

Max laughed again. The rodent had clearly steered away from a dark topic. He admired the humour Karl was able to use. He found himself wondering what life on the road was like. "You have a wife or girlfriend?"

"Yeah, you're sitting in her." The squirrel smirked as he climbed into the driver's seat to sit next to the fox. "No time for any real romance—not sure it's my kind of thing, anyway. I know you hear a lot of stories of guys on the road, picking up hitchhikers and...well, you know. Or, having a girl in every city. Now, I won't say I've never, but I don't do it often and I've never found anyone to settle down with. Truth be told, I ain't looking.

"So, you've asked me a good couple of questions—my turn. You out of the closet?"

The fox grinned at him and nodded. "Yeah, you see this shirt? My Mom got it for me to march in a pride parade."

"That must be nice. My parents...well, let's just say, if I'd had to come out, I'd have needed to get back into the military so I could borrow a bulletproof vest," laughed the squirrel, and then he gave a shrug of his shoulders. "My Pa didn't raise no dirty faggot." Something in the squirrel's eyes told Max he wasn't really laughing. There was more to that story, but now was not the time to press for the epilogue.

"Well, attitudes are changing, even in the south," Max muttered reassuringly and finished off his mug of soup. "Thanks, I really needed that."

"You're welcome, nothing better than hot soup on a cold day," observed the trucker. They sat in silence for a few minutes, just watching the snow fall. Eventually, Karl broke the silence with another question. "So, do you have a fella of your own?"

"Not anymore." The answer burst out before he had any chance to think of it, and the bitterness and anger in his voice were plain to hear.

"Ah, he cheat on you?" It wasn't a bad guess, though, the

relationship had been open and they'd both been free to fuck around.

"Nope, he…" sighed the fox. He fixed his eyes on the snow. The white world did feel strangely comforting. He realised he'd have to tell someone—besides, it wasn't like Karl knew anyone he did. "You…ever try any bondage?"

"You mean like furry handcuffs and stuff? Not really, no. You?" Karl's voice let Max know the squirrel clearly knew what the answer was.

"Well, the handcuffs weren't furry, and rope works better if you know knots…"

"And all you canids are experts at knots," snorted the rodent with a laugh, and Max found himself laughing and blushing.

"Yeah, well my boyfriend, Kyle—he may have been a rhino, but he knew his knots too," Max replied, and his chuckling died. "Stupid bastard tied me into his sex swing, said he just needed to go get some whipped cream from the store…I thought at first it was all just part of a game. Kept telling myself he was going to burst in the room with a cocky smile, sure, I'd be mad, but he'd fuck me to some great orgasm or something to make it all worth it. Then, well, you can only fool yourself for so long. By the time the third hour hit I was trying to wriggle free. My wrists are still sore from it—pulled out a lot of fur there too. Of course, Kyle is an expert at knots." The last part was spat out bitterly. Karl was clearly smart enough to keep his mouth shut.

"I spent…I dunno how long just alone, running through everything, every single scenario in my head. Was Kyle dead, or in hospital in a coma? Nobody knew I was there if he was dead or in a coma—fuck, I was so stupid. I just let him tie me up and leave. I trusted him and the stupid fucker…He could have told the police who arrested him, got someone to come 'round. But, no, that would be too embarrassing for him. Instead, he chose to tell no one, just wait for his mother to get him out and give him a lift home. Of course, she didn't know, so he couldn't hurry her along. Bastard went to Walmart with her, picked up some fucking ice, and he got the whipped cream!"

Max knew he was speaking far louder than he should, but he could feel himself trembling with anger. "He thought…He thought I was going to fuck him after it. Seven hours thinking I was going to die, strapped to a sex swing, that my mother… was going to…and he…he…he…"

The trembles turned to sobs, his words had long since passed the point where they could be understood between sobs. A warm pair of arms were pressed around him. Max accepted the hug, returning it with desperate tightness, burying his face in the squirrel's broad chest. His large stomach and chest were comforting—the warmth of another body and the sound of a heart beating rhythmically helped to soothe his nerves.

Outside the truck, the snow continued to fall, the wind whipping it around the mountains and the trees. Inside the cab, Max just wept as Karl held him, not saying a word, no laughing, no judgment, and no unwanted words of advice.

Eventually, when he had no more tears to cry, the fox pulled away from the warm arms reluctantly. "Sorry, I just…It was just yesterday, and…"

"It's okay. I know this might be hard to believe, but I think I can understand," said the squirrel, pulling out a box of tissues from his glove box. The trucker's top was soaked with tears and…well, other facial fluids best not mentioned. He offered some to the fox and then did his best to clean up. "Not knowing if you have been left behind, if you are going to die or not. Your boy chose to leave you behind, then expected everything to be okay? That's just…I've travelled the length and breadth of this nation, and I've seen a load of dumb shit. However, every time I hear something and think, 'Okay that's the dumbest thing anyone could ever do,' somehow, someone always manages to prove that, no matter how far you dig down into dumb, some stupid fucker can always dig lower."

Max laughed as he wiped his face clean. "Oh, yeah, I'm not even finished college and I think I figured that one out. Still, I'm sorry, it's not exactly cool to unload everything on a random nice guy."

"Don't worry about it," Karl replied with a reassuring smile. "Honestly, Kyle seems like an ass. You can probably do better than him."

"Sure, any guy who isn't going to leave me tied up for more than six hours," snorted the fox with a chuckle.

"Well, you could aim a slight bit higher," Karl replied with a slightly uncomfortable smile on his face. "Pretty sure a good-looking boy like you is gonna have his pick of the fellas."

Max squirmed in his chair, and his face flushed with the warmth of a blush. The words were welcome—it was nice to hear something positive about himself after spending twenty-four hours calling himself every name under the sun. "Thanks. For what it's worth, a good-looking guy like yourself could probably do very well with the fellas too."

"Oh, I know," Karl replied glibly, waving a paw over his ample stomach and the drying stains on his sweater. "All of this is hard to resist, for guys and girls alike."

The fox laughed, but only a little. He had a lot of friends who were very into the daddy type guys, and, at that moment, he could understand why. Karl had saved him, fed him, made him feel comfortable, and held him when he needed it. What's more, he was pretty sure Karl wasn't entirely straight. "Well, you'd be surprised, is all I'll say."

"Maybe," replied the squirrel quietly as if he was thinking over something. Max was hoping he might be picking up on the slightly transparent flirting.

"So, you ever think of settling down somewhere? Finding a nice girl?" It wasn't a great question and certainly lacked the wit that foxes were known for. Sometimes, stereotypes are hard to live up to: He had a horse friend, Martin, and his penis was slightly smaller than the average fox's. Nothing wrong with it, a good length, but the pony always got a slightly disappointed look from his lovers when they found out. However, Max was genuinely interested in knowing more about the guy he was there with. Besides, he had his potential paramour exactly where he wanted him—in a tiny, inescapable cab. He could take his time.

"Well, I actually have a place down outside Dallas. Nice house and a few acres of land. I tend to spend a month or two there every now and then," Karl replied, looking out over the snow. "This job pays pretty good, especially if you are willing to do the real long-haul stuff. I don't spend all my money on girls, or drugs, or family. I paid off my mortgage and paid for my rig. Little tip for life: buy, don't rent. Renting, you pay the same, but have nothing to show for it afterwards."

"Noted," Max replied. It didn't seem like bad advice.

"As for a girl," Karl continued, turning to give Max a sad smile. "I am on the road ten months of the year, sometimes more. That ain't fair for anyone I settled down with. Maybe in a few years, I'll quit driving. Start up a small dairy and make some artisanal cheeses." The last part caught the fox by surprise.

"Artisanal cheeses?" he blurted out far louder than he intended. His tone was similar to the tone of someone asking why someone was refusing to accept their twenty million dollar lottery win.

"What? What's wrong with making cheese?" The squirrel leaned in towards him. "It is really more of an art form. There's thousands of different cheeses. I have tried them all over the country, and a few in other countries too. Plus, have you seen how much people charge for the artisanal stuff?"

Max laughed a little and shook his head. "Somehow, I can't see you as a cheese maker."

"Well, you never know, until you know," Karl replied with a laugh. "Plus, I have a selection of cheese and biscuits back there that would knock your socks off."

"There are way more fun ways to knock my socks off." It was a come on, as obvious as an elephant cannonballing into a swimming pool.

"Mm, I am aware," replied the squirrel with a confident look that made Max's cock twitch in his pants. "I've done it before, after all."

Max noticed the squirrel was leaning towards him. He had slid closer to Karl without conscious thought. "You have…with guys?"

Karl reached out a paw and lightly caressed Max's cheek, and the palm felt warm against his cheek. Suddenly, he was diving forward, his lips meeting Karl's in a soft kiss. He heard the squirrel moan deeply and the pressure on his lips increased. The passion of the kiss grew by the second, and his paws reached out to the warm body of the squirrel. His fingers brushed over the warm, soft bulk of his ample stomach.

A tongue wormed its way into his mouth and he sucked on it, his own tongue dancing with the invader. His paws stroked down eagerly to Karl's crotch and it was Max's turn to moan. Like any good child of Texas, Karl was packing a weapon of impressive size and capability. His fingers traced around the swollen length, trapped in the denim. Then, they moved eagerly to their flies and unbuttoned them just as fast as they could. All the while, the two kissed passionately.

His stomach was growling with hunger, and he knew exactly what he was hungry for. Max's fingers reached into the warm cave of Karl's jeans. It took the effort of mere moments to find the open fly of the squirrel's boxers. He shuddered against the older male as his paw closed around a thick and meaty shaft— just what he was hungering for. With a deft and practised motion, he pulled the hefty pole out through the open flies, keeping the head covered with his palm as button or zip scrapes were not usually welcome on a cocktip. Although the fox would have been sure to kiss any injuries better, it was best to protect the cock rather than make apologies afterwards.

The trucker gasped as his manhood was freed, a pleasantly musky scent filling the small living cabin. Max broke the kiss and moaned deeply as he looked down at the pink maleness that poked out. It was easily one of the thickest he had seen, and definitely on someone who wasn't one of the larger species. There wasn't a heartbeat of hesitation. His head just dived down, his warm, soft lips kissing the cocktip in greeting.

"Oh, go easy. It's been a few weeks," Karl moaned down at him. A broad smile spread across the fox's face. He kissed the tip again, tasting the musk and sweat of a long day sitting behind a wheel, wrapped up in layers of warm-weather clothes. Max loved a cock with flavour, and this one seemed full, potent. A strong musk mixed with the bitter tang of sweat and the odd sweetness of aged port.

With zeal born of the desire to prove he was a good lover, maybe more to himself than to Karl, he pressed his muzzle down slowly. Inch by inch, the thickness slid between his lips, his tongue welcoming the warm flesh, squirming against the length. His nose took in deep lungfuls of his lover's scent, drinking in the stink of lust and desire that his mate was giving. Just as his nose pressed inside the jeans he felt the cocktip pushing to the back of his throat, and he stopped, his mouth filled with thick cock. Max closed his eyes and just basked in the moment, it was all he wanted right there.

"Oh, fuck!" exclaimed the squirrel. Max felt two gentle paws stroking and caressing his cheeks, moving slowly up to his ears and hair. "That feels so good," the older male panted down to him, and he knew it was no lie as the thickness throbbed in his mouth and some bitter drops of precum were released onto his tongue, and Max promptly swallowed. He gave a deep huff, blowing warm air into the open flies and making the older male moan once more. Then, he began to pull back, savouring each wonderful inch of the delicious sausage as it pulled free from his lips.

He opened his eyes when just the cock head remained, pulling at his lips. The sight before him was wonderful. Quivering pink flesh glistening with the moisture from his mouth. His tongue lapped and teased, circling around Karl's coronal ridge, the tip teasing the frenulum and meatus, then across the glans in slow broad strokes. Each motion gained a new moan from the trucker, Max savoured them all, devouring them as a hungry man devours a snack.

There was nothing like the feel of a hot cock in his mouth—it always felt so right. He knew that this was where he belonged, and, most importantly, there was no other place he wanted to be. His mouth drove down again, hungrily taking the length to the full, while, above him, sweet gasps and cries of bliss fed his ears. He didn't stop this time, his muzzle gliding up and down the length smoothly. Karl's paws kept up their work stroking his vulpine ears tenderly and ruffling his head fur.

"Oh god!" whimpered Karl as the squirrel bucked up into Max's mouth. Max could feel the cock throbbing under his tongue, and the paws on his head were no longer stroking, they were holding. He loved that feeling, of someone taking control, taking charge. It was reassuring—all he wanted to do was bring pleasure to his partners. If they took control, he knew they would get everything they wanted from him. Which, in turn, was everything he wanted from them.

The thick meat began to slip back and forth under the motions of its owner. Max held still and just enjoyed the sensation of the cock tickling his lips, the taste of precum flooding his tongue, and the sounds of pleasure coming from above him. It all combined inside him to arouse his own lusts and desire even further. His cock was straining inside his jeans, disregarded, but not entirely forgotten.

"I can't...Oh, shit!" cried out Karl, and Max's lips tightened around the older male's shaft. The squirrel was moments away from his orgasm, and the fox was desperate to make those moments full of wonder. His tongue writhed powerfully, he sucked firmly, and he squeezed the maleness with his lips. Max's reward was a loud cry of pleasure, the throb of that hot meat in his mouth and the flood of potent seed that rushed down his hungry throat.

While his lover cried out in pleasure, lost to the bliss of the moment, Max bobbed his head slowly, squeezing the cock between his lips, making sure to milk every last drop he could from Karl. It certainly had been a while for the older male— either that, or he was naturally a high-yield kind of guy. By the time Max pulled off and let the half-hard cock slip free from his lips, the flow of seed had completely stopped.

Max looked up at Karl and winked as he visibly swallowed the last of his seed. It was a show. Karl would know he swallowed for the lack of a puddle of spunk anywhere in his cab. However, Max had found that most males enjoy the sight of their lover drinking it down. With a smile and a tremble of pleasure, Karl showed that, in that respect, he was like most males.

"Thank you," the squirrel whispered down to him.

"Thank you," Max replied earnestly, and he didn't just mean for saving his life. For listening to him, for showing kindness, and for making him feel attractive in a moment when he felt more vulnerable than he had ever done. However, his own cock was throbbing inside his jeans, letting him know he wanted more. Sitting up, he glanced back into the cabin at the small bed. "Maybe we could…get an early night."

It was as plain an offer as any fox could ever make. However, to hammer the point home he grabbed one of Karl's paws and pulled it down to his hips. Then, he looked deep into the squirrel's hazel eyes and gave him a grin only a fox could pull off. It implied so much more than the look or the paw: it said, in neon words fifty feet tall, 'I am going to fuck your damn socks off, curl your toes in a way no lover ever has, and leave you praying we don't get rescued for a week, just so you have time to recover.'

"It…has been an awful long day," agreed Karl with a grin that Max read clearly as 'yes, fucking, please!' The squirrel's paw gripped his hip tighter for a moment as he leaned close to whisper, "I am sure that under the circumstances we can share the bed. There's room for two if we press real close."

That was all the encouragement Max needed. he practically dove over the seat and his paws tore at his clothes, pulling off his last pair of sweatpants and the jeans underneath, along with all the remaining t-shirts. His pure white and naked body hit the bed less than a minute afterwards while Karl just stared in slack-jawed approval.

The squirrel moved slower, but more deliberately. He climbed over into the back and then reached out to pull some black curtains shut behind him, closing out the white light from the blizzard, along with any cold air. Max got to watch as he pulled off his sweater and the shirt underneath in one smooth motion, that broad belly and chest being exposed at once. If

Max hadn't known of his military history, he would have still guessed they guy had once been very fit. His neck and shoulders still showed muscle, although his stomach was soft and pudgy.

Karl stripped off his jeans and boxers to show that the squirrel did indeed have an impressive set of nuts on him. Definitely enough stored to keep a hungry fox fed through the winter. The red fur on his back and flanks was contrasted sharply by a creamy white of his chest and inner thighs. All of it was capped off with a long and flowing tail that seemed to dance with his every movement.

As for Max, his slender body writhed on the bed, his own cock almost painfully erect and drooling pre as only canid cocks can. Karl paused and Max watched as Karl's eyes took in every inch of him. The fox squirmed a little under the gaze, and yet he knew he loved it. Without a further word, the squirrel grabbed Max's ankles and lifted the fox's legs. Max yipped a little, the sudden dominance of the rodent surprising him, and arousing him all the more.

"Gonna guess a guy who just finished dating a rhino don't need much in the way of preparation," Karl grunted as he climbed onto the bed, his paws holding Max's ankles firmly. Max blushed under his fur and found himself nodding. His heart was beating rapidly, his knees were pressed down, and he closed his eyes, just bathing in the feeling of pure submission. He loved this feeling of helplessness—it was strange how being held down made him feel freer than anything else.

A warm mass pushed to his pucker, and his entire body trembled in anticipation. His breath was coming in rapid pants, his paws clawing desperately at the woollen blanket. Seconds seemed to pass like hours. Karl was holding still, and he didn't know why. He opened his eyes, preparing to beg for it if he needed to. However, the second his mouth opened, Karl struck with a strength of hip that comes from climbing in and out of a high cab all the time. Any words on Max's lips died and were reborn as a deep, feral cry of pleasure.

The thickness filling him was wonderful. It spread a

warmth from his tail to the tips of his ears. Karl moaned out loud as he clenched down, his ass desperate to hold that length inside him. Groaning with pleasure, the squirrel leant over him, the large stomach pressing down on his white legs. The pressure and feel of heat above him made Max whimper with carnal desire.

"Oh, fuck!" he whimpered in delight, trapped beneath a guy he had known for only a few hours.

"That is the plan, boi." Somehow, Max was able to hear the i in boi—the rodent growled it with the pure assurance of a dominant male who didn't just think he was a great top, he knew it for a fact. It made Max's insides quiver with delight and lust. He licked his lips and bucked up against the thrusting maleness, clenching down around it. "Oh…fuck!" Karl gasped in surprise at the sudden tightness.

With a slightly smug grin, the fox winked and replied, "that's the plan, sir!" As he said 'Sir,' the fox clenched down again, making the squirrel moan in pleasure once more. His moment of success was short-lived as two strong arms grabbed the woollen bedclothes and he looked up into two eyes glowing with pure bestial lust. In the half a heartbeat it took for Max to realise he was staring into the eyes of a male lost to his lust, the thick cock was pulled firmly from his ass. In what felt like a single instant, it was returned with so much power that the squirrel's hips slapped off his.

Max's squeals filled the cabin as Karl let loose on him. The thick cock plundered his hole like Karl owned him. His insides were ablaze with the pleasure of the rough breeding, and he gave in to his own instincts, bucking up against his lover with a passion only animals could match. He wanted that thickness inside him—he ached for it, and he revelled in every delicious moment, every firm smack of hips, the feel of a heavy set of nuts smacking off of his rump.

Each powerful thrust sent powerful waves of pleasure through the fox's body. His paws clawed desperately at the bed, his cock aching, trapped between him and his lover, like the teasing of Tantalus, so close and yet always out of reach. It sang to him, begging him for release. All he could do was cry out in delightfully impotent bliss, taking the breeding like he had learned.

Karl hadn't needed ropes, or handcuffs, or swings. He just held the young male down and was taking his pleasure from him. Max whimpered, lost to the pleasure, feeling so powerless and yet so safe. His eyes closed, and he felt a warm nose press to his forehead. His cheek and muzzle fur were getting soaked with the moist, panted breaths. Karl's voice was lifting louder than his, and, with each desperate thrust, the squirrel wriggled his hips, grinding his cock around inside him as it desperately tried to bury it just a little deeper.

With each thrust, Max could feel the pressure inside him building. His helpless cock was screaming at him with so much need, he knew all he had to do was get hold of it. His body wriggled and writhed, but Karl held him down firmly. The rodent moaned louder, his chest pressing down more like a wild animal holding his mate in place. Each moment felt like an eternity of torturous pleasure, the feeling of bliss raging against the desperate need for release.

Just as the fox felt like he would explode for the aching desire inside him, Karl cried out, his thrusts getting shallower and much faster, his hips thundering home with desperate and bestial desire. The squirrel drove into him without mercy, and that was all he could take. Flood of endorphins washed through his mind, wiping it as white as his fur. His cock throbbed, untouched, jetted his cum up onto Karl's stomach. While inside him, he could sense the warmth of another man's seed as it was planted as deep as the squirrel could thrust.

Max gasped desperately, dizzy with the powerful sensations as Karl thrusting slowly came to a halt. As he basked in the glow of the moment, his eyes felt heavy and before he knew it, he slipped off to sleep.

With a yawn and a stretch, Max blinked his way back to consciousness, pausing mid-yawn as his nose picked up a wonderful scent. Bacon, the second-best kind of meat to wake up to. He opened his eyes and saw Karl a few feet away at the stove with a small pan and heard the sizzling sound of bacon being fried. "Morning."

"I tried shaking you, shouting, and threatening to dump you out into the snow. That, you sleep through, but I start cooking some breakfast, and you wake up just in time to get some breakfast," Karl replied with a chuckle and looked back to add, "Typical sneaky fox, making sure I make him breakfast."

"Can't blame a vulpine for wanting a good breakfast after what you did to me last night," Max replied with a wink as he sat up in bed.

"Good thing I have enough bacon and eggs for two," laughed the squirrel as he began to scoop something out of the pant and onto some plates. "According to the radio, they are working on the road—expect to have it cleared by this evening. How do you like your eggs?"

"Sunnyside up. So, we won't be stuck here another night?" Max asked, trying to mask the disappointment in his voice.

"Nope. Assuming your car works after spending a couple of days buried under snow. If not, you can arrange a tow, and I can give you a lift to college," Karl announced with a wink as he expertly cracked an egg into the pan.

"Then what?"

"Well, it's been a while since I even thought about college, but I assume you try to learn something," Karl replied with a smile and a wink. Max got the message. The trucker had told him he wasn't looking for anything long term. He sat in silence, taking a plate of bacon and eggs when Karl pressed it into his paws. The squirrel opened the curtain and he looked out at the white world. The frozen landscape looked so serene and empty.

"Learn something," Max chuckled, thinking he had learned a few things in the last two days. "I think I can probably manage to do that. Though…if you ever happen to be passing my way…"

"I'll give you a call," laughed the squirrel. "If nothing else, you are better than a hot water bottle to keep a man warm.

Besides, after my years out of the military, it was nice to be back in a foxhole once more."

"Oh, fuck! That was bad," snorted the fox, but he laughed anyway. "Of course, we still have a few hours, if you feel like going over the top again, Marine."

"Well, we are pretty much stuck," Karl replied with a smirk. "So, I got nothing and no one better to be doing."

"Couple of days locked up, having sex with a good-looking guy," Max muttered out loud as he realised his plan had worked out after all.

IT'S THE LITTLE THINGS
Tana Simenses

Tana Simenses, as in "Canis Simensis", as in no "vulpes" in the species name. I absolutely assure you that Tana is not a fox, despite what many people believe. Can't trust Wikipedia, either, as they slanderously include "Simien Fox" as an alternative name for the majestic Ethiopian Wolf. Yes. Wolf. They make look like foxes to laypeople but they're most assuredly not foxes. This is not to say the Ethiopian Wolves dislike foxes, because we like them very much. In fact, one would be hard pressed to deny the allure of our vulpine lookalikes and the value their "assets" bring to wolves everywhere. Not Maned Wolves, though, as we are often mistaken for the Leg Fox. I realize attacking another wolf that looks like a fox by calling them "Leg Fox" seems odd considering all I just said, but let's face it: Maned Wolves are just foxes.

Little things matter. The little things I was able to do with the food onboard the ship earned me a lot of little favors. Favors like skipping out on unloading in my favorite little port town. A couple of the guys made little jokes or gave knowing looks as I made my way ashore. The way the orange hue of the setting sun lit the buildings of the serene town made me smile to myself.

Most of the stores had already closed down the evening— one of the drawbacks to small town life, I suppose. Of course, the couple of pubs were packed full of sailors like me who needed to unwind. My routine was a little less simple, and my feet carried me right on past the noisy bars and inns and towards the houses.

It was the little things like the yellow door of his house and the way he always answered it moment I knocked. It was how genuinely happy he looked to see me.

It wasn't any different that time.

It was the little things. The little tuft of fur that always stuck up on his neck that I couldn't help but put back in place with a tender lick. That faintly spicy, vanilla-like scent that my nostrils caught a clear whiff of as I buried them into the whimpering fox's fur. The oversized canine of his that poked out as his lips curled up in a smile. The way the short vulpine looked up at me. Yes, it was those little things that kept me coming back to the little port town where Sean lived.

I could have moved on to bigger and better things. The guys bugged me for awhile about it; wondering why I'd turned down a much more comfortable route in warmer climates and with better pay. Not that they wanted their cook to go, mind you—I was the best damn 'chef' (as they generously called me) that any of those poor sods had ever had, but it wasn't right of me to stay on like I did. They figured it out, eventually. Nothing specific, but what other reason than a crush or a lover would someone have for doing what I was?

It was the little things. How his kisses inexplicably tasted just a little bit like strawberries, and how his paws grabbed at my hips as I pressed him against the brick wall of his small house. It was the way his tail spiked up and twitched with excitement as my fingers took hold of his petite but shapely ass. It was the way my big shaggy grey-furred belly pressed against his eerily-soft white one.

Sometimes we shared dinner first, whether going out or me attempting romance and cooking Sean something. Tonight wasn't one of those nights. Tonight, we'd barely said hello before the touching and kissing and pants-tightening started, and if I had had any hesitation, it was whisked away by him whimpering out "please, Kevin" as our bodies pressed together. I liked seeing our differing shapes come together—another of those little things, maybe.

I was a raccoon, and a kinda chunky one at that. My dad had shared some wisdom with me once: never trust a skinny chef. I liked to think he'd have been amused to see me become one. Nevertheless, I was very conscious of that fact. There have always been the chubby chasers, sure, but I always found it a little hard to believe a cute little guy like Sean would actually find me attractive. I got the feeling I wasn't quite his type, and he really wasn't quite mine, either; it was just a drunken bar hookup that started this, after all. His neckfur was out of place, again, and I lapped it back down like usual. I wanted him right there against the wall—fuck being romantic and sappy and going to the bed. Of course, he didn't exactly keep his lube out on the living room table, so when he broke away from the hungry kissing and groping and beckoned me to his room, I didn't protest.

We left our clothes in a succession of outer to underwear on the path between his living and bedroom knowing full well that gathering up all the articles after sex was going to be annoyance, but also not caring in the heat of the moment. The little fox almost leaped onto his bed, and I was right behind and then on top of him. The bed creaked in protest as I added my weight to it. It'd be alright, though—it certainly wasn't going to be the first time we'd tested the sturdiness on that poor frame. It wasn't that I was *that* big, really—it just seemed like it with as petite as Sean was. While any normal person would be inundated with the smell of aroused fox, and, trust me, I was, I couldn't help but smirk at the background odor of freshly laundered sheets. He washed them every time when he expected my ship to put in, and that cheap, pungent detergent had become something I looked forward to.

Sean wasted no time flipping over onto his belly, which gave me a much-appreciated view of his ass with his fluffy tail draped over top. I didn't waste time, either; giving Sean a few pats on the butt and motioning upwards to let him know I wanted the fox on all fours. Yeah, against the wall would be nice—maybe later. He shivered and lowered his head (and ears) in submission as my meaty paw gave his dangling cock and balls a stroke and squeeze, ending up under his quivering tail. Sean recovered his senses enough to reach into his nightstand drawer and toss me the bottle of lube that he kept there. Same stuff as always, and damn good stuff at that. The clear liquid was cool on my flesh—a result of the whole house being cold and damp—as I spread it generously around my shaft with a paw. It warmed up soon enough, and I bit my lip in anticipation as I spread the lube over my bulbous head (which Sean always found an amazing feature for some reason).

There was plenty of leftover lube clinging to the fur on my paw, so I squeezed it up onto my index finger and sank it right into that inviting opening. He gasped, and the fox just couldn't help but push back against the intrusion. Those needy eyes of his told me he was just as hungry for it as I was. The bottle of lube rolled off the bed and hit his hardwood floor with a sharp, plasticy thud, but neither of us stopped to consider that. Sean wiggled his rump upward while I guided myself against him. He stopped at that moment of contact, breathing heavy and waiting for me to push forward, which I did without hesitation.

I took it slower than my primal urges wanted me to. That fox's ass just felt so goddamn good with the way it just spread open to accommodate me like I actually belonged in there. Whatever noises he was making were drowned out by the low rumble coming from my throat. I didn't make it all the way in on the first few thrusts, but each one got deeper until I'd finally sunk. He lowered his head and buried his face into the pillow almost as if he was afraid someone would hear his yips and moans as I moved inside him. I grasped his hips in my paws and pulled his body against the epicenter of the pleasurable feelings coursing throughout me.

Fuck, I wasn't going to last long. I never did the first time we fucked on a visit; 88 days on the boat'll give one a short trigger. He knew it, and dammit if that sly little fox wasn't trying to get this session over with by squeezing down on me, humping back; all those things that got me off. He knew there was more, better—in his mind— sex coming later. Me? I liked the first 'happy to see you' romp more.

My vision got cloudy, my thrusts lost their rhythm, and my throat let out a growl as I gripped him hard, holding his body against mine as I climaxed. We remained there for what seemed like forever, just panting and giggling little unsaid jokes at each other until I pulled out and rolled off next to him. I'd have offered him a hand or muzzle, but the sticky spot on the bed and his paw said he'd taken care of himself already. Sneaky fox.

As I'd expected, finding my clothes proved a lot harder than taking them off had been, and that one sock in particular was really doing a good job of hiding. Sean wasn't the cuddly sort after sex. The fox had his own routine, and it was no different. "So what's for dinner?" He looked at me with hopeful, perked ears.

"Depends what you have in the kitchen and pantry." Normally, I wasn't big on doing my day job for people, but I made an exception every three months or so. The fridge was mostly beer and leftover carryout, but there was a mostly uneaten rotisserie chicken, apple juice, and tortillas. "Hm." My pondering got Sean all cute and curious, and I made a show of raising my brows and looking through his cupboards and pantry. Garlic cloves, vinegar, oil, onions, some dried chipotle…actually, I could work with that. I set a pair of onions down on the cutting board and waved him over. "Cut these up."

Sean took a knife and started to remove the outer layer.

"Like, diced up?"

"Yep." I got to work on the chicken and made a nice little apple chipotle sauce. The ingredients in that fox's kitchen would have made a lot of chefs scoff, but I was used to working with dried spices and canned goods on the boat. There was something I liked about making mediocre elements into something tasty. I had to hold back a chuckle when Sean proudly slid me the board of onions. His idea of cutting up was crude, but it'd work.

I did the cooking alone, though, and he knew that. My fox, if I could even call him mine, was content with watching his show on TV while I made dinner. The shredded chicken tacos with sauce came out pretty good, which he reminded me of between seemingly every bite that he had.

We'd never said "I love you" to each other and probably never would. He never asked if I had flings in other ports, but he probably suspected. He wouldn't have been wrong, either: there were others. There weren't others that I cooked for, though. There weren't others that I lied awake in my bunk at night thinking of. There damn sure weren't others that I'd passed up a 'better' route for. I couldn't place my finger on why he was different. Maybe it was just those little things, after all.

After dinner, but before our paws started wandering again, my phone rang. Ship was headed out early to avoid a storm, and they needed me back. Sean wasn't happy about it, but we said our goodbyes and shared a kiss.

I liked that little town of his. The cold, damp, northern air felt good in the nostrils. It was clean, not like a lot of the more industrial ports we stopped in. Then, just one little thing caught my eye on the way to the boat. It was a quaint, log cabin restaurant with a sign hanging by a string in the window.

Hiring One Experienced Cook
Inquire Within.

For someone who lived a life of constant routine, I have to admit the best things that'd ever happened to me came about because of sheer impulsiveness. I joined the merchant marines instead of finishing school. I introduced myself to Sean all those stops ago on impulse, and I was about to be rash once more. Worst case scenario, my ship would come back around in a couple months, right? Well, no—they'd be furious with me and probably not let me back on at all in the future. Hell with it. I dialed up my fox with a stupid grin on my face. I didn't even know if I'd get that job. I just knew he'd be surprised to see me calling.

"Take it you're back on the boat?"

My goofy grin wasn't going anywhere, and I hoped he could hear it through the phone. "Sean? Could I stay with you awhile? I know it's crazy, but I don't want to leave this time."

There were a few little moments of silence as he was surely trying to process what I was asking. "I'd love that, Kevin."

"And, I love you. See you in a bit."

ABOUT THE ARTIST
Joseph Chou (Drkchaos)

Joseph is a hobbyist illustrator specializing in pencils, acrylics, oil paints, and various digital mediums. He is fairly quiet within the furry community, and goes under the guise of a red fox dubbed "Fenrir." His works usually focuses on landscape/mood pieces, or fantasy/medieval settings. Recent artworks done by Joseph include pieces for Arcana *edited by* Madison Scott-Clary, Infurno, *and* Seven Deadly Sins: Furry Confessions Anthology, *all published by Thurston Howl Publications. He also worked on illustrating Weasel Press's E-zine* Typewriter Emergencies. *Joseph enjoys online gaming with friends, collecting board games, reading novels, and cooking new recipes. When not doing things at his leisure, he works as a researcher/chef for a major food company. Joseph lives in sunny Southern California with his dog, Garrus.*

ACKNOWLEDGMENTS

"The Treachery of Images" by WhiteClaw. © 2018.

"Ghosted" by Lou Treble. © 2018.

"Cages and Jaguars" by Kuroko. © 2018.

"Spicy with a Hint of Fox" by Colin Leighton. © 2018.

"When the Needs are Denied" by MikasiWolf. © 2018.

"Orientation" by TJ Minde © 2018.

"What I Do For Love" by Patrick Lambert. © 2018.

"Diary of a Slutty Fox" by Ferric. © 2018.

"Unexpected Gifts" by Jelliqal Belle. © 2018.

"Black as Midnight, Red as Blood" by Miles Reaver. © 2018.

"Arctic Fox" by Sisco Polaris. © 2018.

"It's the Little Things" by Tana Simenses. © 2018.

www.ingramcontent.com/pod-product-compliance
Lightning Source LLC
Chambersburg PA
CBHW051132020726
47501CB00005B/1470